The Whole Sky

Book Two in the Love Under the Arizona Sky Series

Hilary Dartt

Also by Hilary Dartt

The Whole Sky

Book Two in the Love Under the Arizona Sky Series

Hilary Dartt

For my three kids.
You inspire me.

Chapter One

R ose Coffey was becoming a master at making the best of a situation ... and she was exhausted. Even a master sometimes breaks, especially at two-thirty in the morning. For the fifth night in a row, the sounds of Rose's inconsiderate college-student neighbors woke her.

Each night, it started the same way. Tires crunching on the gravel parking lot as these kids — young adults, really, and shouldn't they start acting like it? — came home. Headlights sweeping across her blackout curtains, coming through the cracks despite her best efforts to close them as snugly as possible. Car doors slamming shut. Voices. Sometimes talking, sometimes singing, almost always laughing.

There was typically one considerate kid in the bunch, shushing the others. More often than not, someone bumped into the wall of Rose's apartment as the group made their way to the metal staircase, which was completely unforgiving when it came to noise.

Directly above her bedroom, at their front door, her apartment mates fumbled with the keys, stumbled into their apartment, and slammed the door. If Rose's daughter, Celeste, didn't wake up as a result of any of that, she began to stir as the college students settled in upstairs. Sometimes they thumped around the whole place, a herd of elephants overhead. Sometimes they turned on music. On this particular Wednesday night, they started what sounded like a racquetball game.

"What is that, Mommy?" Celeste asked, her voice croaky with sleep.

"Oh, I don't know. It sounds like they have an enchanted ball up there, and they're playing catch."

"An enchanted ball?"

"Yeah." Rose infused her voice with cheer and calm. "It's like magic."

Celeste sighed and rolled onto her back, away from Rose. Moonlight came through a crack in the curtains, illuminating Celeste's wide-open eyes. "I mean, that sounds like a lot of fun. It's just, it's the middle of the night."

From the mouths of babes. "I know, it does make it hard to sleep." Rose had discovered recently that one of the most difficult things about being a mother was the constant need to make everything seem like it was okay. To not fall into pieces, even though she wanted to. In that moment, Rose wanted to fall apart. She'd worked *so hard* to save for the security deposit on that apartment, because it was supposed to be new and quiet and safe. And she kept them on such a tight budget to be able to afford the rent payments. She felt like she couldn't win. All she wanted to do was give her daughter a good home, a home where she could have the essentials. And one of those essentials was a good night's sleep.

"Mama, are you crying?"

Rose felt a tear escape the corner of her eye. She hadn't even realized. "No, sweetie. My eyes are just watering because I'm tired."

"I'm sorry." Celeste rolled towards Rose and laid a hand on her cheek. "I'm tired too. Let's go back to sleep."

Rose remained wide awake, but Celeste drifted off for a little while, until a huge *thud* shook the walls. It was so loud and so thunderous, Rose had to remind herself earthquakes don't happen in Arizona.

Celeste startled awake, her eyes wide. "What was that?"

Shaking her head, Rose said, "I don't know. But it was really loud."Rose decided then and there that they couldn't live like that any longer. "How would you like an adventure?" she asked Celeste.

"You know I love adventures," Celeste said. "But it's the middle of the night. Maybe we should adventure tomorrow. Shouldn't we be sleeping?"

"We *should* be." Hearing the exasperation in her voice, Rose took a deep breath to calm herself. "But, since we're not sleeping anyway, what do you say we go on an adventure?"

She turned the bedside lamp on low.

Even the dim light made Celeste squint as her eyes adjusted. "Okay," she said, her eyebrows knitting together in doubt. "I think someone might be on the crazy train."

"Oh, honey, I've been on the crazy train for a while. Now, I'm going to give you your very own ticket."

Celeste giggled at that.

As Rose got their things together, she thought about where they could go. She knew she could call either of her best friends, Taylor Cole or Jessie Monroe. They had told her innumerable times she could call or come stay, whenever she wanted (or needed) to. But she didn't want to burden them. And she knew from experience that being woken out of a sound sleep in the middle of the night felt like a burden.

She folded the outfit she'd chosen for Celeste and put it in the suitcase, and then did the same with clothes for herself.

She could call her parents, but she couldn't stand the thought of them thinking she wasn't making it, wasn't doing a good job raising her child.

Toothbrushes, toothpaste, and a roll of toilet paper, just in case, went into the suitcase.

You could call Jared, a mean voice piped up from the back of her mind. She slammed shut the suitcase and zipped it, her movements hard and jerky. *No.* She would never call Jared. When she'd finally gathered up the courage to leave him, he'd tried to convince her she wouldn't survive without him. It almost worked. She had almost stayed with him the last time because of how incompetent he'd made her feel.

She wouldn't call anyone, she decided. She would rely on herself.

So, car loaded and Celeste buckled into her booster seat, Rose headed for the only place she felt totally capable: Prescott High School.

Rose was great at two things: being a mom and being a teacher. During her five years as a high school English teacher, she'd gained more confidence more quickly than any other time in her life. The building felt like a home away from home — and, for one night, it was going to be.

"What are we doing at your work?" Celeste wanted to know.

"Having an adventure!" Rose used her key to unlock the main building's side door.

She let Celeste in ahead of her, then locked the door behind them. She'd already decided the teachers lounge would make a perfect camping spot. It had two couches, a microwave, a fridge, and a sink. She flicked on the florescent light, which gave off its typical humming sound.

"It feels creepy in here," Celeste said.

Rose happened to agree. "I think it feels cozy. Look. We can each sleep on a couch. And there's a microwave. And the bathroom is *en suite*."

"What is en suite?"

"It's a fancy way of saying it's connected."

"En suite." Celeste imitated Rose's French.

Noticing the dark smudges under her daughter's eyes, Rose felt another pang of guilt. "Here, let's get your sleeping bag set up."

They unrolled Celeste's mermaid sleeping bag and she wiggled into it. "Good thing I'm still wearing my pajamas."

"Good thing," Rose said. She brushed Celeste's hair away from her face and kissed her on the forehead. "Go ahead and go to sleep. I'm going to be on the other couch."

"Are you going to turn off the light?"

"Yep. Right now." Rose flipped the switch, shook out the blanket she'd brought for herself, and lay down on the couch. Within seconds, she heard Celeste's breathing become deep and even. A clock ticked from its spot on the wall, next to the door. The sound, which normally would drive Rose batty, lulled her into a deep sleep. Her alarm went off at five-thirty the next morning. Zero hour started at six-thirty, and generally, the teachers showed up at six-fifteen. Rose folded her blanket and got dressed, then microwaved the breakfast sandwiches she'd packed.

Naturally, Celeste had a hard time waking up. Rose really couldn't blame her, and did her absolute best not to rush her through the morning routine of dressing, eating, and brushing her teeth — but the closer it got to zero hour, the more stressed Rose felt. She left Celeste in the teachers lounge while she made a trip to the car to load the sleeping bag, blanket, pillows, and suitcase. By the time she returned, Celeste had eaten only a few bites of her breakfast sandwich, and hadn't put on her shoes. The clock next to the door read twelve minutes after six, and Rose knew the zero hour teachers could show up any minute. She knelt in front of Celeste and slipped her shoes onto her feet, then stood and hoisted her onto her hip.

"Mommy!" Celeste said. "You're so silly! Why are you carrying me like a baby?"

"I just don't want you to be late for school."

Fortunately, Celeste couldn't yet tell time and wouldn't realize they had an hour to kill. They made it all the way through the building without seeing anyone, but when Celeste pushed on the door that led outside, she pushed it right into someone coming in. That person pulled the door open and stepped back. Rose was about to offer a hurried thanks, and then she saw his shoes, and lost all coherent thought.

"Johnny Mac." She recognized his shoes only because she'd memorized every detail about him. The brown loafers were one of twelve high-dollar pairs of shoes he wore to school. Delirious from exhaustion, Rose allowed her gaze to travel from Mac's shoes to his thighs, his package, his trim waist, and his chiseled chest, finally coming to rest on his gorgeous, gorgeous face. She could get lost in those deep green eyes. Her own face flamed when she snapped out of it and realized what had just happened.

"Morning, Ms. Coffey. To what do I owe the pleasure, this early in the morning?"

Face still hot with shame, Rose spluttered, "I — my daughter — we —"

"We had a campout here." Celeste's voice was so loud and clear, there was no way to pretend she'd said anything else.

Mac raised his eyebrows, and Rose let out what she hoped was a believable laugh. "Oh, honey! You tell such wonderful stories!" She turned her attention back to Mac and said, "We had a campout in the living room last night. And when it was time to leave for school, we realized we left Celeste's water bottle in my classroom yesterday. She needs it for school."

Mac smiled at Celeste, warm and genuine. Rose's heart melted. "You know, you're lucky to have such a nice mama, that she would come early to school just to get your water bottle. Have a great day, both of you. I've got to go in and teach."

With that, he was gone, leaving behind a leathery scent that made Rose weak in the knees. She made a beeline for her car.

"You're so silly, Mommy! Why did you tell that guy we didn't have a campout?"

Rose didn't know what to say. She buckled Celeste into her booster seat. "I don't know." She got in the driver's seat and started the car. "Here, I'll put on your favorite station."

Rose turned on Celeste's kids' station and turned up the volume, hoping that would keep Celeste from asking any more questions. As they drove away from the high school, Rose's heart rate finally slowed down.

Although Mac was the absolute last person she wanted knowing she was in such a desperate situation, she also felt a thrill at their interaction. She'd lusted after him for years since he returned to Prescott from San Francisco, but never had the guts to actually converse with him. The fact that they'd exchanged more than a few words would stay with her the rest of the day.

Chapter Two

Mac couldn't think of a better way to start his school day than to run into Rose Coffey first thing. He was exhausted. The only way to get the morning chores done at the farm was to be up and walking the property by four a.m. As he walked to his classroom, he thought back to that morning, which already felt like a lifetime ago.

Each morning, he let himself enjoy one leisurely cup of coffee before heading outside to do chores. He leaned against the kitchen counter, holding a coffee mug in both hands. His mom, accustomed to rising early after all her years running the place, came in and poured herself a cup. Her movements, slow and unsteady, and her gnarled, twisted hands, made him sad every time he noticed them. That's why he couldn't give up the farm, no matter how much he wanted to.

"Good morning, Sonny," she said to him, just as she had every morning since he was knee-high. She leaned her head on his shoulder, just briefly, a half-hug for two half-awake people.

"Good morning, Mama. How are you feeling today?"

"Plucky. Fresh as a spring chicken." She went to the fridge to get the cream.

He smiled. She didn't mean it, but she'd never admit as much. Eleanor MacKinnon never complained.

"Don't forget to milk Cookie this morning." She poured the cream and stirred it into her coffee. "And make sure Henrietta comes out of the coop. You know she's been a bit broody. And —"

"And make sure the goats didn't chew through the fence."

"Right." His mom put away the cream and then leaned against the counter next to him. They faced the window overlooking the farm. Not that they could see anything out there now. The sun wouldn't rise for another hour and a half or so. But he could picture the property, his childhood home, with clarity. Two decent-sized corrals, with the goat pen on one side and a chicken coop on the other. In the southeast corner, a lush garden, which he had to remember to weed. And, in the southwest corner, his mom's pride and joy: her flower garden. Although she could hardly do any of the farm chores anymore, she'd never give up that flower garden.

"You know, you don't have to keep the farm," she told him for the millionth time. "I know you didn't move to the big city with dreams of coming back to Podunk Arizona."

He sighed. It was an ongoing conversation. "I know I don't."

She said he didn't have to keep it, and he said he knew, but he was afraid selling the farm would break her heart, especially since she'd already lost her husband. He didn't want his mama to die of a broken heart.

"I'm going to head out," Mac told Eleanor.

She reached up and ruffled his hair. "I remember the days when I could kiss you right on top of your head. You wouldn't believe how fast a lifetime flies by."

That thought fresh in his mind, Mac noticed his footsteps felt heavy as he walked out to the barn. Although all the chores had felt like drudgery when he first moved back home from San Francisco two years before, Mac had come to like the routine. The motion lights flicked on as he approached the barn, and he saw Cookie raise her head, ears pricked. She met him the milking area, and leaned into his touch when he scratched her neck.

"I can't believe I've become attached to a cow." Her ears twitched and she blinked. "You being coy with me?" he said.

He set up the stool and bucket and got to milking. The rhythm of the job calmed him. And, he thought, maybe that was why his mom felt so attached. Not just to the property and the animals, but to the rhythm and routine. The place had a breath of its own, he thought.

At times, the breath felt like his albatross. San Francisco, with its sleek buildings and fast-paced lifestyle, felt like a whole different world.

The milk began to feel fill the bucket, thick and foamy. Cookie stood still, patient. Once he was done milking her, he got on to feeding her and the goats. He checked for eggs in the coop, and had to reach under Henrietta's warm, feathered body and shoo her out of the nesting box.

It used to be, when he was a teenager, his mom would have breakfast waiting for him when they came in from doing chores. Not anymore. He didn't mind — he'd lived on his own and actually enjoyed cooking — but keeping up with everything felt like a *lot*. Before he'd moved home, it was just him. He could happily dump some cereal into a bowl, pour milk over it, and shovel it down before leaving for work. But he was feeding his mom, and even though *she* didn't feel like he owed her, he did. The way he saw it, she deserved a good, hot breakfast every day.

She came into the kitchen again as he was washing his hands. "What's on the menu this morning?"

"Well, we have about a million eggs. Are you tired of scrambles yet?"

Eleanor laughed. "I have to admit, we've had a lot of scrambles lately. But you know I love using what we get from the girls. Have you ever thought about selling our eggs?"

She'd brought it up before, and Mac thought it was a good idea. It was also another item on a very long list of to-dos.

"We definitely have enough to sell." He left it at that.

He supposed he could bring eggs to work. Farm fresh was popular now, from home décor to the farmers market. People would probably jump at the chance to take home farm-fresh eggs. Mac sighed.

"What's weighin' on you, honey?"

Mac did something then he'd only done twice in his life, both times as a teenager. He lied right to his mom's face. "Oh, just thinking about midterms. They're coming up."

After eating breakfast, he'd showered, kissed his mom on the cheek, and left for work, where he almost ran right into Rose Coffey as he entered the building.

She was a sight for sore eyes, and he almost told her so. Fortunately, he caught himself. He'd noticed Rose as soon as he came to work at the high school. Her wild, curly, blond hair drew his attention, and her picture-perfect face captured it.

"Focus, Mac," he said to himself now, as he sat at his desk and stared down at the blank piece of paper in front of him. He really did have midterms coming up, and he'd hoped to work on the test before students showed up that day. *Chemistry Midterm*, he wrote at the top of the page. Try as he might to stop it, his mind wandered back to Rose.

Something about her behavior that morning seemed off. He couldn't quite put a finger on it; they hadn't spoken much and he didn't know her as well as he'd like to. Which also meant he didn't feel comfortable coming right out and asking her.

Typically, he had no trouble talking to women. Friends in San Francisco teased him about it. They'd go out to a bar, and within a few minutes, Johnny Mac would be talking to a woman. His friends called him a lady-killer, Casanova, a playboy ... even though he rarely asked anyone out (and he never took women home).

But Rose Coffey was a different story. He found himself tongue-tied around her.

The first time he'd mustered up the courage to talk to her was at a staff meeting. Ernie Vasquez, the principal, was a stickler for those meetings, which gave Mac weekly opportunities.

Every week, he promised himself he'd talk to her, and every week, he couldn't bring himself to do it ... well, not beyond a casual and stilted, "Hi, Rose." The school year started in August, and the calendar showed December by the time he struck up a real conversation. It was spirit week, and the staff meeting happened to fall on Ugly Sweater Day. Ernie turned the meeting into a holiday party, and after he gave a short, festive version of his weekly principal spiel, Mac spotted Rose alone by the snacks. He decided to go for it. After all, he had a conversation starter. "Nice sweater." He immediately kicked himself, wishing he'd been smart enough to come up with a more original topic.

But she didn't seem to mind. In fact, if he wasn't mistaken (or kidding himself), he would swear she actually blushed.

"Thanks." She looked down at the sweater as if she were seeing it for the first time. "I chose it because it lights up. Want to see?"

Boy, do I. "Sure."

She pinched the hem, and little Christmas lights lit up all over the ugly Christmas tree that took up the entire front of the sweater. Then she looked up at him, waiting for his response. Her smile was so adorable, he almost couldn't speak.

He managed, "That's really cool," and kicked himself yet again for yet another stupid, unoriginal remark. Her friends came in then, and she went to join them at the photo booth, leaving him holding a roll of prosciutto and Havarti, wishing his lady-killer skills applied where she was concerned.

One day later that school year, he'd caught her alone in the teachers lounge and asked, "All ready for finals?"

Her eyes widened in shock, and she looked at her watch. "You scared me! It's only March. We have two months 'til finals, and I haven't even started thinking about them, yet."

Mac had simply turned and left the lounge, unable to recover.

Even in the present, a year and a half after that blunder, he felt the embarrassment from the top of his head to the bottoms of his feet. He looked down at the notes he'd started for his midterm, and groaned. He had only a couple minutes until class started.

After that horrible interaction with Rose, he'd resolved to watching her from afar, learning what he could about her without being creepy or acting like a stalker. One day, he told himself, he'd gather the courage to ask her out.

He knew she was the junior and senior English teacher and a single mom. She drove a bright blue SUV, and parked in spot twenty-eight in the lot. No matter where she was going or what she was doing, Rose always looked rushed, and she arrived out of breath. She ate homemade lunches and although she sometimes went out with the other teachers to celebrate birthdays or promotions or engagements, she always stuck to one drink, *if* she had anything other than water.

Physics Midterm

Mac rubbed his forehead. Seeing Rose that morning, unexpected as it was, had been delightful. And, apparently, it had thrown him off for the rest of the day. His classroom door opened, and three of his students came in.

"Good morning," he said, standing up from his desk to shake their hands. It was a ritual he'd started on his first day of teaching. And if Mac knew anything, it was that ritual could could bring him back to earth, where he needed to be for his students.

He could (and would) daydream about Rose Coffey later.

Chapter Three

Rose and Celeste spent five more nights at the high school without incident, staying at the apartment until just before bedtime, and then sneaking into the teachers lounge.

The following Wednesday morning, in the seconds after Rose's alarm went off, she heard the school's exterior door opening. The creaking of the hinges always seemed like a nuisance, until that moment, when it warned her someone was about to come in and discover them. She didn't bother waking Celeste. Instead, she loaded herself up like a pack mule: Celeste in one arm, her suitcase, blanket, and sleeping bag somehow stuffed under the other, and a backpack slung over her shoulder.

Rose ran down the hall to the nearest exterior door, Celeste and all their belongings bouncing against her body. The sun's first rays shone up from the horizon, but the campus was dim as she made her way to the student parking lot, where she'd parked the night before, knowing staff members wouldn't see her car in the morning.

Still feeling rushed and urgent, even when she reached the car, Rose put Celeste in the backseat, crammed the rest of their stuff in, too, and drove back to the apartment, heart racing as she did her best to adhere to the speed limit. Only once they were safely inside did Rose breathe normally. And also, realize she might finally fall apart.

Her voice cracked when she said to Celeste, "Be right back. I have to go to the bathroom," and she locked herself in there and cried. She couldn't believe what her life had come to. Maybe she really *couldn't* do the whole single-parent thing on her own. Maybe she really *wasn't* capable.

"Mommy?" Celeste's voice sounded tiny and worried on the other side of the door.

"Just a minute, honey." Rose blew her nose and turned on the tap. She cupped her hands, fill them with cold water, and brought the water to her eyes, hoping to at least reduce any puffiness. She repeated the process a few times, then pressed a towel against her face. When she opened the door, Celeste stood there looking up at her, those dark smudges painfully pronounced.

"I have to go potty."

Rose put a hand on Celeste's head. "Go ahead. I'm all done."

By the time she got back to school that morning, Rose still felt less than human. Typically, seeing Taylor and Jessie in the parking lot boosted her spirits. That day, it filled her with dread. Her eyes still felt sandy from crying and lack of sleep, and she was certain they would notice immediately. She took her time parking, gathering her things, and getting out of the car, hoping the girls would head to their classrooms without her, but knowing they wouldn't.

Sure enough, by the time she finally opened her car door, her friends had walked over. They each gave her a hug, and she thought maybe she'd escaped any scrutiny. But then, they both stepped back and examined her, frowning.

"Rosie, are you okay?" Jessie said, and Taylor said, "You don't look so good."

Rose laughed, the sound bordering on maniacal, and then, without warning, she burst into tears. Her friends exchanged a worried look, and then wrapped their arms around her.

"What's wrong?" Taylor said, and Jessie said, "What's going on? Is Celeste okay?"

"Celeste is fine," Rose wept, her voice muffled against Taylor's shoulder. "She's just fine. We are fine. It's just the living situation."

She disentangled herself from her friends and dug a napkin out of her purse to blow her nose and wipe her eyes.

"Your living situation?" Taylor's forehead wrinkled. "But I thought you loved your new apartment. It was the apartment of your dreams."

Rose nodded, blotting at her eyes. "I *do* love it. It's so cute, with its little reading nook, and I love the view of the lake, and I planted that little herb garden in the kitchen window."

"Well, then what's wrong?" Jessie put her hand on Rose's shoulder.

"I've tried everything. I got the blackout curtains, the noise machine. I tried to get Celeste to wear earplugs. I've even talked to them."

"To the earplugs?" Jessie asked.

"No," Rose wailed. "To our neighbors. They are seriously the nicest kids. Young adults. They're just inconsiderate. They come and go at all hours of the night and I haven't gotten a good night's sleep in I don't know how long."

"Oh, Rosie." Taylor put her arm around Rose again. "Why haven't you told us?"

Because I don't want you to think I'm failing.

Rose checked her watch. "We'd better get in there. The bell's about to ring."

"Okay," Jessie said. "But first, tell us why you didn't tell us until now."

Rose turned to Taylor. "You've been so busy getting your business going, and," she said, turning to Jessie, "You've been stressed about Midge, and spending so much time helping her. I didn't want either of you to worry. You've already both been so much help, packing us up and moving us so many times."

As much as Rose had dreaded the conversation, letting her feelings spill out, *finally*, felt so good. Cathartic. She let herself sob another couple of minutes while her friends held her. Then she said, "I've got to pull myself together. That was the first bell."

Jessie rubbed her back, vigorously, as if thawing her out. And Taylor pulled a package of Kleenex out of her purse and handed one to Rose.

The three of them fell into step, Rose's friends flanking her, their camaraderie bolstering her. As they walked, Taylor said, "I think this calls for a planning session. We've got to get this figured out. You can't keep living like this."

They don't know the worst of it.

"I agree," Jessie said. "When is your lease up?"

Rose sighed. "It's up in a month. I just hate the thought of moving again. I felt like we were finally getting settled in, you know? I'm just so disappointed. Not just in the apartment, but also in myself."

Both Taylor and Jessie rushed to reassure Rose that terrible neighbors were not a reflection of Rose's character or life skills.

She giggled at that. "No, that's true. I guess I just wish I could get out of apartment living."

"Well, maybe we can find you a house to rent. At least you wouldn't be sharing walls with anyone, then."

Rose nodded. "I've been looking. I just haven't been able to find any in my price range."

"Ah," Taylor said. "But you have not employed the research skills of the Prescott High School librarian."

"Well, that's true." They'd reached the entrance to campus, and Principal Ernie Vasquez greeted them by name. Making a conscious effort to immerse herself in the normality of the school and all its routines, Rose took a deep breath. She would get through this day, just like she got through all of the others. One class at a time.

Taylor and Jessie split off from Rose, and as soon as she was alone, she heard, "Good morning, Ms. Coffey."

Rose figured the voice, which belonged to Johnny Mac, was a figment of her imagination. When she turned and saw it was him, in reality, saying good morning to her, she wished she could pull her limbs inside her shell, like a turtle, and scuttle into hiding. Taylor's words, *You don't look so good*, echoed in Rose's mind.

"Good morning, Johnny Mac," Rose said, wishing she could

come up with something clever or creative to say. A few options presented themselves. *Nice day. How about those Cardinals? Aren't you usually heading to the teachers lounge at this time, pouring your third cup of coffee?*

But she couldn't say any of those things. Everybody knew the weather was a conversation starter for dull people who couldn't think of anything else to talk about. And the Cardinals? She didn't even watch football. She only she knew it was football season because some of her students had been wearing Cardinals gear. And, if she asked him why he wasn't in the teachers lounge, he would then know that she kept track of his schedule. Rose's thought process had used up all the time it took her to pass Johnny Mac, and she realized she still had a goofy smile glued in place. Well, the moment was over, and she could now spend any spare time during the day thinking about what to say the next time they ran into each other.

Rose and Celeste planned to meet Taylor and Jessie at Rita's Diner that evening. Rose had briefly considered coaching Celeste not to say anything about the campouts, but decided against it. Coaching her daughter to lie — even by omission – seemed like questionable parenting. Instead, she resolved to direct the conversation, and hopefully avoid any talk about their clandestine campouts.

"Sit anywhere you like, gals," Rita called to Rose and Celeste when they walked in.

"Ooh," Celeste hollered. "The corner booth! The corner booth!"

Something about the corner booth, and the way they had to scoot all the way around the table, got Celeste really excited.

"Okay, but remember," Rose started, and Celeste finished, "*Walk* across the restaurant. Don't run."

Jessie and Taylor came in just as Celeste was opening the package of crayons that came with the kids menu. Celeste held up the red one. "Jessie, I challenge you to a game of tic-tac-toe!"

"You're on!"

Rose smiled at Jessie, who was always game for tic-tac-toe. As competitive as she was, she made Celeste earn any wins.

"So how was the rest of your day?" Taylor asked as she slid into the booth.

"It was better, thanks," Rose said. "It was good to get in the routine. And, you know, our conversation this morning? I think I really needed that. I've been putting on a brave face, but it's been getting to me."

"Mommy cried in the bathroom this morning," Celeste said, her voice serious as she carefully drew an O on the tic-tac-toe board.

Rose shrugged. Celeste's ability to listen in on her conversations, and reveal some of her secrets, failed to surprise Rose anymore. "I did. But I'm okay."

Before Celeste could reveal anything else, Rose changed the subject. "How's it going with the barn?"

That tactic worked. Taylor's eyes lit up as she described the progress on her new business. Rita came to take their orders, which was really just her confirming they wanted their usual, and then Rose asked Jessie about how things were going with her neighbor, Midge. Jessie talked about that until the food game came, and they all tucked into their meals.

"Remember what we talked about this morning?" Rose said.

Her friends nodded, and Rose was grateful they caught onto the fact that she didn't want to spell it out in front of Celeste.

"I was thinking," Rose said. "I'll go ahead and start doing some research."

"Research about what?" Celeste wanted to know.

"Oh, it's a grown-up topic," Taylor said. "We'll tell you more when you're older."

Celeste seemed to accept the explanation. She shrugged and nodded and went back to working on the maze on her menu. Without warning, she blurted out, "Guys! Has my mom told you about our campouts?"

Equally amused and curious, Taylor and Jessie looked at Rose.

"No, she hasn't," Jessie said. "But that sounds like a lot of fun."

"Not as much fun as you would expect," Celeste said.

Rose couldn't help it. She burst into laughter. "Well, I'm sorry to hear that," she said to Celeste.

If she could change the subject quickly enough, Taylor and Jessie would just assume Rose had planned campouts for fun, in the living room or something, and Celeste hadn't enjoyed them much. She floundered for a minute. Then she finally said, "I guess there's nothing else to say about that."

She didn't miss the way Taylor and Jessie looked at each other, but fortunately, Rita came over with refills and the bill. Rose threw some cash on the table, said goodbye to her friends, and practically scooped up Celeste and ran out of the diner.

Chapter Four

For the past few days, since Mac had seen Rose that morning in the quad and been completely frozen, unable to start a conversation, he had hoped for another chance. Rose had proven elusive, sticking mostly to her classroom or the library, and usually hanging out with one or both of her friends. It was lunchtime on a Friday, and Mac could barely keep his eyes open. He yearned for a nap. The couches in the teachers lounge beckoned him, seducing him with their soft, flat sleeping surfaces. But, he knew that if he went to sleep at noon, he wouldn't wake up for his last three class periods. So, he took his burrito out of the refrigerator, planning to douse it in hot sauce.

"That'll wake a guy up," he said to himself.

Please tell me your own classes don't bore you to sleep," someone said. If he wasn't mistaken, the voice belonged to ... "Ms. Coffey."

"Johnny Mac. Don't worry, I talk to myself all the time."

He smiled. "Just keeping myself awake, that's all. And, maybe going off the deep end a little. Lack of sleep."

Sympathy etched in her features, she sat down at the table. "I hear you. I haven't been sleeping well, and I keep thinking I'll get used to it, but I haven't."

The microwave beeped, and Johnny took his burrito out and put it on a paper plate. His heart beating faster at the idea of sharing a meal with Rose, he sat down across from her, acting as if it were the most comfortable, natural thing in the world. He started to ask her why she wasn't sleeping well, and they both started talking at the same time. "Why aren't you sleeping well?" he said, and she said, "Why are you so tired?"

She laughed, and the sound eased the pressure in his chest. "You, first," she said.

"I was going to say ladies first."

She shook her head, her big brown eyes serious. "No. It only makes sense for you to go first, because your exhaustion was the topic of our conversation. Then we can switch topics, to my exhaustion."

Mac used a plastic knife to cut his burrito in half. "Fair enough. Since you're the English teacher, I'll leave you to organizing our conversations from now on."

"Good man. So?"

Mac sighed. "My dad's passing two years ago left my mom in charge of the family farm."

"I'm sorry about your dad." He saw her hand move toward him, across the table, as if she wanted to comfort him. But she stopped the movement short.

"Thank you." He swallowed the tightness that formed in his throat whenever he thought about his dad's passing. "I was living in San Francisco at the time. Completely different life. I lived in a high-rise apartment. I didn't have a car. Anyway. My mom, she can't run the farm anymore, not on her own. But she loves that place."

He paused, and she said, "I take it that's where you grew up?"

Mac nodded, the tightness returning in his throat. "Yeah. And when I turned eighteen, I couldn't wait to get out of there. I wanted to go off to the military, and then straight to a big city. So that's what I did. Then my dad died, and my mom was left alone. It wasn't even a choice I had to make. I came back to help her, so she could stay on the farm."

Rose did reach out and touch him then, just a hand on his forearm. Her eyes blazed with emotion when she said, "I bet it means a lot to her."

The ferocity in Rose's voice, borne from being a mother, herself, affirmed he'd done the right thing by coming home.

"Thank you," he said again. "I wouldn't change things, but the farm is hard work, especially since I'm doing it on my own. My mom, she tried to help at first, but with her arthritis, it's just too much. She won't give up her flower garden or her greenhouse, but there's the milk cow, the chickens, the goats, the vegetable garden ..."

Rose's eyes went round. "Holy cow! That's a lot!"

"Yeah. I've been getting up at four a.m. every day to do the chores before I come to school. And then when I go home, I have to feed the goats and milk the cow again. And usually there are a few other things to attend to. Depending on the weather, I might have to water the vegetable garden. Depending on the goats' behavior, I might have to repair a hole or two in the fence."

"No wonder you're exhausted." She wrinkled her nose.

"And," Mac held up the hot sauce, "that's why I am dousing my burrito in hot sauce. To keep me awake through my last few classes of the day."

"Well, now I feel like a big baby for complaining about how tired I am. I'm just dealing with noisy college-student neighbors."

"Oh, yes," Mac said. "The beauty of apartment living. That's one thing I don't miss. But being a parent, having a little kid, that increases the intensity, right? If it was just you, you could put in earplugs, whatever. But I'm sure you're worried about the noise waking your daughter, and then you're worried about her not getting sleep." Rose exhaled. "Exactly."

"Hey, did you bring a lunch?"

Rose shook her head and looked away. "No. I totally forgot to pack one today. I'm sure I could grab something from the cafeteria —"

"Here. Take half of my burrito. I don't think I can finish this whole thing anyway."

"I couldn't possibly. You can definitely eat that whole thing. I've seen the way you eat! You know, the talk around the water cooler is that you work out, like, a ton. I'm sure you need the calories to fuel that. I'll just grab something from the cafeteria."

Mac felt himself blushing. "There's water-cooler talk?"

"Yeah." Her attempt not to smile was adorable. "I know. We don't even have a water cooler. You know what I mean."

"I insist. Take it." He stood up and retrieved another paper plate from the cabinet, put half the burrito on it, and slid it across the table.

"Thank you so much." Her voice was thick with emotion. Over a burrito? Her reaction was another clue that she wasn't telling him everything about whatever she was going through. He filed away that little tidbit.

"You're welcome. Now, I'm going to go to town with the hot sauce. Don't judge me. You're welcome to use it, if there's any left."

"I think I will use it after you're done. Maybe it will help me power through for a couple more hours, too."

Rose wasn't shy about eating in front of him. She grabbed her half of the burrito and took a good, healthy bite. Mac let out a little laugh, and Rose said, "Sorry. I was hungrier than I realized."

He waved her off. "It's fine. Trust me, I love a pretty girl who can eat."

Mouth full, mid-chew, Rose froze. "Did you say a pretty girl?"

Mac felt the heat rush up his neck and into his face, and half hoped Rose would attribute that to his overabundance of hot sauce. There he was, finally talking to her, after all this time, and he'd called her pretty. These days, women could take offense to something like that.

He decided he may as well be honest. "I did." He shrugged. "You are."

For a moment, he worried he'd made a mistake. Rose didn't say anything right away. She chewed, looking thoughtful. Mac could hear the clock ticking. He imagined it was counting down to his demise. He couldn't even take another bite. Finally, she swallowed. Then she unscrewed the lid of her water bottle and took a long drink. Set it down.

She looked right at him. "I can't remember the last time someone said that to me without an ulterior motive."

Mac's breath rushed out in relief. "You're welcome. It's true."

"Just so you know," she said, "you're not half-bad, yourself."

To hide his smile, Mac took another bite of his burrito.

"And," Rose said, "I think it's really sweet that you're helping your mom with the farm. Sweet isn't even the right word. You're a really standup guy. I only hope my daughter takes care of me like that when she grows up."

"Oh, I have a feeling she will." Right then and there, he experienced an urge to get to know Rose, and her daughter, better.

They both dug into their burritos again, and while he chewed, Mac considered asking her out. Before he could swallow his food, the biology teacher, Susan Kemper, and the physics teacher, Craig Jansen, came into the lounge.

"Afternoon, Rose," Susan said. "Mac."

"Afternoon," Rose and Mac responded. Mac decided he liked being paired with her that way.

"Afternoon," Craig said. "Mac, I brought that tool you wanted to borrow. I put it on the table at the back of your classroom."

"It's not a chainsaw, is it?" Rose wanted to know. "Now sitting at the back of the classroom for a student to find?"

Craig turned toward her, his expression friendly. Mac felt a prickle of jealousy. *This is new.*

"Definitely not," Craig said. "It's a fancy welding helmet. I'm sure someone could figure out how to use it as a weapon, but hopefully they'd need a little more time than what's left of the lunch break."

"A welding helmet, huh?" Rose said, turning to Mac. "That sounds serious."

"Craig was nice enough to let me use it to do a fence repair. We have one goat who can squeeze through an opening in the fence. I've tried a few repairs, but they haven't worked."

"Time to bring out the big guns," Craig said.

"Quite the handyman, huh?" Rose said.

Finally, they were having a real conversation. Mac felt hopeful.

He would definitely not risk rejection in front of his colleagues. But, he promised himself, he would ask her out. Soon.

Rose finished her half, and she wiped her face and hands with one of the fast food napkins stacked on the table. She took the next one off the stack and set it down next to his plate.

"Thank you so much for lunch," she said. "It's been a rough couple of days — weeks, actually — and that gesture really meant a lot."

"You're welcome."

They sat there at the table, gazes locked, smiling at each other, for a long moment. Then, the end-of-lunch bell rang. Mac heard the two science teachers talking, but his focus remained on Rose. She snapped out of it first and held out her hand for his plate. He handed it to her, and she got up and threw away the two plates and their napkins. He held open the door. As she walked past him, offering a funny little curtsy and a "Thank you," he inhaled the scent of her perfume. It was light and citrusy and created a pull below his belt. Her classroom was in one direction and his was in the other, and although he wanted, badly, to offer to walk her to hers, he decided against it. He'd already shared his burrito and hot sauce. Escorting her fifty feet down the hallway might be a little weird. They both paused, awkward, outside the teachers lounge door.

"Have a good day, Rose."

In response, she offered him the most genuine smile he'd seen on her. It made her eyes crinkle at the corners. "You have a good day, too, Johnny Mac."

With that, their impromptu lunch date was over. And although Mac felt disappointed the lunch break wouldn't go on for another couple of hours, he also realized he was walking down the hall to his classroom with quite a spring in his step.

Chapter Five

Rose spent the rest of the school day feeling like a giddy teenager. A fun, fizzy energy filled her torso, and she kept having to hold in giggles. She couldn't believe she'd just sat and had lunch with Johnny Mac, the leading man in many of her dating fantasies. Not only that, but she'd eaten lunch with him. His lunch.

After she left Celeste's dad, Jared, a few years before, she'd sworn off men. But that didn't mean she didn't notice them, want them, even daydream about them in some cases. Just like she'd spent the last couple of hours noticing, wanting, and daydreaming about Johnny Mac. She managed to make it through the last lesson of the day. Relief set in when the final bell rang.

"Have a good weekend!" she called to her students, who were just as eager to get out of there as she was. The shuffling of supplies into backpacks and the immediate crescendo of conversations and laughter signaled the weekend. She watched her students leave and then shut her classroom door.

She went through her typical Friday ritual of straightening the books on the shelves, erasing the whiteboard and writing the following week's dates and bell work, and watering her classroom plants. Then she gathered her planner, her water bottle, and her Shakespeare anthology, and put them in her bag.

Out of habit, she checked her phone, which she normally left on silent during the school day. The staff at Celeste's school knew to call the classroom if they needed her. The notification she saw on her screen made her stomach churn as if she'd taken a giant gulp of spoiled milk. *New Notifications: Jared Rochester.*

"I could've sworn I blocked him." Her voice sounded thick and strange in the empty classroom. Not just call, but also a text message. She could delete the notifications and the text. But he was if he was reaching out, it could be important. Right?

"Wrong." She'd promised herself after the last time that she would never talk to him again. Yet here she was, contemplating opening his message. Her thumb hovered over the notification bubble. She shouldn't even look at it. But he was Celeste's father. She didn't want to cut him out of their lives completely. While she stood there, immobile behind her desk, her classroom door opened. Taylor and Jessie walked in, just as they did most Fridays.

"Rosie?" Jessie spoke first.

"You look like you've seen a ghost," Taylor said.

Rose blinked. She looked first at Jessie and then at Taylor. "It's Jared."

"Is he dead?" Jessie demanded, a wicked gleam in her eye. She rushed to say, "Sorry. I'm just kidding. What about him?"

"He just texted me."

"That bastard!" Jessie said.

"What did he say?" Taylor wanted to know. Rose held out her phone, which displayed the lock screen and the unopened message. "I haven't looked yet."

"I would advise you not to," Taylor said.

"I know, you're right. In fact, I thought I had blocked him. I was just about to delete it when you guys walked in. It's just—" she set the phone on the desk, face down—"he's Celeste's father."

"Sperm donor, more like," Jessie said.

"I know." Rose forced a smile. "And yet, I'm so tempted to read what he sent me. He always starts out with these sweet messages, like, 'I miss you,' or, 'I was just thinking about you.'"

Jessie crossed her arms and looked at the ceiling, praying for patience. "Yep. That's how he tries to weasel his way back in."

"I know," Rose said again. Then she wondered why, if she really knew, she still hadn't deleted the message.

"Rosie —" Taylor said, and Jessie cut her off. "Want me to delete the message for you?" She held out a hand, palm up. "We can all pretend this never happened."

Rose shook her head. "I'll do it."

Taylor strode across the room and put her hands on Rose's shoulders. "Listen to me. Every time you even consider looking at a message from that jerk —"

Jessie interrupted again. "Jerk." She scoffed. "That's putting it mildly."

Taylor shushed Jessie and looked, hard, into Rose's eyes. "I want you to remember that night you called us, the first time you were scared of him. I want you to remember why you left him. I want you to picture Celeste's adorable little face and ask yourself if you really want her to grow up with a so-called *father* like that. Do you remember?"

Rose remembered. She closed her eyes to block out Taylor's words, but all that did was conjure images of that night. She'd asked Jared to watch Celeste for a couple of hours, so she, Taylor, and Jessie could do their traditional back-to-school shopping trip. He agreed, and Rose thought his willingness signified he was such a great partner.

It was the first time she'd asked him to stay home with Celeste while she went out, and if it went well, she figured she could do it once in a while.

It didn't.

Taylor and Jessie cooed over Celeste for a few minutes when they picked up Rose, and then they were off to the mall, where they went to a couple of stores before making a pit stop for snacks at Wooly's. Because it was a weekend, the restaurant was packed. The hostess offered them a seat at the bar and they ordered a round of margaritas and a plate of shareable nachos. A few of their teacher friends showed up about halfway through, and they all took pictures together. Someone — Rose couldn't remember who — posted some of the pictures to social media. Before they left the restaurant, Rose checked her phone. Jared hadn't called or texted, so she texted him: *How's it going there?*

He wrote back: *Fine.*

She would later learn that *fine* didn't really mean fine. Everyone said to be careful when a woman used that word, but apparently, she should have treaded carefully when Jared used it, too. Blissfully oblivious and enjoying her three hours of baby-free time, Rose and her friends hit another couple of stores before heading home. The girls dropped her off with happy waves.

Inside, she found a very unhappy child, and a very unhappy Jared. Celeste stood in her playpen, her hands gripping the top rail so hard, her tiny knuckles were white. Her face was bright red and wet with the combination of tears, drool, and sweat. Jared sat in his recliner, head tipped back, legs outstretched, a beer in one hand.

At first, Rose thought he was sleeping. "Jared?"

He turned his head toward her, slowly. His eyes were glazed over. "Little brat has been crying ever since you left. She hates me."

"I'm sure she doesn't hate you —"

Jared was out of his chair and towering over Rose before she even realized he'd gotten up. His pointer finger was inches from her nose, and she could feel his split on her face as he yelled at her. "She hates me! She just kept saying, 'Mama, Mama, Mama.' And crying. All she does is cry."

Rose backed away, moving toward her daughter. "I'm here now. Let me get her settled down." She lifted Celeste out of the playpen and her screams subsided into quiet, pathetic, hiccuping sobs. Jared came toward her again, moving so fast, she thought he might hit her.

"I will never babysit her again," he said. "You understand me? You will never leave her with me. Ever again."

Something caught her eye on the kitchen counter. She looked past Jared and realized he'd stacked his empty beer cans there — at least eight of them. She knew better than to say anything.

He attacked again. "That's right. I had a few beers. I saw that post. You said you were going out shopping, but you were actually out drinking. You left your child here, miserable and crying the entire time, so you could go out drinking and partying with your friends."

"I — we didn't —"

He cut her off. "There's no use denying it. I saw you there, a drink in your hand and a smile on your face."

Arguing was futile. "I'm just going to put Celeste to bed."

"You do that."

She crept out of the living room and into Celeste's bedroom, where she spent the night on the floor.

Yes, Rose thought, opening her eyes and blinking, relieved to find herself in her classroom again, and not in that tiny apartment she'd shared with Jared. She remembered. Like it was yesterday. She took a deep breath and said to Taylor, "You're right. I'll delete it right now." And she did.

Still, as she went about the rest of her after-school routine, picking up Celeste, grabbing groceries for dinner, tidying up the apartment, cooking, and making her way to their high school campout, she experienced flashbacks of other situations with Jared.

It was summertime when Celeste was learning to walk. She was about about eleven months old, and Rose stayed home with her while Jared went to work. One day, Celeste fell and hit her mouth on the edge of the coffee table. Her lip bled and swelled, and by the time Jared got home, she looked like she'd been in a fight.

"What happened?" he demanded, accusatory.

Rose thought he was joking, insinuating she'd done something to hurt the baby. Smiling, she said, "Oh, you know, the perils of learning to walk. She hit her face on the table. Got herself good, poor baby."

Jared's expression showed no trace of humor and his voice was a low growl when he said, "You let this happen."

Fear prickled along Rose's spine and up the back of her neck. "I couldn't have prevented it. She just lost her balance."

He picked up Celeste, and Rose had to stop herself from snatching their daughter out of his arms. "She's bleeding."

"Well, she was, but it's stopped now."

"I don't know if it's safe to leave her with you. You seem to be missing that protective maternal instinct. I never should have trusted you to be the mother of my child."

His cruel words caused her to recoil. How could he believe that? Since the moment she'd found out she was pregnant, she'd considered motherhood a privilege, an honor ... and protecting her unborn child was her first duty.

At the library, she checked out all the books on how to have a healthy pregnancy, and followed all the advice. She didn't miss a single doctor appointment. Took her prenatal vitamins every single day. Doubled her water intake. Played classical music for the baby through headphones pressed to her belly.

At that moment, Celeste screamed and reached for Rose. Jared's energy probably scared her as much as it scared Rose. Instead of handing her off, though, he marched out of the house. Rose followed him, and stood in the driveway, frozen in disbelief, while he buckled Celeste into her infant seat, got in the car, and drove away.

Another time, Celeste's teething had kept her — and Rose — awake night after night for what felt like weeks. In reality, it lasted only about six days. On the seventh night, Jared woke Rose at three a.m., his grip on her upper arm so painful she gasped. "How could you sleep through this?!"

Only then did she realize she'd slept right through Celeste's shrieking cries.

"I'm sorry," she managed through gritted teeth. "I'll get her."

She wanted to ask why he couldn't get up with Celeste, just this one time, after Rose had done it every night for the past week. But instead, she scuttled out of the bedroom, wanting to avoid a confrontation.

After she'd soothed the baby and gotten her back to sleep, she returned to the bedroom, where Jared sat on the edge of the bed waiting for her. The way he looked up at her, from under his angry eyebrows, gave her the creeps. "You'd never be able to parent that baby without me."

Rose knew that wasn't true ... and was starting to believe that maybe parenting that baby without him was the only way to keep her safe.

Five years later, modern-day Rose tucked their daughter — *her* daughter — into bed on the couch in the teachers lounge at her place of work and wondered, not for the first time, if Jared was right.

If she were truly capable of raising a child, wouldn't they be going to bed in a nice, cozy house? Wouldn't she be planning a home-cooked breakfast instead of heating frozen breakfast sandwiches? Wouldn't she feel like she had it all together instead of experiencing a constant struggle?

As she lay down on the second couch, listening to Celeste fall asleep, she realized she didn't know. Maybe Jared had been right all along.

Chapter Six

The end-of-day bell rang, and Mac practically sprinted down the hall and out the door of Prescott High School's main building. He couldn't wait to get home, change out of his work clothes, and crack open a cold one. Maybe even two cold ones. Outside, the sun practically blinded him. The weather was unseasonably hot. Summer was over, but the thermometer in Mac's car told him it was ninety-one degrees.

If he were still in San Francisco, the end of September would mean he could put down the top on his car. But not in Arizona. He turned the air conditioner on full-blast and rolled down his windows, just to let in some fresh air until the AC got going.

He'd promised his mom he would make chicken fried steak for dinner, and his mouth watered thinking about that. The crispy breading, the juicy steak, the gravy saturating the mashed potatoes. He backed out of his parking spot and waved at a couple of his fellow teachers as he drove off campus. The air coming out of the vents finally felt cold, so he rolled up the windows and turned up the music. The song that came through the speakers was about living as if you knew you were going to die. He took it as a sign: he had to ask Rose out. Yes, he decided, he'd give himself one week to build up the courage, and then he would go for it.

Although Prescott *was* completely different from San Francisco, as he drove through its quaint, bustling downtown, with its austere courthouse, the lush green lawn surrounding it, and the hustling busy-ness of a city center, he felt energized. He belonged in a city. It didn't have to be San Francisco, he thought. But the closeness of all the people in the metropolis made him feel like part of a community, part of something alive.

Stopped at a red light, he watched a family — two parents and two kids — playing Frisbee on the grass. They were all pretty good, except the mom, who threw the Frisbee over the head of every person she threw it to. Mac felt himself smiling as he watched the family laugh. The son, who Mac guessed was probably around thirteen, made a show of jumping as high as he could, arms outstretched above his head when his mom was going to throw to throw the Frisbee to him. All four of them seemed to have a fit of the giggles. Someone honked, and Mac realized the light had turned green.

Within a few minutes, he was out of the city and turning onto Williamson Valley Road, which would take him into the country. As the houses started thinning out and the land spread into wide pastures punctuated by roomy ranch-style houses, Mac started to feel claustrophobic.

Pop!

As if the universe itself for trying to prevent him from leaving the little city center, a tire went flat. His car veered to the left, toward oncoming traffic, and he fought to straighten the wheel and pull off the road, onto the shoulder. He put on his hazards and got out to assess the damage. The left front tire was shot. Completely flat. There was no way it was repairable. Mac groaned. Swore. Putting on the spare tire would add twenty minutes to his trip home. Mac wasn't a big crier, but he felt like he could burst into tears right then. All he wanted to do was go home and have his beer. He opened the trunk to get out the spare, and almost screamed when he realized the four-way wrench wasn't there. *Shit.* He'd left it at the farm when he changed his mom's tire the week before. He could kick himself.

Typically, he was very organized, fastidious. But lately, he'd been so discombobulated. His new life had so many moving parts, and obviously, he couldn't keep track of them all. He didn't want to bother his mom, so he called for roadside assistance and waited. A couple of farmers stopped to offer their help. But now that Mac knew firsthand how much they had to do when they got home that evening, he thanked them and sent them on their way.

Plus, neither of them could resist making cracks about his fancy car and delicate tires. He didn't care. He could've bought a truck when he moved out to Arizona, but his hot rod was one piece of his city life he couldn't bear to part with. An hour and a half after he made the call, the roadside assistance people showed up. They changed the tire in about seven seconds, and Mac made a mental note to put the four-way back in his trunk.

By the time he got home, he was sweaty and cranky. His mom greeted him in the driveway and noticed his mood right away. "Everything okay?"

"Just got a flat tire, that's all. It's fixed now, though. I'm just going to sit down and have a beer before I start the chores. And then I'll make you dinner, okay?"

"Okay, hon."

Inside, he grabbed a beer first thing, then took off his work shoes and flopped onto his dad's old recliner. Despite its age and and the worn leather on its arms, the chair was about as comfortable as a chair got. Afraid he might fall asleep if he reclined, Mac sat upright and took a swig of the beer, relishing the way the bubbles popped on his tongue.

Eleanor hovered in the kitchen doorway, a mother bird wanting to make sure her baby bird was all right. She'd always had a sense about these things, Mac thought, and he wished she'd outgrow it like he'd outgrown talking about his feelings.

"Your day go okay?"

He sighed. "It did. I'm just tired, that's all. Still recovering from the flat tire. Well, from waiting in the heat for ninety minutes."

"You did bring a city car into the country, you know." Her voice was gentle and teasing at the same time, and he offered her a small smile.

"I know. I just couldn't give it up, though."

"You can drive your dad's old truck any time," she said. Again.

"I know."

She broke eye contact and went into the kitchen.

"I'll at least start fixing supper while you relax. That way, when you come back, you can just do the big stuff."

Mac acquiesced. He knew the small stuff, like chopping vegetables and getting out jars, hurt his mom's hands, but also knew he had to let her do it. At least, once in a while. "Okay," he said. "Thank you, Mama."

He listened as she opened and shut the fridge, got out the cutting board and knife, and started chopping. Usually when they had the you-can-drive-the-truck conversation, he told her he couldn't bear the truck's squeaks and creaks. That he loved the speed and race-car handling of his beloved muscle car. That he couldn't stand to go slow, and was accustomed to zero-to-sixty in four seconds flat.

The truth, though, was that that truck was his dad's baby (much as his car was his). The old rust bucket smelled like Johnny Mac, Senior. No one had bothered to remove this things: the Leatherman tool he kept in the glove box, the old fleece-lined jacket laid out on the back seat, the soda can he spit his sunflower seed shells into.

Driving that truck would be like spending time with his dad's absence. And he just couldn't do it.

He finished off his beer and on his way through the kitchen to throw away the bottle, he stopped and kissed his mom on the top of her head, just like she used to do to him. She chuckled, and the sound followed him back to his bedroom, where he changed into his jeans and boots.

As much as he told himself he dreaded the chores, Mac felt calm settle over him when he went outside and got to work. His body ached from exhaustion, and so did his mind, if that were even possible. But the rhythm of feeding, watering, and milking numbed both his bones and his psyche. The racing thoughts that occupied his brain throughout the day fell away as the chores forced him to focus on the present moment. All the tension had mostly unraveled and he had almost finished the chores when he saw Pinky, his mom's favorite goat, had escaped from the fence once again. In the second after that, he realized he'd forgotten the welding helmet Craig Janssen had brought to the school for him. He had to repair that fence, tonight. Even if he put Pinky back in the pen, she would escape again before he even returned to the house. He groaned. Then called, "Pinky! Get back in here."

The goat's giant, soft ears perked up and turned toward him. She blinked and hopped away. Mac and his mom had spent a lot of time laughing at Pinky's hopping. Even in his frustration over forgetting the welding helmet, Mac found himself smiling. "You're a real pain in the butt, you know that?"

The goat hopped some more. Mac shook his head and resolved to go back to the school.

True to her word, Eleanor had chopped all the potatoes into nice, small cubes, and she'd set the water to boil.

She was nowhere to be found, so Mac hollered, "Thanks, Mom," and she hollered back from the other end of the house, "You're welcome, Sonny!"

Mac opened the fridge. His mouth watered as he gazed at the steaks. He'd committed to going back to the school, getting the helmet, and fixing the fence. But he would eat, first. And, to save time, he'd grill the steaks instead of battering and frying them. His vision of an early bedtime floating off into space, he put the potatoes into the pot of water on the stove.

Then, even though he wanted another beer, he grabbed a sparkling water out of the fridge and took the steaks out to the grill.

Again, as much as he told himself he was a city guy, looking out over the property during the golden hour — as the sun made its descent, washing the scene in its glow — he felt that calmness settling over him. Living on the farm didn't have to be permanent, but maybe he didn't have to be in such a rush to get back to the hustle and bustle.

When Mac and Eleanor sat down at the kitchen table, he told

her, "I'm going to have to run back over to the high school. I forgot that darn welding helmet, and Pinky's already out."

Eleanor shook her head. "I sure love that goat, but she is a real pain in the butt. Do you think the fence could wait 'til tomorrow?"

Mac stabbed a piece of his steak with his fork. He shook his head. "No. Did you hear those coyotes last night? If she stays out, whether it's because she's a pain in the butt or because she can't get back in, she's dinner for those guys."

Eleanor nodded. "Your daddy used to declare war on those coyotes. You remember that?"

Mac smiled. "I sure do. I don't think I'm willing to go quite as far as he did. But I do want to keep Pinky safe. So I'll run back in after dinner."

"I appreciate it. Want me to go with you? Keep you company?"

He hated the idea of dragging her out that late, but also knew she was lonely. She hadn't been getting out to the Bingo games and book clubs she did before his dad died. The little errand would be good for her.

"Sure. That would be nice. We can take a ride with the top down."

At the school, Mac took the bus route and drove right up to the building. "Want to come in with me?"

To his surprise, she did. "Someone could really stand to grease those hinges," she said when he unlocked the door and pulled it open. "Remind me tomorrow morning and I'll send you with a can of your daddy's grease."

Inside, they walked down the hallway, their footsteps in sync and echoing off the linoleum tiles and cement block walls.

"Somebody here?" Eleanor said. "There's a light on just down the hall."

"That's the teachers lounge," Mac said. "Somebody probably just left the light on. I'll go turn it off, and then we can head upstairs."

He picked up his pace, his long legs propelling him forward and ahead of Eleanor. When he reached the teachers lounge door, he looked in through the window before opening it.

He yelped when he saw someone in there, and that someone looked up from the couch, eyes round, mouth open in shock. That someone was Rose Coffey. And she was wearing pajamas. Pajamas that lit his fire. Literally. He could feel the heat traveling from his core to the tips of his fingers and soles of his feet.

Chapter Seven

Mac's, tall, broad-shouldered silhouette appearing in the window of the teachers lounge door startled Rose. She jumped, adrenaline surging through her veins, making every nerve ending stand at attention. Mac pulled open the door, and as relieved as she was that the intruder wasn't a serial killer, she was also completely mortified it was someone she knew — even more so that it was Mac, the central figure in so many of her daydreams.

He said, "Rose!" just as she said, "Mac!"

She put her hand on her chest, and could feel her heart beating against her palm.

They both said, "What are you doing here?"

Mac, his handsome features twisted in confusion, pointed toward the staircase in the hall behind him. "I was just going to my classroom to get something I forgot. That welding helmet we talked about at lunch. Not a chainsaw."

Rose felt her own face contort into a grimace. "We were just having a camp out."

When Mac noticed Celeste, he startled just as much as Rose had a minute before. Rose glanced down at her daughter, glad to see that she was still asleep despite the intrusion. Looking back at Mac, she couldn't quite read his expression. She didn't spend too much time trying though, because the door opened wider, and Mac stepped aside quickly as if he had just remembered someone else was with him. Rose wondered briefly if it was a woman — a woman he was dating — but got her answer when the opener of the door squeezed past Mac and Rose got a good look at her.

"Rose, this is my mom, Eleanor. Mom, Rose Coffey, English teacher extraordinaire."

Did he consider Rose extraordinary? Wait. That shouldn't be her focus. Oh, great. Not only did Rose have to face Mac, but now she had to face his mother, too.

To Rose's surprise, Mac's mom smiled warmly. "Hello, Rose. It's lovely to meet you."

She spoke in a hushed voice, her gaze resting on Celeste for a couple of seconds. When she looked at Rose again, Rose felt like they were connecting, mother to mother. She would have expected judgment from someone discovering her in that awkward situation, but there was none. Rose searched her mind for something to say. Something clever, funny maybe, to break the ice. The clock ticked, punctuating the silence. Rose stood up and smoothed her pajamas, as if running her hands over them would somehow make her look less ridiculous. Her nervous system had finally caught up, and shame set in, fast and hard. Her face flamed and her palms were sweaty against the fabric of her pajamas.

This is awkward.

Eleanor gathered her wits first. "Why are you sleeping here, Ms. Coffey, if you don't mind me asking?"

Rose saw nothing but kindness in the woman's features. "Kind of a long story."

Mac and his mom continued to look at her.

"It's the only quiet place we've been able to find," she started ... and then found that the words flowed out like water. "We have college students for neighbors. I've tried everything, but no matter what I do, we can't sleep through their noise. Then Celeste is tired the next day, which is pretty much every day, and it's hard to get her ready to go on time. Then she has a rough day at school, a rough evening at home, and —"

"It turns into a vicious cycle," Eleanor finished. The unexpected understanding made Rose's chin tremble.

Do not cry.

"Apartment living isn't really the best when you're right next to a college." Mac's voice was soft and quiet. "My first apartment in San Francisco was right across the street from a community college. I don't think I got a solid night's sleep more than two nights in a row for as long as I lived there."

Rose's voice cracked when she said, "We've tried several apartments. I thought this one was going to be it."

Mac pushed the door open a little farther, and gestured for his mom to go in. He followed her and, to Rose's dismay, they both sat down at the table. As soon as she'd seen them, she'd hoped for the quickest possible conversation. But now it seemed like they planned on hanging around.

Mac put his elbows on his knees and leaned toward Rose. "How long has this been going on?"

Unable to bear eye contact, Rose looked at Celeste, who lay on the couch as peaceful as could be, her arms flung overhead and her mouth open just the tiniest bit.

"A couple weeks," Rose whispered. She looked up at Mac's mom, and then at Mac. "I thought it would be for just one night. But it was so quiet here. We finally slept. And it felt so good. And then, each night, at the apartment, I would tell myself, you've got to sleep here tonight. But we'd have dinner, and I'd be so tired I just craved sleep." Her laugh sounded almost like a whimper. "And we would find ourselves here again."

"How much longer on your lease?" Mac asked.

"I can get out of it in a month," Rose said. "And I'm sure I could find another apartment. It's just that we've tried so many different apartments. And I'm starting to think we're doomed. Or that finding someplace quiet is actually impossible."

With that statement, much to Rose's embarrassment, she burst into tears. Fortunately, she thought darkly, she had lots of practice crying without waking her daughter. Eleanor was at her side, perched next to her on the couch, her arms around Rose's shoulders, a second later. She made gentle shushing noises and rubbed Rose's upper arms. "It'll be all right, now. We'll help you. You don't have to do this alone."

Her kindness made Rose cry even harder. "I'm so sorry. I didn't want to get anyone else wrapped up in my problems. Taylor and Jessie, they've offered to help a million times. But they've already done so much. And I couldn't possibly ask you to help."

"Why don't we pack up your things?" Mac said. "Mom and I will take you over to the Hassayampa. It's nice and quiet, especially during the week."

Rose sniffled. "I can't afford that place. The rent for my new apartment is already stretching our budget as it is. Hotels costs even more."

"Don't worry about that," Mac said. "We'll take care of it."

"I couldn't possibly ask that of you."

"Honey, you stop that, now," Eleanor said. "You didn't ask. He offered. Now, let's pack your stuff up and get you to a place where you can get a good night's sleep."

Having someone (or two someones) there to tell Rose what to do, to take charge, felt so good, Rose found she couldn't do anything other than obey Eleanor and Mac. Together, they packed up the few items Rose had brought to the school. Mac filled his arms with the majority of the stuff, handing Eleanor a couple of things to carry.

All Rose had to carry was Celeste. This little sharing of her burden made Rose's soul feel so much lighter. Guilt remained, a lead weight in her belly. But, finally sharing her big secret was someone (or two someones), made Rose feel like she could breathe just a little easier. When they got outside, Mac looked around. "Where's your car?"

Sheepish, Rose looked at the ground. "Student parking lot."

Mac just nodded, as if he understood why she'd parked there. "If you give me your keys, I'll go get it so you don't have to carry Celeste all the way up there." Rose dug her keys out of her purse and handed them over. He jogged off, and after Rose and Eleanor watched him for a couple of seconds, Rose said, "I can't tell you how much I appreciate your help."

"We're part of a community," Eleanor said. "It's what neighbors do for one another."

Rose and Mac parked side by side in front of the hotel. Eleanor offered to stay with Celeste while Mac and Rose checked in. Despite all the chaos, Celeste was still asleep, and so deeply that a little string of drool hung from one corner of her mouth. It would be nice to be able to carry her straight up to the room and tuck her into bed.

Rose nearly went weak in the knees, imagining the luxury of climbing into a real bed ... and not just any bed, but a hotel bed, perfectly made with its clean sheets and downy pillows.

For a moment, when Rose and Mac walked into the hotel lobby together, she pretended they were a couple.

Leaning over to whisper in her ear, he said, "I asked for a room on the top floor, so you won't have neighbors pounding on your ceiling all night."

Rose wasn't sure what gave her the chills — his breath in her ear, or his thoughtfulness.

Mac gave his name at the check-in counter and asked them to add Rose's to the reservation. When the receptionist asked him for a credit card for incidentals, he didn't even hesitate handing his over. The receptionist handed the keys to Mac.

Still side by side, they walked back out to the cars. Rose expected Mac and his mom to leave right away, but Mac said, "Let me help you up to your room. You have a lot to carry."

Rose opened her mouth to protest, but he held up a hand. "First of all, you really do have a lot to carry. Second, my mom is right there. She will literally disown me if I don't walk you to your room."

Rose could feel Eleanor's eyes on them, and she wondered what the other woman was thinking. She certainly didn't want Mac's mom to think she was seducing him, so she could use him for his money. Or his hotel reservations. Also, she didn't want Mac to get in trouble with his mom.

"Come on. You'll actually be doing me a favor if you let me help you. I'll only have to make one trip."

"All right," Rose said, resigned.

She loaded Mac up with the suitcase, Celeste's special pillow, and the backpack. Then she got Celeste out of her booster seat and wished Mac's mom a good night. The weight of Celeste's body, warm and droopy on her own, made Rose crave sleep.

Once they were inside the elevator, Rose said, "Thank you so much for putting us up in a hotel. You didn't have to do this, you know."

Mac shrugged. "I know, but I want to."

The elevator stopped and its robotic voice announced they'd reached the fifth floor. Arms full, Mac gestured with his head for Rose to go out ahead of him. She did, and followed the signs to her room. She and Mac stood outside the door, facing each other. "Thanks again. I don't know how I'll repay you."

"That's not necessary. It's just an act of kindness."

Rose nodded. She unlocked the door and pushed it open, then stuck out her foot to hold it. "I've got it from here," she told Mac. "I'll just lay Celeste down and come back for all of the stuff."

Mac gave her a single nod and set down her things. Rose was grateful her arms were full, because she wanted to thank Mac with a hug. Maybe a kiss, maybe more. But none of those seemed appropriate at the moment. So, she offered him a smile, hoping it expressed her gratitude.

His gaze held hers. "I hope you sleep well, Rose."

Then he was gone, leaving behind his pine-tree scent and a wistfulness Rose didn't experience often. She watched him walk down the hall and wished she could call for him to come back.

Chapter Eight

All the way back down the hallway, inside the elevator, and through the hotel lobby to his car, Mac thought about Rose. That first morning he'd seen her leaving the school as he was arriving for zero hour, he sensed something off. He'd been right. Rose said she and her daughter had slept at the school for a couple of weeks — so that encounter must have followed one of their first nights in the teachers lounge. Celeste had mentioned a campout, but Rose had changed the subject.

When he got in the car, his mom said, "She seems nice," as if they had just met Rose at a picnic or run into her at the grocery store, not as if they had discovered her sleeping at the school.

"She is. Very nice." He started the car and only then did he glance over at his mom, who sat there in the passenger seat with a cat-that-ate-the-canary smile.

"What are you smiling at?"

"Oh, nothing. Only the fact that you were so distracted by Ms. Rose Coffey that you left the welding helmet at the school again. We never even went up to your classroom."

Mac groaned and rammed his forehead against the steering wheel a few times. "We'll just have to go back. We can't have Pinky out all night."

"Tell me more about this Rose." His mom leaned her head against the headrest as he started the car and pulled out of the parking spot.

"If we're being honest, I wish I knew a little more about her. She's an English teacher, single mom. She likes spicy food."

"How long have you had your eye on her?"

Mac looked at his mom just long enough for her to flash him a smile before he returned his eyes to the road. "Why would you think I have my eye on her?"

"Oh, I don't know. Maybe it was just how you had your eyes on her all night."

"You can't blame a guy. We walked in on her basically breaking and entering at the school. She was wearing pajamas. And, she's practically homeless. If anything, I had compassion for her, not eyes on her."

Eleanor shrugged. He caught the movement out of the corner of his eye. "Okay, Sonny. Whatever you say." It was her typical response during any conversation where they shared two different viewpoints. Instead of arguing, she would just say, "Okay, Sonny," and leave it at that. The pattern was both endearing and infuriating.

"Want me to run you back to the house before I go get that helmet?" Mac tried a change of subject.

"No thanks, hon," his mom said. "I wouldn't want you to waste all that gas driving home and then back into town and back again."

Mac nodded. That was reasonable. Even if he felt the need to be alone at the moment, to examine the feelings he experienced whenever Rose was present.

The school was still quiet and deserted. Mac jogged up to his classroom, grabbed the helmet, and jogged back down the stairs. In the hallway before he reached the door, he spotted something on the floor. In the dim light from his phone flashlight, he recognized it as a ratty stuffed animal ... maybe a rabbit? Or a puppy? The stuffed animal may not be recognizable, but Mac knew it belonged to Celeste, and he knew he had to get it back to her as soon as possible. The last thing he wanted was for her to realize it was missing and cause Rose yet another sleepless night. He wished he'd gotten Rose's phone number. Knocking on her hotel room door at night would probably scare her, give her an adrenaline rush, and prevent her from sleeping afterwards. Still standing in the dark hallway, Mac dialed the number for the hotel and asked to be put through to her room. She answered right away, her voice uncertain.

Mac couldn't help himself. He pictured Rose, sitting on the edge of her bed in those pajamas. He could almost feel the soft, creamy skin on her thigh, how the weight of her breast would feel in his hand.

He could definitely feel the tightening of his pants. He cleared his throat. "Ms. Coffey. Rose."

"Mac?"

"Yeah." His mom would hate that he'd just drawled, "Yeah." He cleared his throat again. "Yes. I realized after I left the hotel that I'd forgotten to grab that welding helmet."

"Oh, I'm so sorry." She grimaced. "I guess we were a pretty big distraction."

Again, Mac imagined her skin against his palm, and thought she couldn't be more right. "No, I'm just forgetful," he lied. "But that's not the reason I'm calling. I went back to get it, and I found a stuffed animal on floor. I figure it belongs to Celeste. She probably dropped it on the way out."

Rose gasped. "Oh, you found Bumpy. Thank goodness. She hasn't noticed yet that he's missing, but I know if she did, it would be full-on panic mode."

Mac couldn't believe the level of pleasure he felt at her gratitude. "I'll bring it over real quick, if you don't mind."

"No, no, that's okay! You've already done so much. I'll just get it from you tomorrow. If she does realize, I'll just tell her you and Bumpy are having a sleepover."

Weighing the pros and cons, Mac wavered. Keeping the stuffed animal overnight meant Celeste might wake and realize it was gone. It also meant an excuse to talk to Rose the next day. But, that was selfish. "I insist. Knowing you've been struggling to sleep for the past couple of weeks, I couldn't, in good conscience, keep this ... whatever it is overnight, knowing Celeste might wake up and want it."

Rose chuckled, and the sound sent another wave of pleasure through Mac's body, skittering over his skin. "I appreciate your delicate handling of Bumpy's description. He's a bit worn out, isn't he?"

Mac found himself laughing, too. "I didn't want to offend you, but when I picked him off the floor, I thought, what the hell is this?"

Rose's laughter, wind chimes on a warm spring day, came through the earpiece. "I know," she squeaked. "She loves that thing. I've tried to get her to let me replace it, but she won't. It's probably carrying about eight thousand different germs."

Mac's smile was making his cheeks hurt. "I'll run it over. It's really no big deal."

They hung up and still grinning, Mac jogged out of the building and back to his car.

"What are you so smiley about?" his mom wanted to know. He held up the stuffed animal, and his mom eyes widened.

"I take it that well-loved, yet unidentifiable creature belongs to Rose's daughter."

"Yes, it does. And to prevent what Rose described as full-on panic mode, I'm going to run it back to the hotel."

He handed the stuffed animal to Eleanor, and she set it in her lap, facing forward as if it were alive.

A few minutes later, Mac knocked on Rose's hotel room door, and the sight of her when she opened it took his breath away. She was so, so beautiful. She'd pulled her hair into a bun on top of her head, and despite the attempt to tame her curls, a handful of them escaped, spraying out of the bun. Her eyes, an unusual shade of all kinds of brown, danced with humor, and Mac could see laughter lines around them. He wished, so desperately, that he could reach out and touch her.

"Special delivery." He held up the stuffed animal. She took it from him, and he could have sworn that she intentionally brushed her fingers against his. She held the stuffed animal against her chest, making him jealous. "Thank you so much. Crisis averted."

"You're welcome. I really hope you get some sleep."

As he walked down the hallway and back to his car once again, he knew one thing for certain: he wouldn't be getting any.

* * *

The interaction with Rose reenergized Mac and he found himself whistling as he dragged the welder out near the fence, hooked it up to an extension cord, and adjusted the helmet to fit him.

Just before he put on the helmet to get started, he heard his mom's voice. "I can't remember last the last time I heard whistling like that out here."

Mac smiled at her. "I'm just glad to be getting this done. We'll keep our little escape artist safe."

As if on cue, Pinky bleated at them from the other side of the fence.

"We'll see who gets the last laugh, Miss Pinky," Mac said to the goat.

"Since you have your work cut out for you, I'm going to go ahead and go to bed," Eleanor said. "I'll see you in the morning."

"Good night, Mama."

He fired up the welder and put on the helmet. Pinky had the good sense to keep her distance, but she watched him, ears twitching as the sparks flew. Once he finished the repair, Mac lured the little goat over with a special treat. Fortunately, Pinky wasn't feeling too frisky anymore, and she allowed him to lead her back through the gate and into the safety of the goat pen.

After putting away the supplies, Mac found that as soon as the task no longer occupied his mind, his thoughts wandered again to Rose. He wished she'd gotten her number. He would give anything to be able to text her, to tell her he'd repaired the fence and say goodnight. Walking back up to the house, he thought that he'd like even more to occupy the same space as her. To tell her goodnight in person, press his lips to hers, stretch his body out next to hers. But, she was vulnerable, he reminded himself as he let himself in through the kitchen door. And he didn't plan to stick around forever. The first chance he got, he'd head back to San Francisco. She deserved more than that. The only fair thing to do was to keep his feelings from her. And take a cold shower. That's just what Mac did before finally falling into a dreamless sleep.

The next morning when Mac came back into the kitchen at five after doing the chores, Eleanor presented him with a basket. She'd filled it with muffins, fruit, bottled juice, ground coffee, nuts, and chocolate bars, and she'd placed a bouquet of flowers on top.

"For Rose," she said. "And her daughter, of course."

"Mom." Mac drew the word out into two syllables like he had as a kid. "This is so sweet of you. But I can't bring this to her at school. Not only will it give her the wrong impression, but also, it will make people suspicious."

His mom had the audacity to look amused. "And what is the wrong impression? That you're head over heels for this woman?"

Mac made a dismissive gesture with one hand. "I won't even dignify that with a response."

"Tell her it's from me. I don't want you getting credit for my thoughtfulness, anyway."

Mac shook his head. "*You* bring it to her. *You* tell her it's from you."

"That's actually a good idea. I'll take it over to the hotel right now, before she goes to school."

Why didn't I think of that?

"You didn't think of that, my boy, because you haven't started thinking outside the box, yet. I have a sense that when it comes to Ms. Coffey, that's what you're going to have to do."

"I'll take it to her." He snatched the basket from his mom and turned around as if to leave right away. Then he realized Rose was probably still asleep, and he needed to shower and change before he left the house. So he set it the on the counter again.

"After I shower," he snapped.

His mom laughed in response. "Oh, what a good idea."

Chapter Nine

Rose couldn't believe how refreshed she felt after sleeping in the cool, dark hotel room, between the crisp white sheets, her head on that just-right down pillow. Because it was so dark and quiet, she was able to get up and shower without waking Celeste. When she finally sat on the edge of Celeste's bed and rubbed her arms to get her up, Celeste yawned, opened her eyes, and said, "I slept good, Mommy!"

Thanks to Mac.

"Me, too."

"This is a really nice hotel," Celeste said, as if she had any frame of reference.

Smiling, Rose brushed Celeste's hair away from her face. "It sure is. And even though it felt kind of like a fairytale to sleep here, now we have to get up and get on with real life."

She laid out Celeste's clothes and went back into the bathroom to do her makeup and hair.

"Someone knocked on the door," Celeste called a minute later, her voice singsongy and unconcerned.

Rose's heart practically leapt into her throat. Who would be knocking on the door before six in the morning? *Jared. He found out where we are.* She pushed that thought from her mind. "I'll get it, honey. You just keep getting dressed."

Hands shaking, Rose opened the door. "Mac." Her heart had caught up to her nerves, and pounded hard against her ribcage. She realized she'd forgotten to be conscious of her half-ready state, but as soon as Mac saw her, his gaze raked down her body. She saw lust flare in his eyes, and she saw him consciously tamp it down. Seeing his reaction to her, like that, sent a warm bolt of lust through her body. It settled between her legs, and she wished she were alone in that hotel room. She definitely would have invited him in. *Who are you kidding? You'd be too scared.*

She'd been so focused on Mac's face that she hadn't noticed he held a large basket in his arms, which he now lifted toward her in offering. "Special delivery."

"I could get used to special deliveries from you." She took the basket and let her fingers rest on his for a moment.

He dropped his hands, then leaned against the door jamb and crossed his arms. "If we're being honest, my mom made this basket for you and Celeste. I just offered to bring it to you since I was coming into town for zero hour."

Without warning, Rose's eyes prickled with tears. "Thank you, both. Will you please tell your mom I really appreciate this? I was just thinking about what I was going to feed Celeste for breakfast. I had some frozen breakfast sandwiches, but they're still in the teachers lounge freezer."

Mac smiled. "My mom's baking is one hundred percent better than any frozen breakfast sandwich."

His reaction, and his pride in his mom's baking, warmed Rose's heart, and she told him as much. "You guys are obviously close. It's really sweet."

"We've spent a lot of time together since my dad passed."

"I can tell how close you are. And I don't think I said it before, but I'm sorry about your dad."

Mac shifted, stood up straight. "Thanks. It's been nice to spend time with my mom, though. And her baking." He winked. "Now you get to experience it for yourself."

"Thank you again. I can't wait."

"You're welcome." With obvious reluctance, he pointed down the hallway. "I've got to get to zero hour. So I'll see you later."

It was only after he was gone, and she and Celeste each had a muffin and some fruit, that Rose remembered she wanted to talk to Mac about one more thing. She'd just have to catch him at school, and hope no one overheard them.

Rose knew from half-stalking Mac that his prep period was right before lunch. So, if she could find someone to come in at the end of her fourth-period class, just for a few minutes, she could sneak up to his room to talk to him. She arranged for one of the teacher's aides to come in, and gave her kids an assignment to keep them busy.

As she walked up to Mac's room, she had to resist the urge to look behind her to see if anyone had noticed or was following her ... which was ridiculous. Teachers walked around the building all the time, visited one another, discussed how they could make their lessons overlap. Really, the English teacher visiting one of the science teachers shouldn't be a big deal. Still, every time Rose heard footsteps or a door opening, she flinched and looked around.

When she finally reached his classroom, she saw through the window that he was sitting at his desk, his forehead resting in one hand. He sat so still, she thought he must be distressed. She knocked quietly on the door, but he didn't look up. She knocked a little louder, and he did a full on startle, arms flailing, legs flailing, eyes wide. Just as suddenly as those movements happened, he stilled his body and smiled at her. When she came in, he burst into laughter. "You caught me sleeping."

"Sleeping? Is that what normal people do during their prep period? I always thought we were supposed to grade papers or write lesson plans."

"It's what I do, these days. I can't seem to get through without a nap."

"No judgment here," Rose said, holding up her hands. "As you know, I've slept on campus, too."

Mac smiled at her, and she smiled back.

"Anyway, now that you've startled me awake and given me an

adrenaline rush that will keep me that way for the rest of the day, how can I help you?"

Again, Rose looked around, to make sure no one was within earshot. She walked up to the desk closest to Mac's and sat down in it. "I know I probably don't have to say this, but I was hoping you'd keep this whole me-sleeping-at-the-school, you-putting-me-up-in-a-hotel thing between us."

Something passed over his features then, and Rose wished she knew him better so she could define it. Was it hurt? Irritation? Surprise?

He pressed his lips together, inhaled. "Of course, Rose. You're right, you didn't have to ask me. But I understand where you're coming from. And of course I will keep it between us. And Celeste. And my mom."

They both smiled at that, and Rose found herself wishing she could stay in his classroom with him, through the lunch period. The bell rang and Rose stood up. "Thank you for hearing me out. And for saying you won't tell anyone I've been having clandestine campouts with my daughter in the teachers lounge. And thank you for delivering that basket this morning. And thank you, again, for putting us up in a hotel. I slept better than I have been a long time."

Mac stood, too. "You're welcome. Please let me know if there's anything else I can do."

Rose nodded. Mac nodded. They stood there, unmoving. The sounds of two thousand students being released to lunch crescendoed, and Rose looked at the classroom door. "I'd better go. My lunch is downstairs."

"Okay," Mac said. "Thanks for stopping by."

Rose paused before leaving the classroom, and looked both ways through the window before opening the door. She slipped out, only to hear someone calling her name right away.

"Jessie!" Her friend caught up to her. "How are you today?"

"More importantly, how are you? I just saw you sneaking out of Johnny Mac's classroom." She wiggled her eyebrows at Rose, and despite Rose's protests that it hadn't been a romantic meeting, she felt her face burning.

Fortunately, Principal Vasquez chose that moment to catch up to Rose and Jessie.

"Ms. Coffey! A word?"

Rose's armpits prickled with sweat, and her heart raced. Had he somehow discovered she been sleeping in the teachers lounge? What if there were cameras? She'd never considered that. Jessie, apparently unbothered by Ernie's request, bumped her shoulder against Rose's. "Later."

"Bye, Jess." Rose knew darn well that Jessie's "later" meant she expected Rose to tell her later why she'd been in Mac's classroom — not that she'd see her later. Rose's palms were now slick with sweat. Panic forced her to stop walking, and students adjusted their paths to go around her.

Ernie inclined his head. "Let's walk. Lunchtime is short, and I'm sure you have a meal to eat."

Rose's mouth had gone dry. She licked her lips nodded. "How can I help you?" she said as they fell into step, finding a spot in the tide of students making its way down the hall.

"As you know, homecoming is coming up."

Oh. Homecoming.

Relief replaced fear, making Rose's vision black around the edges. Trying to be discreet, she inhaled through her nose and exhaled through her mouth. "Yes. Homecoming is coming up." She added a laugh, and it sounded high-pitched and awkward.

"Have you seen the theme for this year?" His tone was casual, but she knew he was dead serious about teachers reading his weekly email updates. She was almost positive she'd seen *something* about homecoming, but she'd been so distracted, she hadn't really paid it much attention. "I admit, I saw something about it in one of the weekly emails, but I don't remember the details."

She grimaced at him, hoping she looked somewhat apologetic. He waved a hand at her. "Doesn't matter. The theme is heroes from literature. And, who better than the English teachers to step in as advisors for each class?"

"Who better, indeed?"

"Great." Ernie clapped, just once, clasping his hands under his sternum. "I've assigned you to the junior class. What do you think about, say, Shakespeare?" Before she could answer, he said, "I've made up a schedule. I'll email it to you. First meeting is next week."

"Great!"

And then Ernie was gone, and Rose walked the rest of the way to the teachers lounge, wondering how, with everything she had on her plate, she'd agreed to that. Still, this could be a fun distraction.

After school, Taylor and Jessie came into Rose's classroom.

"Well, what happened?" Jessie asked. "You look about hundred percent better today than you did yesterday. Did you finally get a good night's sleep?"

"Yes," Rose said, hearing the gratitude in her own voice.

Her friends both smiled.

"What changed?" Taylor said. "Did you soundproof your ceiling? Call the police on your college neighbors? Dig an underground bedroom?"

Rose froze. She couldn't tell them what had changed. She couldn't admit that, number one, she'd been sleeping at the school, and number two, Mac had caught her and then put her up in a hotel. It was humiliating on so many levels.

"I don't know," she lied. "Everything just miraculously fell into place. Even if it's just for one night, I'll take it."

Jessie raised one eyebrow. "I have a feeling there's something you're not telling us."

Rose should have known. The three of them had been best friends for years. Of *course* Jessie would know if she wasn't being entirely honest. "What do you mean?"

"You come to school today looking like a million bucks. After looking like a disaster — sorry, but true — the past few weeks. And then, I see you today, sneaking out of Johnny Mac's classroom —"

"What?" Taylor's eyebrows were practically in her hairline. "Sneaking out? That sounds very sneaky."

"Exactly," Jessie said. She held up her pointer finger. "Sneaking out. If she were there on school business, she would have walked out, all casual. But no. She was sneaking out. I saw her through the window. She looked up and down the hall, to see if anyone would see her coming out. And then when she did open the door, it was like she tried to turn herself into water, slide out, be invisible."

Rose shook her head. "You are so full of it. I looked both ways because the lunch bell rang, and I didn't want to get trampled by students."

"Ah." Jessie raised an eyebrow.

"It's true! Besides. I was talking to Johnny Mac about official school business. I was asking for his help with the homecoming float. Principal Vasquez asked me to be an advisor."

There. That should do it.

"Aha!" Now, Jessie was using her pointer finger again, this time pointing it directly at Rose. "Ernie didn't ask you to be an advisor until after I saw you sneaking out of Johnny Mac's room. Ergo, you were not talking to Johnny Mac about homecoming. You were there for another reason. A sneaky reason."

Taylor looked from Jessie to Rose and back to Jessie again. Rose knew she was caught, but she kept trying anyway. "Ernie asked me earlier."

"Did not."

"How do you know?" Rose said.

"Because I eavesdropped. I pretended to walk away, but I stayed close enough to hear what he was saying to you. Which means, you're not being truthful with us. And I want to know why."

Chapter Ten

During the next week, Mac didn't see as much of Rose as he would have liked. He still hadn't come up with a clever way to ask for her number so he could ask her out (and he realized he could ask her out in person and that his own anxiety was putting up the you-must-ask-for-her-number roadblock).

Between her regular duties and her new homecoming duties, plus her rushing to get Celeste after work, she always seemed too busy to chat. And Mac's never-ending list of farm chores and various repairs kept him equally occupied.

When he realized exactly one week had passed since he made the hotel reservation for Rose and Celeste and he still hadn't talked to her, he forced himself to find an opening. He knew her prep period was right before his. So, just as she'd done the week before, he arranged for someone to sit with his class under the guise of having to go to the office to make copies. On the way through, he swung by Rose's classroom. The door was open — he noticed she didn't usually close it until the end of the day — and she sat at her desk, a huge book open in front of her.

He knocked on the door jamb as he walked in and said, "Oh, so this is what normal people do during their prep period. They read. They're productive."

She looked up at him, smiling, and he was insanely pleased that she got his joke.

"I don't know if I would consider myself a normal person. But yes, I try to be productive during my prep, since it's one of the only times I get peace and quiet during the day."

Just as Rose had the week before, Mac sat in a desk right next to hers. Before he could say, "Listen, I've been trying to come up with a way to ask," or, "I was wondering if I could get your digits," or something actually clever, she said, "You're probably here for an update on the living situation. I wanted to let you know that I've put in applications at seven different places. Four houses and three apartments."

No wonder she'd been MIA. She was hustling, looking for a more permanent living situation. He wanted to say, "No wonder I haven't seen you," or, "Actually, that's not why I'm here. I'd pay for a hotel for you forever." Instead, he said, "Wow, you've been productive. Let me know how those turn out."

"I will." She smiled at him, and the way her eyes crinkled at the corners, and the little dimple that appeared on one side of her mouth, made him feel all warm and fuzzy inside. And apparently, stupid. Because he couldn't find the words to say what he wanted to say.

"Anyway. Between that and all of this homecoming stuff, I've been really busy. Can you believe they expect me to help supervise the building of a float?"

"I'm sure you're capable," Mac said. "Plus, can't you turn all your juniors into little minions and have them do your bidding? Surely there are a handful of students who can use power tools."

Rose looked thoughtful. "Ah, yes. And I hadn't thought of this until now, but I'm sure I could ask parents to help."

Suddenly, Mac pictured bare-chested single dads, with six-packs and tool belts, instructing Rose on how to run a drill. Jealousy surged through his veins. "I could help. I'm great with power tools. And, I was on my class's homecoming committee, all four years. We won best float my senior year."

Rose's eyes lit up. "Really? You'd help?"

"Sure." He shrugged as if it were no big deal. He stopped himself from saying something cheesy like, "If it means getting to spend more time with you," even though that's what he was thinking. She jumped out of her chair, came around her desk, grabbed his hands, and pulled him to standing. Then she flung her arms around his waist.

"Thank you, thank you, thank you." Her voice was muffled because her cheek was pressed against his chest. He wrapped his arms around her shoulders in reflex and found he didn't want to let go. She fit so perfectly in his embrace.

"You're welcome." He practically saw the light bulb illuminate above his head. "Maybe I should get your number. That way, you can tell me when we have meetings, and we can talk about the materials we need."

She gave him one more squeeze around the waist, and then stepped back and grabbed her phone off her desk. "Great idea."

He gave her his number, and he heard his phone ding a second later. He pulled it out of his pocket and read her message. *Thank you. I seriously owe you.*

His heart did a little pitter patter, and he saved her as a new contact and stowed his phone in his pocket.

"I'd better get going. I've got someone sitting with my class so I can go make copies."

Rose nodded. "And I've got to get through this scene in The Tempest before my next class comes in. Maybe I can even squeeze in a nap." She winked at him, and the warm and fuzzy feeling intensified. He didn't know what he just gotten himself into — adding homecoming float building to his long list of obligations was downright crazy — but he was pretty certain it was going to be worth it.

* * *

The next morning when Mac's alarm went off, his eyes felt dry and gritty. He couldn't remember the last time he'd felt so bone-weary. His new lifestyle was catching up with him. Turning off the alarm, he rolled out of bed and made his way to the bathroom, where he put the shower on its coldest setting.

Sure enough, the shower woke him right up, and he felt almost human when he walked into the kitchen and poured his coffee.

"Made the coffee strong this morning, huh?" His mom came into the kitchen, sniffing the air.

"I did."

"You're looking pretty tired there, boy." Eleanor cupped her hand around the back of his head and looked into his eyes. "You know, they say country life is the simple life. But it can also be a hard life. Maybe we should hire someone to come around, help out with things."

Mac shook his head. "It's okay. I've just got to toughen up. Maybe the city made me soft."

Eleanor poured her coffee. "Maybe. But it wouldn't hurt to have some help." She blew across the top of her mug to cool the coffee.

"Give me some time," Mac said. "If I can't get it together, get accustomed to the schedule, we can hire someone."

Eleanor's face contorted when she sipped the coffee, and Mac laughed. "That bad?"

"It smells strong, but that? That is like mud!"

"Well, hopefully it'll get me through the day. You can water yours down."

He headed outside, his mom still muttering under her breath. His limbs felt heavy sluggish as he slogged through the chores. Pinky came trotting up to the fence to greet him, and he ran his hand over her head and down her neck. "You really are a sweet little pain in the butt," he told her. She blinked in acknowledgment and bounced away.

"I'll have to leave right after we eat," Mac told his mom over pancakes and bacon a little while later. "I've got to get to school a little early today."

Traffic was sparse when he hit the road at half past five. The full moon was still up, and it cast the shadows of bushes onto the road, creating an eerie abstract landscape. The morning felt soft and peaceful, and Mac found himself thinking about Rose — again. He finally had her number, which was a victory in and of itself. But, having it meant nothing if he didn't do anything with it.

It probably wasn't yet appropriate to text her good morning or good night, but he could always text about homecoming. Business could lead to pleasure, right? His mind heard the word *pleasure* and immediately drew up some vivid images featuring Rose. The thought of giving her pleasure ignited a thrill in his belly. He envisioned taking her into the bedroom, undressing her, one button at a time. He imagined slipping his hand under her shirt, feeling the satin or lace of her bra, her breasts full beneath it. He heard a groan escape from his own mouth.

The next thing he heard was the screeching of tires and the crunching of gravel. He snapped awake. Through the windshield, he saw the world spinning. No, his car was spinning. His muddled brain struggled to put together coherent thoughts. *Spinning out. Damn tires. Fell asleep. Still spinning.* As suddenly as Mac had jolted awake, the car came to rest on the side of the road, miraculously facing the direction he'd been going. Mac shook his head, fast. It wasn't difficult to discern what happened. Overtired, he'd fallen asleep, hit the gravel and spun out.

He took a few deep, cleansing breaths, envisioning the oxygen flowing through his veins, giving him energy. All he had to do was get to work. As he sat there, mustering up the energy to drive to Prescott High School and get through another day, he considered that maybe his mom was right. Maybe they *should* hire someone. Maybe there was no way he could grow accustomed to the farm schedule while still working full-time. And maybe he shouldn't try.

The only thing that kept him from jumping at her idea to hire someone was pride. And Mac was starting to see ego had no place in his life. Still. Whoever they hired had to be someone they could trust. Mac's mom was vulnerable. The property overflowed with valuable tools and equipment. Not to mention all the living creatures. Mac sighed and put his head back on the headrest. A truck blew past him, creating a wall of air that made his own car sway. He really should get going, get off the side of the road. He realized then that the truck had pulled over in front of him, and the driver was now walking toward his car. He rolled down his window and the man, a cowboy type with a giant belt buckle and even bigger mustache, put his elbows on the windowsill. "You all right? I saw the skid marks."

Mac nodded. "Thanks, man. I fell asleep. Spun out. But I'm wide awake now."

The cowboy laughed, and when he spoke again, his expression showed compassion. "It's happened to me a time or two. Once, I woke up just as I was going off the road, heading straight for one of those steel fences. I was pulling a horse trailer, too. If I'd hit the fence, I could've killed my horses. Something woke me up just in time. I've always said it was divine intervention. Anyway. Stay safe."

He rapped his knuckles on the windowsill and went back to his truck.

And then it hit Mac: his accident wasn't an accident at all. It was divine intervention. The universe was pointing him toward a solution. He'd been driving along, thinking about how tired he was, and then, *bam*! He was thinking about Rose. Yes, he was thinking about pleasuring her, he thought, a slow smile spreading across his face. But he was thinking about *her*. She would be perfect. She needed a place to stay. A quiet place, where she could keep her daughter safe and healthy. And Mac and his mom needed help. If they split the chores, the burden would be only half as big. They would both have more time for the things they needed to do. Suddenly energized and wide awake, Mac pulled back out onto the road. He couldn't wait to share this idea with Rose.

Chapter Eleven

Just before the end of fourth period, Mac came into Rose's classroom. Her smile was quick, involuntary. So was the pitter patter of her heart. What was it about this man that evoked such a strong reaction? He smiled too, and she glanced at the clock, willing the bell to ring. It did, a few seconds later, and Mac came up to her desk as the kids filed out of the classroom. Quite suddenly, his expression looked serious.

"How can I help you?"

"I was just wondering." He shifted his weight from one foot to another. "Have you heard back from any more of those rentals?"

Oh. So he was there on business. "No, not yet. But, don't worry! Someone has to let me move in." There was that awkward fake laugh again. The sound faded, leaving what was surely a grimace on her face.

"Actually, that's what I wanted to talk to you about." Mac leaned against her desk. "I have a proposal."

Rose's heart went from pitter pattering to thundering. A proposal? What could it possibly be?

"You probably know I lived in San Francisco before moving back home to Prescott a couple years ago."

Nodding, Rose licked her lips.

Mac continued, "I had a pretty simple life back then. A single guy, all I had to think about was myself. And then my dad died. I moved back here. You know, my mom said this morning that people call farming a simple life. And in a way, it is. In the city, there's public transit, so many nightclubs, so many things to do. It's busy, busy, busy. Here, it's not like that so much." He paused, and even though he smiled at her, she thought he looked sad. "When I moved here, I thought I would be bored out of my mind." He stood, started walking around the classroom. Rose's gaze followed him. "I'm anything but bored. I'm dead tired. I wish someone had told me how much work this life is. I wouldn't give it up, wouldn't trade it. At least, not right now, while my mom's still alive."

At the end of a row of desks, he stopped walking and stood with his back toward Rose, his hands on his hips. Although he faced a bulletin board where Rose had pinned up quotes from famous writers, she was pretty sure he wasn't seeing it. She took the opportunity to admire the way he filled out his pants. After a beat, he spoke. "On the way to school this morning, I fell asleep."

"Fell asleep?" That jolted Rose out of her admiration and into alarm. "On the way to school? Were you driving?"

Mac turned, and this time his smile showed amusement rather than sadness. "Yes, yes, and yes."

Rose rushed across the room and grabbed one of his wrists in both of her hands. "Are you okay?"

"I'm okay."

She dropped his wrists, put her hands on top of her head. "I feel partially to blame for this! You worrying about Celeste and me has probably not helped your stress level. And stress makes you feel tired."

Taking her shoulders in his hands, he looked into her eyes. "No. That has nothing to do with you. It's hard to run a farm and work full-time." He dropped his hands and began pacing again. "For a few months, my mom has been trying to talk me into hiring someone to help out around the farm. But I keep saying no. It's hard to find someone trustworthy. As much as I want to help, I'd rather do it myself than worry about having someone else in the house and on the property." He'd made a lap, and started another. "But after I spun out on Williamson Valley Road this morning, I had an epiphany. This is where my proposal comes in." Suddenly, he was in front of her again. He blinked, but didn't speak.

"Well? Don't hold out on me."

"No. This is crazy. I can't believe I thought it was a good idea."

Charmed, Rose laughed. "Now you *have* to tell me. At this point, I would consider almost anything outside the realm of crazy. Remember, you're talking to the girl who brought her five-year-old daughter to sleep at her place of employment for several weeks."

"There is that."

A few seconds ticked by.

Finally, Mac spoke. "Here goes. What if you and Celeste came to live at my house, on the farm? We have a spare bedroom. I could really use some help around the place. There's just so much to do. Instead of paying rent, you could help out. How you help is up to you. If you want to do farm chores, like weed the garden, harvest vegetables, milk the cow, you can. Or, if you want to cook and clean, you can. My mama just can't do much anymore. And I've discovered that I certainly can't do it all. As much as I would like to, it's just not feasible anymore. So. That's my proposal. Move in, help me out, and enjoy the so-called simple life."

Rose couldn't believe what she was hearing. She couldn't speak.

"It's all right if you don't want to. I understand. I mean, we don't know each other very well. It's just an idea. Listen, you don't have to answer right now. Why don't you think about it? See if you get any more responses to your applications. And then you can decide." He sounded manic. "No pressure whatsoever. If anything, my little episode this morning proves that I really need to hire someone. So if you decide you don't want to move in, then I will hire someone else. Get references. That sort of thing. But I thought I would ask you first."

Speechless, Rose nodded. "Okay."

Mac turned on his heel and left her classroom. Rose watched the door shut behind him, thinking that if nothing else, she definitely wouldn't mind seeing him every day.

Chapter Twelve

"I did something crazy today," Mac said to his mom that night at the dinner table.

Pausing in the middle of cutting her chicken, she looked up at him and raised an eyebrow. "And what was that?"

"I asked Rose Coffey to move in here." To her credit, Eleanor didn't appear surprised. "I think that's a great idea."

The response gave Mac such a shock, he laughed out loud. "Good. I probably don't need to explain my reasoning, but I will, anyway. It seemed like a win-win. She needs a place to stay, and we could certainly use an extra pair of hands around here."

Eleanor nodded. "Agreed. And what a wonderful way for that little girl to grow up. Imagine everything she'll learn from being on the farm."

"Thank you, Mama. I wasn't sure how you'd feel about it."

Eleanor smiled and Mac thought he detected a hint of deviousness. "So, what did she say?"

"To be honest, I was so nervous to bring it up, I panicked after I made the proposal. I didn't really even give her a chance to respond. I blurted out the idea and then told her she could think about it. Then I hightailed it out of her room before she could say no."

His mom's eyes twinkled. "Well, I sincerely hope she says yes.

Not because I sense a certain chemistry between you two. Not at all."

It was Mac's turn to raise an eyebrow at her. She pointed her fork at him. "Not because of that. But because I do think it would be good for all of us. She seems like a really nice person, and her daughter is adorable. I think we would like having them around."

"I agree. And, of course, I will keep you posted."

"Of course."

Chapter Thirteen

That night after Rose tucked Celeste and Bumpy into bed at the Hassayampa Inn, and then nestled down into her own bed, Celeste said into the dark, "Mommy?"

Rose's eyelids felt heavy and her voice came out thick when she said, "Yeah?"

"I love this hotel." Rose heard the short inhale and long exhale of Celeste's yawn.

"Me, too."

"But, do you think we'll ever have a *real* house? Maybe one with a yard?"

Rose's heart nearly broke. "I think we will. I will do my very best to make sure that happens."

"Thanks, Mommy."

Rose had nearly drifted off when Celeste said, "I love you, Mommy, and if we live in a hotel forever, that will be okay, too."

"Thanks, sweetheart. I love you, too."

The next morning, Rose contemplated Mac's offer.

In the shower, she thought about showering at Mac's house. When her mind veered to thoughts of what it would be like to shower *with* Mac, she gave herself a stern talking to and thought about her conversation with Celeste the night before. Mac lived on a farm, she thought as she scrubbed her hair. He certainly lived in a real house, with a yard. Celeste would love that. While they waited in line at the coffee shop in the hotel lobby, where Rose would buy Celeste a breakfast sandwich and orange juice, she thought about how good it would feel to sit down to a home-cooked meal at real kitchen table every morning and evening. The idea of staying there, with Mac, was so tempting. And, she thought as she drove away from Celeste's preschool after dropping her off, the farm was probably quiet. Luxuriously quiet. Mac lived out Williamson Valley Road, where the parcels were big and spread out, and the houses were far apart. Rose imagined she wouldn't hear a single college student, laughing, yelling, or dribbling a basketball on the floor.

One point of concern kept niggling at Rose's brain. She was attracted to Mac. His long legs, his trim waist, his muscled arms. How could she possibly live with a man that attractive, and not think about kissing him? Or, down the road, sleeping with him?

When she arrived at the high school, she went directly to her classroom. Seeing Mac in all his handsome glory would only muddle her mental clarity. She busied herself organizing the worksheets she'd copied the day before. While she stacked and separated and piled, she thought about Mac ... some more.

She could tell he found her attractive, too. She'd seen the way he looked at her. But acting on that attraction would be a terrible idea. If she and Celeste were staying at Mac's house, and she and Mac started a relationship, and that relationship went downhill, then what? She and Celeste would be homeless. Again. And in that case, Mac wouldn't put them up in a hotel for a second time. They'd be back at square one, having to find a place they could afford, in a good part of town, without college neighbors. The first bell rang and Rose sighed.

If she decided to take Mac up on his offer, and that was still a big *if*, she would have to ban herself from ever acting on her attraction. At this point, she would consider his proposal as a last resort. She was still waiting to hear back from a couple of the rental agencies. She would see what they said and then decide what to do.

Knowing she had a backup option, Rose spent the rest of the day feeling pretty positive. During breaks between classes, she found herself humming, and a handful of students commented that she seemed particularly chipper.

Everything changed at the end of the school day, when she checked her email. And there it was in black-and-white: proof that she couldn't provide for her daughter on her own.

* * *

Dear Ms. Coffey,

We received your application for our rental property. Thank you so much for applying, but we are sorry to say we don't have a space for you at this time. Good luck in your search, and we hope that if you have rental that you'll consider us if you have rental needs in the future.

Sincerely,
The Team at Premier Rentals

* * *

Rose's phone clattered onto her desktop. She sank into her chair and put her head in her hands. That's how Taylor and Jessie found her. Absorbed in her own misery, Rose didn't hear them come in, but she heard their concerned voices as they rushed her desk. She lifted her head, almost too ashamed to make eye contact with them. "You guys are probably so tired of finding me upset like this."

"We are." Jessie settled a hip onto the edge of Rose's desk. "But not for the reason you're thinking. We're just worried about you. We don't like seeing you stressed."

"I'm so sorry. This is probably causing you guys stress."

"No, it's not." Taylor, too, rested a hip on the edge of Rose's desk. "I mean, a tiny bit, but we're okay. We just want you to be okay."

"I want to be okay, too." Rose's voice caught on the word, too, making a pathetic squeak.

Finally, after keeping secrets from them for weeks, she told them everything: how she'd pulled out all the stops to make her apartment quiet — and failed; how, desperate, she'd secretly holed up in the teachers lounge; how Mac had discovered her there; how she'd been applying and applying for new rentals with no luck. Her friends were quiet, listening. Even if Taylor and Jessie couldn't help her come up with a solution, just talking about what was going on gave Rose some relief.

"And, there's one other thing."

"Oh, geez," Jessie said. "There's more?! No wonder you've been so stressed."

This was the big one. Rose hesitated, stood up, and blurted out, "Johnny Mac offered to let us move in with him."

"What?" Jessie said, her voice at yell volume and her eyes going round as she, too, stood.

"No, no, it's not like that." The words came out in a rush. "It's not romantic, or anything. He knew I needed a place to stay. He and his mom need help around the property. I could be an extra set of hands and also sleep in a real bed every night."

"I *knew* it!" Jessie pointed at Rose, her eyes alight with victory. "I *knew* you were in his classroom talking to him about something top-secret."

"I was," Rose sat down again. "But it wasn't about moving in. It was about how he had discovered us sleeping in the teachers lounge. I was in his classroom asking him not to tell anyone."

Jessie looked a little disappointed, and Rose said, "Sorry."

"I can't believe you told Johnny Mac you are sleeping at the school, but you didn't tell *us*."

Rose shook her head. "I didn't *tell* Johnny Mac. He found out we were there because he came back to the school late when he realized he forgot a tool he needed. I didn't want to tell anybody."

"And now." Taylor sat up a little straighter. "We know why he found you camping out in the teachers lounge. Because he is now the hero of your story, Rosie. You know what this is, right? It's fate. Just like how Judd ended up working at the school, and how that bank lender was interested in my business idea, but switched banks and then turned up again. Don't miss out on this opportunity. Think about how good it will be. For you, for Celeste, and even for Johnny Mac and his mom. You really can't turn it down."

"Taylor's right, you know. You've been so worried about your living situation and then along comes this proposal. It's the perfect solution. And it doesn't have to be forever. It could just be a place where you get a temporary reprieve from all the stress. You could commit to a certain number of months there. And meanwhile, Johnny Mac and his mom could look for someone to hire. And you could slow down and take your time finding a permanent living situation."

Rose considered. "Well, when you put it that way, it does sound pretty good. You're right, it doesn't have to be forever. Thank you guys, as always, for listening. One day, I'll get my life together, and you'll be listening to happy stories."

"I'm certain of it," Taylor said. "Things always have a way of working out. Remember how many rejection letters I got for my business loan before I finally got an approval? I thought, this is never going to happen. And then, my approval wasn't even a traditional approval. A particular loan officer took an interest in my business and went out of her way to help me. I have a feeling something similar will happen for you. I mean, maybe this is it."

"I want to believe that," Rose said. "But I feel like I have to guard my heart, you know? Nothing ever seems to go right. I'm starting to feel hopeless."

Her friends both reached out to rub her back, and she leaned into the contact. "I know you guys are here for me. And you've been so supportive. Even so, I've felt so alone."

"I think we all feel alone sometimes," Jessie said. "No matter what our circumstances. But I have a feeling things are about to turn around."

"Yes." Taylor sounded certain. "So do I. This living situation is going to be the start of it."

As Rose watched her friends walk out of her classroom a minute later, she hoped they were right.

Her mind (mostly) made up, Rose went and picked up Celeste. They went back to the apartment for dinner and to pack a change of clothes. Over Celeste's favorite — the grocery store's copycat version of restaurant-style chow mien and broccoli beef — Rose asked, "Remember how you asked me last night when we might get to live in a real house, with a yard?"

"Yeah. Why?"

Rose twisted her noodles around her fork. "Well, I have an idea to tell you about. Do you remember Mac?"

"Yep. He's the guy who's letting us stay in the nice hotel."

"Right. Well, he lives on a sort of farm."

Celeste raised her eyebrows and, mouth still full of food, she said, "A real farm? Like, with animals and stuff?"

"Yeah. Cows, goats, and chickens."

"Wow. That sounds like so much fun. Can we go visit?"

"Well, that's what I wanted to talk to you about. See, Mac came to my classroom today and told me how he and his mom need help around the place. She's getting older —"

"Like a grandma?"

Rose nodded. "Yes. Like a grandma. Next time, swallow before you talk."

Celeste nodded.

"So, yes. Like a grandma. She can't do as much as she used to. And Mac has been doing most of the chores by himself. He's also working with me, at the school. So he's really tired. Anyway. He had the idea that maybe you and I could move on to the farm for a while."

Celeste wrinkled her nose. "Like, *outside* on the farm? Because my friend Todd says cows can be smelly."

Rose laughed. "They can. And no. Mac and his mom have a house. They have an extra bedroom or two. We might have to share. But, we could stay there for a while, at least. We could help with the chores."

"Oh!" Celeste put down her fork. "So we would be helping him, with chores, and he would be helping us, because we could live in the house."

"Right."

Celeste shrugged. "That sounds like a pretty good idea."

One of the best things about kids, Rose thought, was how simple they kept things. "I thought so, too. I was hoping you'd say that. But I wanted to ask you before I gave him an answer."

Celeste picked up her fork and copied Rose, twisting her noodles onto it. "Well, I think it's a good idea. You should go ahead and tell him we'll move in."

Rose breathed out a sigh of relief. "Okay. I guess I will."

Chapter Fourteen

Frantic, Mac rushed around the house tidying up, noticing every item that was out of place or looked like clutter. He found a coffee mug on the bathroom counter and couldn't remember who'd used it or when, so scooped it up, only to reveal a stain beneath it.

"You're working yourself into a tizzy over a guest who, I'm sure, won't notice a stray coffee mug or old newspaper." His mom sat on the couch, amusement showing in the arc of her eyebrows.

"I know, I know." Mac scrubbed the stain. "But I just can't stop."

"She's supposed to be here in what? Ten minutes?"

Mac looked at his watch — again. "Yes. Ten minutes. Think I have time to vacuum the rugs?"

"Didn't you already vacuum the rugs?"

The doorbell rang. Mac froze. Eleanor chuckled, and he threw her his darkest look, eyebrows drawn together. That turned her chuckle into a full-on laugh.

"Guess you don't have time to vacuum the rugs. Again."

He growled at her. "I just want it to look nice."

"I know, Sonny. And it does. Trust me. Rose and Celeste aren't going to be looking for specks of dust or out-of-place knickknacks. And if they are, do we want them living here, anyway?"

"No." He sighed. "I guess not."

"Right. You're fine. Now, go. Answer the door."

Like a little kid, he followed his mom's instructions and pulled the door open. As soon as he saw Rose, pretty as a picture in a flowery sundress, he felt all the tension unwind, like a ball of string being untangled.

"Hi."

"Hi, Mr. Mac." Celeste bounced on the balls of her feet. "We're here to see the farm. Can you show me the cows?"

Smiling, Rose said, "Sorry. Someone's a little excited about the animals. She would sleep in a cardboard box if it meant getting access to a yard and some pets. Even if those pets are chickens."

"I understand," Mac said. How was he already smitten with the little girl? "Come in. We can go straight through to the cows."

Eleanor had gotten up and was standing in the kitchen. She greeted Rose and Celeste with hugs, throwing Mac an I-told-you-so over their shoulders.

He gestured at the door on the other side of the kitchen. "That door leads to the back yard."

"And the cows?" Celeste said. She looked up at him, her eyes adorably big in her tiny face.

"And the cow. There's just one. But before we go out there, I'd better tell you a little bit about cows."

He knelt down in front of her, and she looked right at him, serious as could be. "Mommy said you might have to give me safety instructions. Cows are giant when you see them up close. Even though they don't mean to, they could hurt you."

"That's exactly right," Mac said, impressed that Rose had thought of that, and that Celeste remembered. "One really important thing to know is that you should never walk behind a cow. Or a horse. It's easy to surprise them, and the first thing they do when they hear a noise behind them is kick."

"Got it." Celeste nodded, once, like she was committing the idea to memory. "Never walk behind a big animal."

"Right."

"Okay. What else?"

"For now, always stay outside Cookie's fence. Cookie is the cow, by the way. Until you two get to know each other, I don't want you getting too close. She could step on your feet and hurt you. Okay?"

"Okay. Stay outside of Cookie's fence."

"Right."

"What kind of cookie?"

"What?" Mac said.

"What kind of cookie is she named after? Like, chocolate chip, oatmeal raisin, Oreo?"

Eleanor laughed. "Why don't you let us know when you meet her? We just named her Cookie because she's sweet. But I'm sure you can tell which kind of cookie is most appropriate."

Again, Celeste gave a single nod.

"All business," Mac said to Rose.

"All business," Rose said back. "I may have over-emphasized the importance of listening to you." Her lips twitched in the most adorable way.

Mac had never thought too hard about whether he wanted kids — he'd never met a woman who made that path seem likely. But in that moment, looking up at Rose, both of them reveling in Celeste's cuteness, he thought kids were a distinct possibility. He almost passed out.

"You know," he said to Celeste. "For now, let's just say that the most important rule is to listen to me, your mom, and my mom around the farm. Okay? Do what we ask, and remember that everything we ask is for your safety."

When she gave him the single nod that time, her curls fell forward. When she brushed them away from her face, he noticed the little dimples on her knuckles.

"Come on. Let's go."

He pushed open the door, and held it open for Rose and Celeste. As they made their way across the yard, Celeste slipped her hand into his. Surprised, he looked over at Rose, who grinned at him and shrugged.

"That's the barn, over there." Mac pointed to the building, which his dad had painted the traditional red and white. "We've got one cow and six goats, plus a bunch of chickens and three horses."

"Horses?!" Celeste shrieked, bouncing again while still holding onto Mac's hand.

"Horses," he said. "I have a feeling you're going to like them."

"Can we see them first? Pretty pleeeeease?"

How could one kid be so darn cute?

"Sure. We can see them first. Just next to the barn, there, is the chicken coop. You can help me collect the eggs, if you want." More bouncing. Mac went on, "That's my mama's greenhouse, where she grows some of her flowers. And right next to it is the vegetable garden."

Although Mac was having a great time seeing the property through Celeste's eyes, his attention kept drifting to Rose. The golden afternoon sunlight illuminated her white-blond curls. She looked like an angel. The tension he'd seen in her shoulders and around her eyes eased even as they walked around the buildings and the yard.

Celeste was skipping at that point, her movements jerking Mac's arm just a little, and Rose gave him another knowing smile. "She does like to skip," she said. "Sometimes she about tears my arm off. Feel free to ask her to walk if it's driving you crazy."

"It's not," Mac said. "It's actually exciting, how excited she is."

"She's real excited." Laughter tinged Rose's voice. "She's been asking since she woke up — at five-thirty on a Saturday, mind you — when we could come here."

"Oh, no!" Mac said. "You could have come earlier! You could have texted me. I didn't have much going on today."

Again, Rose laughed, and the sound was so carefree, Mac felt his own shoulders relaxing.

"It's fine. A hazard of child-rearing, I'm afraid. I knew better. I should have told her we were coming, like, *right* before we left the hotel. But I was excited, too."

They'd reached the barn. Celeste ran up to the sliding doors, grabbed the handle on one of them, and put all her weight into pulling it open.

"There's a trick." Mac rushed to unlatch the doors. "See? Try again."

She did, and the door slid open, nearly silent on its tracks.

"Can we go in?"

"Of course," Mac said. "Walk though, okay? And talk quietly. These animals haven't been around anyone other than old people. They're not used to all the excitement a kid brings."

"You're not old, are you?" Celeste said. Mac opened his mouth to answer, but she had already moved on. In a whisper-yell, she exclaimed, "There they are! The horses! Can we go up to them?"

The excitement was contagious. "We can." He caught up to her, and took her hand again to lead her to one of the horse stalls. The horse came to the half-door to greet them, his giant head well above Mac's. "This is Old Timer," Mac told Celeste.

"He's giant." Her eyes were wide with awe.

"He is. He's our biggest horse. And our sweetest."

"Then why didn't you name him Cake or something?"

"You'll have to ask my mom. Want to pet him?"

"Yes, yes, yes!" Celeste whisper-yelled.

"Okay. Watch how I keep my hand flat when I reach out. That way he doesn't think my fingers are carrots. You can touch his cheek, here, or his neck." He demonstrated. "He doesn't really like it when we touch his forehead."

Celeste nodded, and, with a gentleness Mac hadn't expected, she placed a tiny hand on Old Timer's massive cheek. Without moving her hand, she turned her head until her eyes met Mac's.

"This is amazing."

One of the goats bleated then, and Rose jumped and put her hand on her chest.

"I know," Mac said. "It sounds like a little kid screaming."

Rose laughed. "It's kind of terrifying."

"If I hadn't grown up with that sound, I would think so, too. Want to come see them? I think you'll find them a lot less terrifying up close."

Pinky seemed to sense a kindred spirit in Celeste. The goat ran right up to her and nuzzled her stomach. Celeste squealed, and Rose said, "You're right. They're pretty cute. Not terrifying at all." She knelt to pet Rooster, a fluffy guy with a long beard. "Although I wouldn't mind if I never heard that sound again."

Next, they visited the chickens and collected the eggs. Mac walked them around the vegetable garden and showed Celeste how to pick tomatoes and zucchinis. She seemed to find that pretty exciting, but literally dropped her bounty when she saw the pumpkins growing at the other end of the garden bed. "Oh my gosh! Are those pumpkins? Actual pumpkins in *real life?*"

Mac laughed. "Yes. Those are real, actual pumpkins. They're not quite ready to pick, but we might be able to take a few in a couple of weeks."

After sprinting the distance between the zucchinis and the pumpkins, Celeste squatted down to get a closer look. "You think we can carve some?"

A rush of emotion making Mac feel warm and tingly, he smiled at her. "Of course we can."

Again, her attention shifted. She was on her feet, pointing at the old tractor across the field. "Is that a real tractor?"

"As real as the pumpkins."

"Wow! Can I see it?"

Rose touched her shoulder to Mac's. "What she means is, can she look at it up close? Can she touch it? Can she climb on it?"

"I figured. And, of course. To all three. Let's go."

Celeste ran ahead of them, and for the first time in as long as he could remember, Mac thought the scene looked pretty magical. The sky was turning shades of peach and purple, and the fields looked lush.

Mac and Rose fell into step immediately. Within a few seconds, Mac noticed they were close enough to hold hands, and he was tempted to intertwine his fingers with hers. But a little voice in the back of his mind whispered, *Not yet.* When he looked over at her, she was already looking at him, and she smiled. He saw genuine affection in her expression, and again had to fight the urge to hold her hand. A desire to be with her, every single day, hit him. If she decided not to stay, it would wreck him.

"Your home is amazing," she told him. She gestured at Celeste, who stood in front of the tractor and was running one hand around the edge of the tire. "I haven't seen this much wonder from her in a really long time."

The flicker of hope Mac noticed a few minutes before grew into a bigger blaze. If Celeste loved the place, wouldn't Rose be inclined to stay?

"It's pretty cool seeing the place through Celeste's eyes," Mac said. "I grew up here, so all this stuff — the horses, goats, chickens, tractors — was pretty much status quo. Watching Celeste see all of this stuff and get excited about it makes it seem magical to me, too."

They'd reached the tractor, and Celeste heard their footsteps and turned around. "Holy moly! This tire is taller than me!"

"It *is* a really big tire," Mac said. "It has to be big, so it doesn't sink into the muddy fields."

"Will you take me for a ride?" Celeste wanted to know.

Mac looked at Rose, who shrugged.

"I will take you for a ride," Mac said. "But it's going to have to be another day. I haven't driven this thing since I came home, and I'm pretty sure it's going to need a new battery."

Celeste's tiny shoulders slumped, producing another laugh from Mac. "I know. I'm sorry. But as soon as I get it fixed, you'll be the first one to go for a ride."

As quickly as disappointment had set in, excitement was back. "Really? I can be the first one?"

"You can be the first one."

As they made their way back to the house, Mac wished he was bold enough to ask Rose what she was thinking about moving in. But he couldn't bear the thought that she didn't want to, especially after she'd seen the place in person. He figured he would see them off now, and then wait by his phone for the next couple of days until she sent him a decision. The kitchen door opened as they approached.

"Do I smell cookies?" Celeste hollered, and Eleanor, who stood in the doorway, laughed. "You do. I always like to make cookies for the kids. I hope you like chocolate chip."

Celeste bounced again, and Mac wondered how Rose could keep up with her energy all the time. "I do! I love chocolate chip cookies!"

"Oh, good. I was hoping you'd say that," Eleanor said. "Come in, come in. I've got them waiting for you."

She held the door for Rose and winked at Mac as he followed Rose in.

Then, over warm cookies at the kitchen table, Eleanor said, "So tell me, girls. What do you think of the place? Would you like to stay?"

Chapter Fifteen

"It's move-in day!" Still in bed, Celeste stretched, her smile almost literally reaching from one ear to another.

"Don't you mean, coronation day?" Rose asked, tickling her.

"Very funny, Mommy. Are you excited to move out of this hotel and onto Mac's farm?"

Following Celeste's lead, Rose stretched too, enjoying the luxury of hotel bed sheets for one last morning. "I *am* excited about being moved in. But I'm not that excited about the actual moving part. It's a lot of work."

"But I'm going to help you!"

"I know you are. And I'm grateful for that."

Less than three hours later, all their belongings were at Mac's house. Rose and Mac stood in the living room, having just stacked the final box after the final car trip from the apartment.

"I can't believe this," Rose said. "I thought we were going to be at that all day."

"I guess we make a pretty good team." Mac looked away immediately, almost as if he were embarrassed.

Rose smiled. "We do."

"It also doesn't hurt that everything you own fits into a couple of carloads."

That comment stung a little — Rose still felt somewhat behind in life, like she should be a homeowner with a real furniture set and a vacuum.

Mac must have read it in her expression, because he rushed to add, "I consider that a good thing. I was the same way when I moved back here from San Francisco. It's nice to travel light. Anyway. I'll give you some time to unpack, get settled."

Celeste followed Rose into the bedroom they would share, bouncing along behind her.

"Is bouncing your new mode of travel these days?"

Giggling, Celeste bounced some more. "Yep. I'm just so happy when we're here, I can't help it. I just want to bounce."

Rose picked Celeste up and hugged her to her chest. "I'm so happy you're happy. I think we're really going to like it here."

"Me, too," Celeste said.

"And I guess squealing is your new mode of talking?"

"Yep." Celeste kissed her on the cheek and then squirmed to get down.

Rose opened one of the giant cardboard boxes they brought from the apartment. "This one is all of your clothes. Why don't you start putting your clothes in that dresser? And I'll work on my clothes."

Instead of bouncing, Celeste slithered over to the box. "Do I have to?"

Rose reached out to tickle her. "You don't *have* to. But I don't think you want to be digging your clothes out of a cardboard box every day."

"Okay, okay. You're right. But if we hurry and unpack, really fast, can we maybe go walk around the yard again?"

"Of course." That was motivation enough, and soon, they were outside in Mac's glorious backyard. Mac had told them to treat the place as if it were their own, but Rose still felt a little strange being out back without him. Celeste, of course, ran around without a care in the world, hooting and hollering like she couldn't dream of being anywhere better. Rose watched from the back patio as her daughter walked around the garden, looking for vegetables ready to pick, kneeling down to pull a weed here and there.

"Seems like Celeste is happy here," Mac said, coming to stand beside her.

Rose turned to him and smiled. "I didn't hear you come up. I was so enjoying watching Celeste enjoy your place."

"Our place," he corrected her.

"Thank you," Rose said, looking into his eyes. There was a moment. A moment where she felt like kissing him would be perfectly natural, the best and only next step in the conversation. He felt it, too. She saw his gaze move down to her mouth and back up to her eyes. The moment lasted for exactly a moment, and then it seemed they shared an unspoken thought. *Off-limits.*

Oh, but seeing that desire in his eyes heated Rose's blood. He wanted her, and it felt so good to be wanted.

"Mommy!" Celeste shrieked. Rose startled, even though she knew right away that it was a shriek of pleased surprise, and not pain or fear. Mac startled, too, and then Celeste yelled, "A kitty! I found a kitty! Come see!"

Rose and Mac exchanged a look, and he inclined his head toward Celeste. "I'm guessing she found Potato."

"Your cat is named Potato?"

Mac shrugged. "You've got to see it to believe it."

They made their way over to where Celeste knelt on the ground outside the barn. And there she was.

"Potato," Rose said. "I get it now."

As the cat rolled in the dirt, purring and making quiet meowing noises, Celeste cracked up. "Her name is *Potato?*"

"You can see it though, right?" Mac said.

Celeste clutched her belly, still laughing. "Yes! But is she always this fat?"

Guilt swamped Rose immediately. What kind of parent didn't teach her child not to tease people (or cats) for being fat? She looked at Mac, ready to apologize, and saw that he, too, looked guilty. He grimaced and said, "She's pregnant."

Rose laughed, and Celeste gasped, clapping both hands over her mouth. She removed her hands right away and said, "She's going to have babies?!"

"And soon, too," Mac said.

Obviously delighted, Celeste reached down to scratch Potato's neck. Potato stood up and arched her back.

"Well, that's exciting," Rose said, and Mac said, "It is. But we're going to have to find homes for them. Hopefully she doesn't have too many."

"Aww," Celeste said. "Can't we keep them?"

"I mean, she could have six or seven kittens," Mac said. "We don't want that many cats running around."

"Can we keep *one*?" Celeste looked up at them with the cutest puppy-dog eyes. Rose and Mac looked at each other again. "We'll see," they both said.

"I'm getting hungry. Are you guys?

"I am," Mac said. "What should we have for dinner?"

"Rita's!" Celeste said.

"I love Rita's!" Mac said, and Rose found herself smiling, again. She loved that his enthusiasm matched Celeste's.

"We do, too," she told him. "Do you think it'll be okay with your mom? I can call it in and go pick it up. As a thank you for letting us stay here, and all your help with moving today."

"You're going to think this is crazy, but my mom has a very specific order. I'll write it down for you."

Thirty minutes later, Rose walked into Rita's. Rita stood behind the counter, her hand on one hip, her gum popping. "Rose Coffey! Don't tell me you're having dinner with Johnny Mac his mom. Do my eyes deceive me? I have a usual for Rose and Celeste and a usual for Johnny Mac and Eleanor. And you're picking them all up."

Rose handed Celeste a quarter, and she ran over to the candy machine as Rose walked up to the counter and leaned against it. "I know how the rumor mill gets going in this town. Surely you already know Celeste and I are staying with Mac and Eleanor for the time being."

"Starting today, right?" Rita raised an eyebrow.

"Right."

Rita moved her other hand to her other hip, and shifted her weight to the other leg. She meant business. "And the first time you order dinner, you order from Rita's. You know my diner is the starting point for romance, right?"

"I may have heard that rumor a time or two." Rose's lips twitched. "But there's not going to be any romance here. It's just two friends, entering into a win-win situation. He needs help around the farm, and Celeste and I need a place to stay."

"And, he needs a woman and you need a man."

Amused, Rose rolled her eyes. "I don't need a man."

"Honey, you need *that* man. You just haven't figured it out yet. Anyway. Here's your order."

She shoved the bags across the counter and gave Rose her total. Rose handed over her card, and when while Rita ran it, she said, "You know, Taylor Cole met Judd O'Connor right here in this very spot. Well, they had a little tussle at the door before he bought her coffee. And the rest is history."

"True."

When Rita handed back Rose's credit card, she said, "Mark my word. This is the beginning of a beautiful relationship."

Rose took the bags, called for Celeste, and went back to the farm. Home, she reminded herself. She had to start thinking of it as home.

Eating dinner with Mac and his mom was way more fun than Rose expected. They laughed and joked and shared stories throughout the meal.

"And this boy," Eleanor said. "He used to like to play tricks on his dad. Every so often, he would short-sheet the bed. Once, he replaced our family photos with celebrity photos. Then there was the time he sent his dad a letter, thanking him for his donation to Guy Rooney's political campaign."

"Dad hated Guy Rooney," Mac said.

"He would get so upset," Eleanor said. "But he could never stay mad for long."

Looking across the table and seeing Mac's mischievous smile, Rose could see why his dad couldn't stay upset for long.

After dinner cleanup, they all went for a walk around the property. Eleanor pointed out spots featured in Mac's childhood: the old oak tree where a tire swing once hung, the path to a wide spot in the creek where he caught frogs, and the pair of trees where he used to hang his hammock.

"Are you getting a little misty-eyed, Mom?"

Even though Eleanor laughed, she swiped at her eyes with her fingertips. "I'll admit it." She looked over at Rose. "They just grow up so fast. And even though these days seem hard, you'll look back and realize how wonderful they are."

Suddenly, Rose was misty-eyed, herself. Celeste chose that moment to slip her hand into Rose's, and Rose gave it a little squeeze. "I think it's almost bedtime."

After going through the usual bedtime routine, Rose laid with Celeste until she fell asleep and then went into the kitchen seeking a glass of wine. Finding Mac there gave her a rush of pleasure.

"Long day." He handed her a glass of wine.

"How did you know I was coming in here for this?" she asked. "Thank you, by the way. It's exactly what I needed."

"You're welcome." He didn't quite smile at her, but in the crinkling at the corners of his eyes, she saw affection and tenderness. "Even though I would say today went relatively smoothly, moving is a big deal. Especially when you have a very energetic five-year-old helping out. So, I did for you what I would do for myself."

He pointed at a bottle of beer on the counter, then lifted it and tapped it against her glass. "Cheers. To new beginnings."

Rose gulped. "To new beginnings."

She took a healthy drink from her glass, and then a healthy breath of air. The space between them felt charged all of a sudden. It was the first time they'd been alone in the house. The first time the room was quiet enough to carry on an adult conversation. The first time Rose really stopped, and felt her attraction for him hit her. And hit her it did. Her limbs felt liquid, and a delicious warmth spread from her heart to her fingers and toes. She felt her head tilt, an invitation. Mac stepped forward, accepting.

"Mommy?"

Rose closed her eyes, then opened them again. "Celeste. Everything okay?"

Her hair messy and her cheek already lined from laying down, Celeste came into the kitchen. "Everything's fine. Only, I didn't get to say good night to Mac."

To his credit, Mac hid his deep breath really well. He turned to Celeste and smiled. "Good night, Celeste. I hope you sleep well."

"Can I give you a hug?"

"Of course." Mac dropped to his knees, and Celeste ran into his arms. Mac hugged her tight. "Now get to bed. We've all had a big day, and we all have school tomorrow." Celeste nodded and bounced away.

Chapter Sixteen

Not kissing Rose was the first thing Mac thought of when his alarm went off the next morning. It was one of the biggest feats of self-control he had ever accomplished. She was just so ... kissable. But, he told himself as he got out of bed, they couldn't become romantically involved. Sticking to that self-imposed rule was going to be very, *very* difficult. Especially if she kept walking around, looking all sun-kissed and content.

Because Rose offered to make breakfast that morning, he'd been able to set his alarm for a full hour later than usual. He felt more rested than he had in days and noticed a pep in his step as he went into the kitchen.

Eleanor sat at the counter, sipping her coffee and reading a magazine. "Sleep well?"

"Like a rock."

That was only half-true. Plagued by unreleased tension, he had taken forever to fall asleep. He'd slept well once he finally did, but he'd never admit any of that to his mom.

He didn't have to, though, because she said, "Hmm," and raised an eyebrow at him. Before he could ask what she was thinking about, she went back to reading her magazine like it was the most interesting thing she'd seen. Mac shook his head, and smiling, went out to do the chores.

The sizzling sound of bacon cooking greeted Mac when he returned. The sight of Rose at his stove, in his mother's apron, her hair piled into a wild mess on top of her head, made his heart stop. His body stopped, too — he froze in the doorway — and then he quickly attempted to recover without anyone noticing. His recovery wasn't as seamless as he thought, because his mom, who now stood at the counter removing muffins from the muffin tin, offered him another raised eyebrow.

Mac pretended to ignore her. He walked right up to Rose and grabbed a piece of bacon off the plate. She swatted his arm. "It's not breakfast time yet!"

He put the whole piece of bacon in his mouth, and made a show of chewing. "Mmm."

Using similarly exaggerated movements, Rose took the plate and moved it to the other side of the stovetop, out of his reach. Mac grinned at her, and way too tempted to kiss her on the cheek, headed toward his bedroom. "Smells good, ladies. I'm going to clean up for the day."

Alone in his bedroom, Mac cursed himself. Taking the bacon was one thing. It could be something a brother did to a sister, or one friend did to another. But wanting to kiss Rose on the cheek? Practically having a heart attack, seeing her at his stovetop? Those were purely romantic. Why did she have to be so beautiful? Why did she have to look so good in an apron? And why did he have to have that visceral reaction to her in his kitchen?

After washing his face and hands, he yanked off his work shirt and replaced it with a clean undershirt. He took off his jeans and put on clean work pants.

When he returned to the kitchen, he didn't miss the way Rose's gaze traveled from his face down to his waist, lingering on his stomach. Yes, he knew he had great abs, and even though he'd worn an undershirt only to avoid getting grease on his work shirt, he may have chosen one that fit a little tighter just to see how she'd react. Her reaction didn't disappoint.

He waited for her to make eye contact again, and let his look smolder a minute before getting plates out of the cupboard. He saw her hide a smile before she turned away. Celeste came bouncing into the kitchen, wearing a sparkly dress, a tiara, and mismatched plastic high heels.

"How do I look?"

Eleanor answered first. "You look lovely, honey. Are you going to be able to play in those shoes today?"

Celeste made a dismissive gesture with her hand, and the movement was so adult, Mac's jaw dropped. "These things? Yeah. I can play in these."

Rose hadn't even looked up. She was scrambling eggs, adding seasoning, slicing chunks of butter into the pan. "Go change your shoes."

Celeste's shoulders drooped. "But, Mom —"

"Go."

Celeste turned around and attempted to stomp out of the kitchen, but lost her footing and fell.

She impressed Mac by playing it off, hopping up and grabbing both high heels in one hand. He thought he heard her muttering about "these damn shoes," as she went back to the bedroom.

"She's a little spitfire, isn't she?" Eleanor said.

Rose nodded. "Sure is. A cute spitfire, but a spitfire nonetheless."

Celeste returned a few minutes later, wearing rhinestoned sneakers with her fancy dress and tiara. They all sat down at the table, and as they passed the serving dishes, the pitcher of orange juice, and the salt and pepper, Mac experienced an unusual feeling settling over him. Contentment.

"Hey, Mr. Mac," Celeste said, and Rose said, "Don't talk with your mouth full."

Celeste gulped down her food and said, "Hey, Mr. Mac. Can I help you with chores after school?"

"Sure," he said. "I'd never turn down help."

"Thanks," she said, and when she smiled at him, a little chunk of egg on the corner of her mouth, he could practically feel her affection across the table, a little zing of energy, a pick-me-up.

He was smart enough to recognize that he wouldn't feel that way with just any woman and child sitting at his kitchen table. No, the feeling was related specifically to Rose and her adorable daughter. He glanced at his mom, and found her watching him. She winked, and he looked away. Whatever she thought she saw, he told himself, they were just friends, sharing a meal. Still, as they cleaned up and prepared to leave for the day, he found himself thinking, *Liar.*

* * *

A ripple of anticipation ran over Mac's skin when he came home that afternoon and saw Rose's car parked alongside his mom's. Although they'd crossed paths a few times during the day, he looked forward to seeing her again at home, talking to her, thinking about kissing her.

Because he most definitely would not kiss her.

Before he made it inside, Celeste came flying out flying down the front path. "Your car is really loud! Are you ready to do chores?" She threw her arms around his knees, and the fizzy feeling of joy bubbled up inside him.

He hugged her back. "Almost. I have to change clothes. I don't want to get my work clothes all dirty."

She stepped back and pointed at his shoes. "You don't want to get your fancy work shoes dirty, either, right? My auntie Taylor says you wear really nice shoes. And a man's taste in shoes really says something about him."

"I'll take that as a compliment. Come on, let's go inside."

She skipped along beside him and thanked him when he opened the door for her. Rose and Eleanor sat at the kitchen table, a plate of cheese, crackers, and cut up vegetables in the middle.

"We're having snacks." Celeste said. "I saved a spot for you, next to me. You might want to change before you eat. In case you get your work shirt dirty."

"Good advice."

He unbuttoned his cuffs. "How was everyone's day?"

"Mine was fair," Rose said, "until I got home, and found your mom here, with this beautiful plate of snacks. That ratcheted things up to excellent. Can I keep her?"

Eleanor laughed. "It's been so long since I got to make an after-school snack. Mac won't let me dote on him. But I figured Celeste wouldn't turn down this spread."

"You're right." Celeste climbed back into her chair and took a noisy drink of her water.

Seeing all three of them, looking as natural as could be, Mac wanted to pull up a chair and join them right away. Something about the calm, content energy, the obvious camaraderie, Rose's appreciation for his mom's sweet gesture, made Mac want to freeze the moment in time. Forever. That thought gave him a start, and he said, "Be right back."

While he changed into an old T-shirt and jeans, he thought about what Celeste said. *My auntie Taylor says you have great taste in shoes.* So that meant to Rose and her friends had talked about him. And, if they discussed his shoes, they'd been talking about him for more than professional reasons. He was still smiling when he walked back into the kitchen. Celeste patted the chair next to her. "You sit here."

Mac did as he was told, and she slid a plate in front of him.

"Well," he said to her. "Thank you. You included a little bit of everything. This looks perfect."

Celeste threw her mom a shady look. "See? I told you he would like it if I made him a plate."

Rose glanced at Mac, hid a smile. "You were right."

When they finished eating, Rose offered to clean up, and Celeste grabbed Mac's hand and pulled him out the kitchen door. Her hand still in his, she said, "What's first?"

All business. He had to admire that in a kid.

"We'll start with the goats."

"Why?"

"They're kind of mischievous," Mac said. "I like to feed them first so they're busy eating while I do the rest of the chores."

Celeste laughed, the sound like music. "That's silly."

"Goats are pretty silly. They like to bounce, like you."

"Why?"

"You know, I've never thought to wonder why. Maybe it's because they're happy."

"Bouncing *is* fun," she said. "What will we do after the goats?"

"Horses and cow."

"Oooh! Why do we do them next?"

Mac pointed to the goat side of the barn and then the horse and cow side. "They're next-door neighbors. Only makes sense to do them after the goats."

"And then what?"

"We'll pick vegetables."

"Why?"

Mac laughed. "Because they're not fragile or hard to carry, like the eggs and milk. We'll put them in a basket and then do the milk and eggs, and then carry everything inside."

"Okay."

Sure enough, the goats bounced all over their enclosure when they saw Mac and Celeste coming.

"You're right! They are really bouncy."

"Yeah," Mac agreed. "They have a lot of energy. Just like a certain five-year-old I know."

Celeste gave him a side-eye.

"I'm just kidding. I mean, you do have a lot of energy. I was teasing you."

"I know. My mom says I'm a mover and a shaker. So, how do we feed them?"

Mac showed her the container where he kept the goat feed and helped her pry off the lid. She asked if she could scoop the food and put it in the bowls. The first time, feed scattered all around the bowl when she poured it. She looked at him, obviously nervous about his reaction. While he did wonder how much her help would cost him, he gave her a reassuring smile and said, "Don't worry about it. It's your first time. Maybe try holding the scoop a little closer to the bowl when you pour it in." The second scoop, which Celeste performed with her tongue sticking out between her teeth, went a little more smoothly, and with the third, she spilled almost no grain.

"Well done," Mac said, and Celeste beamed at him. "Now we do the horses and Cookie?"

"Yep."

She threw quite a few more "why" questions at him as they completed the chores. *Why do tomatoes change color as they ripen, but not zucchinis? Why do cows and goats eat different foods? Why do you have goats and cows? Why do chickens lay eggs?*

Once again, Mac marveled at the energy required to interact with a five-year-old. Celeste was a fun, charming, well-behaved child, but Rose must be a legitimate Wonder Woman.

The smell of onions and garlic greeted Mac and Celeste when they went back into the house.

"Smells good in here," Mac called out.

Rose turned to smile at him from the counter, where she stood chopping vegetables.

She looked at the basket he held and said, "Good. You brought me vegetables. Want to hand me a couple of zucchinis and a couple of carrots?"

Walking up to Rose and kissing her seemed like the most natural thing to do. And again, Mac chastised himself. But he did place the basket next to where she was working and stand close enough that their arms touched, and he reveled in that small pleasure.

Chapter Seventeen

For Rose, living on the farm felt at once enchanting and perfectly ordinary, like she was living in a fairy tale that had long ago been embedded in her genes. The typical daily routine, cooking and cleaning, collecting eggs, feeding the goats — she hadn't tried milking the cow, yet — felt almost ceremonial in its simplicity.

One Saturday afternoon, she volunteered to deep clean the kitchen while Mac repaired the tractor. Eleanor was off at a Bingo game, and Rose enlisted Celeste to pull all the dishes out of the lower cabinets, which she planned to vacuum out. Before she moved in, Rose might have imagined the task feeling somewhat intrusive, but after having lived there a few weeks, she felt a sense of purpose and service as she stacked the dishes in the sink and started vacuuming.

Soon Rose was so wrapped up in the rhythm of her task that she lost track of time. At some point, she realized she hadn't seen or heard Celeste in a while. She called for her, but Celeste didn't answer. She knew she shouldn't worry too much. Celeste had quickly learned the ropes and the safety rules, and Rose was eighty percent certain she wouldn't put herself in harm's way.

"But there's always the other twenty percent," she muttered, turning off the vacuum and hollering for her.

When Celeste didn't answer, Rose went to the kitchen door and hollered again. Almost immediately, she saw Celeste running toward her, her arms spread out wide as if she were flying. "Mommy! Mommy! It's a *really* hot day! Mac is *really* sweaty! I *really* think we should make him some lemonade!"

"Really?"

Celeste responded to Rose's joke with a full-blown belly laugh, and pulled her into the kitchen. "Really."

"I love that you're thinking about doing something nice for Mac," Rose told Celeste as she got out the supplies. Powdered lemonade mix might not be legit lemonade, but it was just as refreshing on a day so hot, heat waves rose from the ground. She and Celeste mixed the powder and water into a pitcher. Celeste insisted on putting some ice in a glass and then pouring in the lemonade. She filled the glass right to the very top — it was literally brimming — and then insisted Rose carry it out so it didn't spill. Rose took a tiny sip when Celeste wasn't looking, and then let Celeste lead her across the yard. "He's over here, Mommy. He's fixing the tractor. Careful! Don't spill!"

Rose didn't see Mac until they reached the tractor, and he climbed out of the cab and stood on the running board.

Oh, my. Celeste was right. Mac was sweaty. He was also very, *very* sexy in his boots and jeans and cowboy hat. He was so hot, he'd taken off his shirt. *And made himself even hotter.*

Rose imagined that if she put a finger on his shoulder, it would sizzle.

Every muscle in that man's torso stood out — his chest, each abdominal muscle, his obliques — and she wanted to get her hands on all of them. His skin gleamed with his sweat, and she pictured the two of them, between the sheets, their bodies slick against one another.

"Mommy!"

Rose realized she'd frozen, lemonade in hand, mouth open. Who could blame her, really? She closed her mouth. "Oh. Sorry." She cleared her throat. "Celeste said you were, um, hot and sweaty. She wanted to bring you lemonade." She held out the glass in offering.

"I asked my mom to carry it because I filled the cup too full."

"That was very thoughtful," Mac said. He hopped down off the tractor with the grace of a wild cat. Then, making eye contact with Rose the entire way, he walked over and wrapped his hand around the glass ... and her hand. "Thank you. It *is* a very warm day. And this will hit the spot."

He took the glass from her, put it to his lips, tipped his head back, and drank. Rose thought that was the sexiest thing she'd ever seen in her life. The sun shone on his torso and beads of sweat ran down into his waistband. Rose's body literally vibrated with need. She briefly wondered if she could send Celeste on an errand for a few minutes, and have her way with him. *It wouldn't take long.* Mac finished drinking, and wiped his mouth with the back of his hand.

"Wow!" Celeste said. "You must have been thirsty! See, Mommy? I told you!"

"You're right. He does look very hot. Er, thirsty." She looked at Mac then, hoping he'd pick up on the accusatory glare she was putting down. He had no right to go around looking like that.

He did pick up on it, because he raised an eyebrow at her and handed her the empty glass. "I owe you."

Those words sent a fresh wave of lust through Rose's body.

"You do. For now though, I've got to get back to the kitchen. I have more cabinets to vacuum. Come on, Celeste."

"Mo-om," Celeste whined. "Can I stay out here with Mac? I can help him fix the tractor while you vacuum the cabinets."

Although it pained her to look at Mac again and not touch him, Rose turned around. "Do you mind?" She hoped her voice sounded less strained than she felt, holding herself back from throwing herself at him. "She *was* really bored in the kitchen."

He smiled broadly as if he could actually read her thoughts. "I don't mind at all."

"Thank you," Rose said, her tone as prim as she could make it.

With that, she ran back inside, grateful for the alone time.

An hour of hard work in the kitchen calmed Rose's system (and her sexual energy) enough that by the time Mac and Celeste came back in (him with his shirt on), she felt like she could breathe again, and was in slightly less danger of combusting.

"The tractor's fixed! The tractor's fixed! Mac said we can take it out for a spin tomorrow!"

"That's amazing," Rose said to Celeste, and then to Mac she said, "It was really nice of you to fix it. I know you might have done it on a different timeline if Celeste wasn't involved."

Mac chuckled, and Celeste, lower lip thrust out in a pout, said, "Hey! Mac told me that tractor is probably tired of sitting there, with no one driving it."

"That's true. I did tell her that."

"Well, I'm sure the tractor will be very happy to get some exercise tomorrow," Rose said.

Celeste nodded, the arch of her eyebrows indicating she felt vindicated.

"Your cheeks are looking pretty rosy," Rose said to her. "Why don't you go relax and watch some TV for a little bit. Cool off." Celeste bounced away, and within a few seconds, Rose heard the opening notes to the theme song for one of her favorite shows.

"The kitchen looks spectacular," Mac said. "I can't remember the last time I saw it this clean."

Rose took off the rubber gloves she'd been wearing and tucked them into their new spot under the kitchen sink. "Thanks. It feels so good to have a space all organized, doesn't it?"

"It does." Mac hooked a thumb toward his bedroom. "I'm going to go shower."

Of course, his need for a shower brought back the image is of his six-pack and the way he looked when he was drinking that lemonade. Rose felt heat pool between her legs. "Okay. I have a few more things to finish up in here."

"Sounds good. And Rose?"

"Yeah?"

"Thanks for that lemonade."

He's doing it on purpose! He knew damn well how good he looked without his shirt on, and he was trying to turn her on! Before she could form a coherent response, he turned around and walked away.

While he was gone, Rose organized the cookbooks in alphabetical order and dusted the knickknacks on the kitchen windowsill. She focused so hard on being completely present in her organization duties that she didn't notice he was back until he was literally right behind her. The front of his body was just a hair's breadth from the back of hers. His hands were on the sink, one on either side of her waist. And his breath was in her ear.

"Rose," he said, and she almost came right there, standing at the kitchen sink with a duster in her hand. "I haven't been able to stop thinking about you. About kissing you. About how much I love coming home to you in my kitchen. Our kitchen." While he spoke, his breath sent shivers over her skin. "Tell me you've been thinking about it, too. That night when we almost kissed — I keep replaying it in my mind."

Rose realized that she'd unconsciously relaxed her arms and leaned against Mac's body. He felt solid and warm and strong.

A loud snore came from the living room and Rose turned to see Celeste had fallen asleep on the couch, arms and legs splayed out in pure exhaustion and comfort. "Celeste is asleep," she whispered, turning the rest of the way around, so she and Mac faced each other. God, he was so handsome up close. His skin was a superb light shade of brown, and his eyes were warm and, at the moment, filled with desire. She put her hands on his hips and he rested his forehead on her hers.

"Now what?" Mac said.

There they were, alone, obviously equally intoxicated with one another. She tipped her face up, brought her lips to his. When they kissed, a sound escaped his throat, guttural, erotic. His hands were in her hair, and his mouth was hungry on hers. A desperate need, a strong longing Rose had never experienced before, overtook her and she wrapped her arms around his waist and pulled him against her. Lust, pleasantly warm and powerful, flowed through her veins. She'd never experienced desire like that, and quite suddenly, she'd give anything to ride that wave home.

The kitchen door opened, squeaking on its hinges, and Mac jumped away from Rose as if she were on fire.

"Hello," Eleanor called as Rose spun around to face the sink again. Mac put both of his hands on his head, and turned around so he was facing the center of the kitchen. Rose stood there, shell-shocked.

"Hi, Mom," Mac said.

Eleanor looked from Mac to Rose and back to Mac again, and a slow smile spread across her face. "Well, hello, you two. I had a great time at Bingo, but I'm all tuckered out. I'm going to go lie down for a while."

Chapter Eighteen

Rose was avoiding him. In the week since they'd shared that kiss — arguably the most mind-blowing, earth-shattering kiss Mac had ever experienced — he had barely seen her. Somehow, she still managed to do all the cooking and cleaning, timing it perfectly with Mac's chores so she was in the house when he was outside, and vice versa. Most days she left before he did and returned in time to put Celeste to bed. From what he could glean from Celeste, the two of them were spending lots of time with Taylor and Jessie.

Which meant their kiss affected Rose as much as it affected him, Mac thought as he lay in bed Saturday morning. He felt himself smiling at that realization. He knew Rose planned to grocery shop that day ... not because she'd told him, but because she'd mentioned it to his mom.

She can't avoid me forever. He pictured himself as a conspiratorial mastermind, drumming his fingers together. She would have to come home with the groceries, and he would be there to help put them away. His bedsheets felt cool against his skin as he stretched, appreciating the luxury of an extra hour of sleep and the delicious memory of that kiss.

Mac wasn't surprised to find Celeste and Eleanor (and not Rose) in the kitchen.

Celeste greeted him by holding up her fork, a couple of squares of pancake stuck to its tines. "Good morning, Mac. We saved some pancakes for you."

"Thank you," he said. "They smell delicious."

"They are."

Mac smiled because he knew Rose would tell her not to talk with her mouth full. "I put syrup on mine. But your mom put honey on hers. What are you going to put on yours?"

At the counter, Mac dished himself up. "Oh, I don't know. Maybe I'll do syrup on one and honey on one."

"You're only going to have two? I'm having four. Your mom had three. My mom had four. Now she's at the grocery store. She said she wanted to get there early, before everyone else."

Celeste was a good source of information and Mac loved that about her. "Okay. I'll have four, too. And that was smart of your mom to go to the store early."

Pancakes, bacon, and eggs on his plate, Max settled himself at the table.

"Good morning, hon," his mom said. "I asked Rose if Celeste could stay here, help me with my garden." She winked at Mac, and Mac knew she'd offered to keep Celeste at the house so Rose could shop in peace and quiet.

"I helped pick weeds," Celeste said.

Nodding, Mac dug into his pancakes. "That's serious business."

Mac ate quickly, hoping to get the chores done in time to help Rose bring in the groceries and put them away when she returned. His plan worked. As he carried the fresh milk and eggs toward the kitchen, he heard the tires of Rose's car crunching on the gravel driveway. *Caught!*

Chuckling at his own conniving, he set the milk and eggs on the counter and met Rose in the driveway. She looked surprised to see him, and this boosted his satisfaction even more.

"Good morning," he said, and she responded in kind, albeit with unnatural cheer.

"Celeste said you wanted to beat the crowds. Did you?"

"I did."

Mac noticed Rose gave him plenty of space as she made her way to the liftgate. He also noticed she was wearing her perfume, something spicy and floral. The scent turned him on. She opened the liftgate and reached in to grab some bags. The curve of her hip would fit perfectly in his hand, and the urge to run his palm from that curve up to her waist almost overtook him. But it seemed they needed to have a conversation before he started putting his hands on her.

"Well," he said, keeping his tone light. "Looks like you did some serious damage."

For the first time that morning, she made eye contact with him and smiled. "I know. I'm used to shopping for two, though I might have gone a little overboard shopping for four."

Not a second after they finished putting away groceries, Rose said, "Unless you guys need me for anything else, Celeste and I have some errands to run."

Mac's heart sank. He'd planned on spending time with Rose, feeling her out, maybe even talking about that kiss and the aftermath. But she wasn't going to give him a chance. No matter, he decided, consciously shifting his attitude. She lived there. She'd have to face him eventually.

After Rose and Celeste took off, Mac asked his mom if she wanted to go to the farmers market.

"Now that it's cooling off a bit, one of those fancy coffees sounds really good," Eleanor said. "Plus, I was thinking about getting Celeste a hat made from alpaca wool. Wouldn't she look cute in one of those?"

"She'd look cute in just about anything. Let's go."

Eleanor didn't waste any time putting Mac on the spot as they drove toward town. "So. How do you think it's going with Rose and Celeste here?"

Hoping to determine whether she was going to ask about what she'd walked in on the week before, he looked at her out of the corner of his eye. Her face didn't give anything away.

"I think it's going well. What you think?"

"Me?" Eleanor put a hand on her chest, the movement exaggerated. That's when Mac knew. She was ready to pounce.

"Yeah. You."

"I'm loving it. Rose is wonderful, of course. She has been a huge help. But, Celeste! There's just something about having a child around."

"I've enjoyed having her around, too," Mac said. "She sure has a lot of energy."

Eleanor chuckled. "She does."

They rode in silence until the fields gave way to the tidy yards just outside downtown. Then, exactly as Mac expected, Eleanor said, "Seems like I might have interrupted something when I came in the other afternoon. It also seems like Rose has been avoiding you since then. What happened?"

Avoidance might work for Rose, but it had never worked for Mac. So he procrastinated, instead. He put on his blinker and took his time looking over his shoulder before switching lanes. He turned on the radio, and then changed the station. Crossing her arms, Eleanor waited. When Mac ran out of tasks he could do while driving, he finally said, "You're right. We kissed. It was —" how much could he say to his mom, without saying too much? "A really great kiss. I know it was great for her too because, you're right, she's been avoiding me ever since. I have a feeling she's afraid that if we get romantic, and things don't go well, I won't want her to live here anymore."

Eleanor uncrossed her arms and put an elbow on the windowsill. She looked over at Mac. "Is that true?"

"I don't know." Mac shrugged. "I mean, if we became romantic, and decided to part ways like two mature adults, of course we wouldn't kick her out. But what if she broke my heart?"

"Or, what if you broke hers?"

Huh. Mac hadn't considered that. He'd become so besotted with Rose, he figured she was the one who'd be doing any heartbreaking.

"Good point."

They'd arrived at the farmers market, and after standing in line to buy their fancy coffees, they perused the stalls. Mac bought some fresh pasta, and Eleanor found an alpaca wool hat for Celeste. On the way home, Mac spotted a pile of junk on the side of the road, with a *Free* sign taped to a bookcase. A separate sign, taped to a lamp on top of a well-used side table read, *Take one thing or take it all.* Mac pulled over just ahead of it.

"I know what caught your eye."

Mac grinned at his mom and got out of the car. He'd stopped due to pure altruism. But, he thought as he threw the old tire into the trunk, now Rose would *have* to talk to him. And that was a pretty great benefit.

Just before dinner time, Rose and Celeste came home. Because Mac wanted to surprise Celeste, Eleanor met them in the driveway and led them through the front door. Mac waited in the kitchen. He heard Celeste's voice in full storytelling mode as she filled Eleanor in on what she and her mom had done that day. He was surprised to feel his stomach aflutter with nerves. There was no way Celeste wouldn't love her surprise. *Maybe you're more worried about impressing Celeste's mom.*

Celeste, always traveling at high speed, reached the kitchen first.

"Mac!" She ran up to him and hugged him hard, as if it had been days, not hours, since they'd seen each other. He hugged her back, and the snakes writhing in his stomach calmed down.

"Celeste! I have a surprise for you!"

"A surprise?" Celeste looked at Rose, her expression saying, *Can you believe it?* "I *love* surprises! Where is it?"

Mac pointed at the kitchen door. "It's outside. Want to see it?"

After a few of her trademark bounces, Celeste said, "I do! I do! Can I, Mommy?"

"Of course." Rose looked at Mac, her eyebrows furrowed like she was trying to figure out what the surprise could might be.

"You can come too, Rose," he said.

With an uncertain smile, she said, "Okay, thanks."

Eleanor watched the whole scene unfold, her eyes twinkling. "Can I come, too?"

Celeste ran up to Eleanor and grabbed her hand. "Yes! Come on!"

Mac held open the door, and the ladies walked out ahead of him. Celeste saw the tire swing in less than a second, and she shrieked, "A tire swing! Is that my surprise? I love it! I love a tire swing!"

She proved it by breaking into a full-on sprint, her little arms and legs pumping faster than Mac had ever seen them. The three adults laughed, and Rose said, "She has wanted her own tire swing for as long as I can remember. You're never going to get her to move out now."

Mac smiled at her. "At this point, I wouldn't mind. But I'm sure her thoughts will change when she hits the teenage years." Still smiling, Rose said, "Thank you. This is really special."

"You're welcome."

"Want a push?" Eleanor asked.

Already clambering onto the tire, Celeste yelled, "Yes! Yes, please!" She giggled as the swing picked up speed, and Mac heard his mom giggling, too.

"This is so good for her," Rose said.

"I think it's good for all of us," Mac said.

After a while, Celeste tired of being on the swing and announced she was going to run some laps. Mac watched as her little legs strode across the expanse of the yard, and her little arms pumped. Quite suddenly, she stopped next to the barn.

"You guys! I think Potato had her kittens!"

She was kneeling on the ground by the time Eleanor, Rose, and Mac made it over there and sure enough, there was Potato, laying on her side in an old wooden produce crate, four tiny kittens nursing.

"Looks like you're right," Mac said.

"This is not what I thought kittens would look like." Celeste sounded uncertain.

Mac's mom chuckled. "They do come out looking kind of smushed. But their eyes will open soon, and they'll get fluffier, and you'll fall in love with them."

Naturally, that prompted about a dozen more "why?" questions before they trooped back inside.

That night, Mac went into the kitchen, poured himself a bourbon on the rocks, and sat at the kitchen table to wait for Rose. He'd given her time to come around, to talk to him on her own. But she hadn't.

He would take matters into his own hands.

She had a single glass of wine every night, but for the past week she'd been drinking it in her bedroom, hand washing the glass in the morning and leaving it on the drying rack.

At the moment, he could hear Rose in the bedroom she shared with Celeste, her voice animated as she read a bedtime story. After the story, Rose would rub Celeste's back for a few minutes before coming out for her wine. Sure enough, a few minutes after Mac sat down, she came through the bedroom door and shut it quietly.

She practically tiptoed down the hall to the kitchen, and jumped when she saw Mac sitting there. "You scared me!" She laughed, but for a split second, the look in her eyes conveyed anything but humor. She looked genuinely scared. "I'm just here to rinse Celeste's water cup, and then I'll leave you alone."

As she stood at the sink, Mac decided immediately to change his tactic. He'd planned on seduction, but he could see the timing wasn't right for that. She still looked frightened, like the raccoon he'd caught in a live trap a few years before. The little rascal had made a nest under the house, and dug through an HVAC pipe to do it. Mac had the dirty task of evicting him, and when Mac found him in the trap one morning, he cowered against the back, eyes wide, body trembling.

Rose's reaction to seeing Mac in the kitchen when she hadn't expected him was concerning.

"Sorry." He kept his voice quiet and gentle and lifted his drink off the table. "I was just having a nightcap. Want to join me?"

The water still running, Rose's body stilled. "I did come in for a glass of wine. I like to have one at night, to wind down." She finished rinsing the cup, turned off the water, and set the cup next to the sink. Finally, she turned to face him, leaning her hip against the counter. "But I don't want to bother you."

"You won't be bothering me at all. In fact, you still look a little shaken up. Why don't you let me get it for you?"

Rose wiped her hands on her pants. "No, that's okay. I can get it."

Mac stood. "I insist. I didn't mean to startle you. Let me get your wine for you. You can decide whether it's chivalry or guilt."

That earned him a laugh.

"Okay. Thank you." She sat down at the table, and Mac poured her a healthy glass.

"What are you drinking?" she asked as he sat down across from her.

"Bourbon," he said. "Want a sip?"

"No, thanks. I'll stick to my wine."

The temptation was strong to dig into Rose's reaction, to find out why he'd startled her as much as he had. But he decided it was better at that point to be direct, and stick to his original reason for waiting her out.

"I can't help but notice I haven't seen much of you this week."

Rose took a sudden interest in her wine, staring into its depths. Mac smiled. Waited.

"I know," she said.

Not demanding an explanation took every ounce of self-control Mac possessed. Instead, he waited some more. At long last, she looked at him. Maintaining eye contact, she took a drink of her wine. Then another. "That kiss," she said. His heart leapt in his chest. It *had* meant something to her. "That was a great kiss." A smile replaced her serious expression, and Mac felt his lungs open up. He could breathe again.

"It was. So why have you been hiding from me ever since?"

Rose's chest heaved with her sigh. "Because it was so great."

To keep from speaking, Mac pressed his lips together. Words threatened to spill out. He bit his tongue.

"Mac," she said. God, he loved the way she said his name. She lifted her glass and took another drink. "Living here, with you and your mom, has been absolutely wonderful. And although I would relive that kiss over and over, and maybe I have, in my mind, I don't want to do anything to jeopardize Celeste and I living here."

"I can understand that," Mac told her.

Her shoulders relaxed. "Good. Then I can stop avoiding you."

Mac took a step of his drink, enjoying the warmth that traveled down to his stomach. "I hope you will. And I hope you'll kiss me again. For the record, I thought the kiss was pretty great, too. And I'm fairly certain that as two consenting adults, we could do some kissing without messing up our living situation. I've enjoyed having you and Celeste here, too. Not just because you've made my life easier, but because I love being around both of you."

Rose nodded. "I'm glad to hear that. I know Celeste can be... a lot."

"A lot of *fun*," Mac said, grinning. "I admit, I've asked myself on several occasions, how you keep up with her. Seriously. You're amazing. You're doing a great job with her."

Something flickered in Rose's eyes, but it was gone before Mac could identify it.

"Thank you," she said. "That means a lot."

"You're welcome." Mac took another sip of his drink. "Does this mean we can try kissing again?"

The sound of Rose's laughter echoed in the empty kitchen, and she clapped a hand over her mouth. Using her thumb and forefinger, she twirled her wine glass by the stem. "I would love to." She looked at him again. "But I'm not sure if it's the best idea."

"You know what my dad used to say?"

"No," Rose said, tilting her head. "What did he say?"

"He said that the worst ideas are often the best ideas."

Another bark of laughter from Rose brought a smile to Mac's face.

"Well, I'm not sure I'm inclined to live life by that philosophy."

Mac chuckled. "Okay, but if you decide you want to test it out by kissing me, I'm totally open to it."

Both of their glasses were empty, and the air in the kitchen felt heavy with expectation.

"Want me to take your glass?"

"I think I'll have another." She handed her empty glass to him, and when he brought it back to her, having refilled his, too, she was standing next to the table.

"Why don't we take this conversation outside?"

Chapter Nineteen

Outside, the evening air felt crisp on Rose's skin. She shivered.

"Cold?" Mac asked.

"No." She smiled, and he smiled back.

"Let's walk." Mac slipped his hand into Rose's, sending a fresh round of chills over her skin.

"You can see the whole sky out here," Rose said. "It's incredible. I've been living in the city for so long, I forgot what it's like to see all the stars."

"It's beautiful. And it reminds me how small we are, in the grand scheme of things, and how short life is. Which is why I think we should do more kissing while we have the chance."

Rose laughed. They stopped next to the old oak tree where Mac had hung the tire swing. "Thank you again for the tire swing. It was a really sweet gesture."

"You're welcome. The tire swing was pretty much my favorite place to hang out as a kid. I thought Celeste would get kick out of it."

"She sure did. And it will definitely keep her busy. Along with the kittens. I have a feeling she's going to fall in love with them."

"Me, too."

Rose took a sip of her wine. Fueled with liquid courage, she decided to come clean to Mac. "I really enjoyed kissing you. I'd like to do more of it." When he smiled, she held up a hand. "But. I feel like there are so many reasons we shouldn't have a relationship."

Mac tilted his head. "What are those reasons?"

All the fears she hadn't expressed came rushing out of her mouth. "First of all, I don't want Celeste to get too attached. Second, we work together. If we break up, we still have to see each other every day. Third, now we live together. If things don't work out, that's going to be real awkward. Fourth, I don't want to rely on you. Not just you, but anyone. I learned early on that people aren't always as dependable as they seem. And if you're suddenly out of my life, then what? I've come to rely on you, and it's hard to go back to being on my own."

She could tell Mac was hiding a smile, and irritation prickled at her consciousness. "What's so funny?"

He reached up and smoothed the crease between her eyebrows with his thumb. "Why does every scenario end with the two of us breaking up?"

Rose hadn't thought of that. "Well, I don't really know. Dating me is one thing. But dating me means you get my daughter, too. It's a lot to take on. I can't imagine an attractive, free-wheeling guy like you would want that commitment."

"It *is* a lot. In a good way."

Again, Rose thought she hadn't considered that angle.

"I'll address each of your points, one at a time," Mac said.

Rose's heart pricked its ears.

"First of all, I'm getting attached to Celeste, too. Even if you and I went our separate ways, I hope you know that Celeste would have only good memories of our time together. Second of all, lots of people work together. And, you know, have relationships." His eyes twinkled with humor. He wiggled his eyebrows.

"You were going to say sleep together, weren't you?" Rose asked.

"I was. But I didn't want to seem crass."

"Carry on."

Smiling broadly, Mac continued. "Third, you're right. If we

went our separate ways and you still lived here, it might be awkward. But, I hope if that happened, we could both be mature about our next steps. Hopefully, with what you've saved on rent by staying here, you and Celeste would be able to afford to rent, or even buy, a nice house in quiet neighborhood. And fourth, I hope you do start to rely on me. I'm a reliable guy. Besides, I think there is a scenario you haven't considered."

"And what is that?" Rose asked.

"What if we *both* get attached? And Celeste, too? And what if it's great? What if it's as great as that kiss? And what if we don't go our separate ways?"

Shock left Rose speechless. She had to admit, he made some good points, and she told him so. Yet ... her points were valid, too.

With her free hand, she reached out and took his. "Will you give me some time to think about it?"

His voice was husky when he responded. "You've been thinking about it all week, haven't you?"

She had been. She had relived that kiss too many times to count. In fact, she was reliving it again, standing out in Mac's yard — *their* yard — under the wide open sky. As if their bodies were pressed together, hip to hip, she felt an urgent heat building between her legs. "You're not wrong."

"So have I." He dropped her hand and tucked her hair behind her ear, his hand coming to rest on her collarbone, his fingertips on the back of her neck. She was aware of exactly where his skin touched hers.

The breath trembled on her lips. He tipped his head toward hers, so their lips nearly touched. Nearly.

"I'll tell you what," he said. "Let's kiss once more, right now. I can tell you're thinking about that."

She nodded.

"And then I'll let you think about it. I just want you to be very, *very* certain of exactly what you're thinking about."

"Okay," she whispered, every cell in her being yearning for another kiss. "That sounds like a good idea."

He brought his mouth to hers. This time, he wasn't gentle. He was insistent, hungry. His tongue was on hers, and his hand slid up the back of her neck to cradle her head. Rose's insides ignited, pleasurable little flames licking at every nerve ending. Although she'd been grateful she had a drink when they first came out — it gave her something to do with her hands — she now wished she could toss it aside and use her entire body to show Mac just how thought-provoking she found the kiss. And then it was over. Breathless, they stood facing each other, his hand still in her hair, her hand gripping the back of his shirt. He smiled, cocky. "There. That ought to do it. Should we raise a glass to thinking about those kisses?"

Suddenly, Rose felt like she had to fight off a wave of giddiness. A laugh bubbled up. "Cheers."

* * *

At their first homecoming meeting, the eleventh-grade students had decided to build the ship from Shakespeare's *The Tempest*. To Rose's surprise, Mac offered to host a float-building session at his house Friday evening.

"We have plenty of space, and this way, you can go in and put Celeste to bed, so she won't be up all hours of the night. Plus, we'll have all my tools here."

Students started showing up at five minutes to seven, two or three to a car. By ten after, Rose and Mac had a group of fifteen kids ready to work.

Mac told Rose he'd made a blueprint, but she was shocked when he unrolled the poster-sized piece of paper and taped it to the barn wall. The drawing was more than just a guideline. It was a literal blueprint, with measurements, lists of specific nails and screws and materials, and suggestions for paint colors.

"Well," Rose told the kids. "It looks like Johnny Mac has made this easy for us."

He held out his arms and smiled. "I live to serve."

Rose told herself that her sudden arousal had nothing to do with imagining Mac serving her. No, it was probably hormones. Or something.

Everyone gathered around the blueprint, and Mac put the kids in groups and assigned each one a job. They split off and began assembling the different components.

Rose and Mac stood next to the blueprint, watching the students work, while Celeste flitted from group to group asking questions. "Why are you using that tool? Why are you building the float out of wood? Why are you building a ship?"

Mac chuckled, and Rose groaned. "She is going to *why* our workers right off the property."

"No she's not. Look how good they are with her."

Sure enough, one of the students, Olivia, was showing Celeste how to hammer in a nail.

"That is really sweet," Rose said.

"Ms. Coffey?" Henry, a student in her fifth-period class, raised his hand.

She walked over to where he stood, holding a drill and a piece of wood. "Henry, how can I help you?"

"I can't get this screw to go in."

Rose ignored the comments from other students ("Henry can't screw stuff," "Henry's having a hard time getting it in"). She showed him how to drill a pilot hole, and watched as he drilled in the screw. By the time she got done with that, Mac was helping another student with the frame for the ship's hull.

During her tenure at the high school, she'd heard nothing but positive talk about Johnny Mac from the students. He was an enthusiastic, hands-on teacher, exploding things and lighting things on fire to keep the kids interested. He told corny jokes, and even though the kids acted exasperated by those jokes, they repeated them throughout the school day. Rose saw evidence of his camaraderie with the kids as he worked with them on the float.

The longer she watched him, the more she started to think maybe he was right. Hadn't he proven already that he was a genuinely nice guy? She watched as he showed one of the kids how two of the frame pieces would fit together, then orchestrated that step by assigning some students to hold the pieces while others drilled them into place. He was authoritative, but not bossy. Knowledgeable, but friendly.

And he showed about as much patience with Celeste as she did.

Only a truly kind person would have put the two of them up in a hotel room, brought back Celeste's ratty stuffed animal, Bumpy, and put up a tire swing. She couldn't deny the attraction between them. Yes, there was the shirtless lemonade-drinking moment. But also, she found herself noticing — and appreciating — his powerful physical attributes throughout the day. At the moment, his biceps flexed as he carried a rotary saw over to the table he'd set up. And his butt in those genes was downright mouthwatering.

What harm could it do to give things with him a spin?

Ah, piped up that old, critical voice in the back of her mind. *Even the nicest guy in the world would quickly get tired of being saddled with a pre-made family.*

"Are you okay, Ms. Coffey?" Henry looked at her, concern etched in his eyebrows.

Rose blinked. "I'm fine. Sorry, just spacing out. What's up?"

"Um, your daughter."

Rose felt a deep sigh starting in her chest. She had worried Celeste might get in the way. "I hope she's not being too much trouble."

Henry laughed. "No. Not at all. It's just that she fell asleep ... in the tractor. I just wanted you to know where she was."

"Oh, good. I thought you were going to say you almost injured her because she got in the way," Rose said. "Thank you for looking out for her. And me. I would've been in a real panic if I couldn't find her."

Henry shrugged. "No problem. That's what I figured. She's a funny kid."

"Yes, she is a funny kid."

Rose figured she'd better get Celeste and take her inside to bed. The longer she slept in the tractor, the harder it would be for her to fall back asleep once she got in bed. When Rose reached the tractor though, she realized retrieving Celeste wouldn't be as simple as lifting her down. She was curled up on the driver seat, inside the cab. Rose would have to climb up to reach her, and then climb down with Celeste in her arms. Just as Rose put a foot on the first rung of the ladder, she felt a hand on her arm.

"Let me help you," Mac said. "It'll be easier if one of us climbs in to get her and hands her down to the other one."

Relieved, Rose nodded. "You're right. Thank you. I was wondering how I would get down, gracefully."

"I was wondering how either one of us would get down safely. Here, let me climb in and get her. That way, if she wakes up, I can hand her right to you, and she won't freak out."

Rose smiled. "Sounds like a plan. Although, I don't think she'd freak out if I handed her to you. She thinks you're pretty great."

Rose was tempted to say, I think you're pretty great, too, but shyness prevented her from vocalizing that sentiment. Celeste didn't even open her eyes as Mac picked her up and handed her down to Rose.

"Thank you," Rose said, settling Celeste onto her shoulder.

"You're welcome." He hopped down from the tractor. "Take your time putting her to bed. I'll hold down the fort here."

Touched by his thoughtfulness, Rose did as he suggested, half-waking Celeste for a quick brushing of the teeth before tucking her in. When she came back outside, Mac was leading the kids through cleanup to the tune of some silly marching song. They sang along, cheerfully putting away tools and stacking boards and rolling up the blueprint. Even though the song was silly, and Mac look even sillier acting out the different verses, Rose thought that was just about the sexiest she'd ever seen him.

Chapter Twenty

There was something special, almost magical, about lifting a sleeping child and handing her to her mother. Celeste's little sigh as she settled onto Mac's shoulder evoked a fresh wave of tenderness and affection. Sharing the duty of caring for a child made Mac feel even more connected to Rose. And, he didn't miss (or dislike) the way she looked at him when she came back from putting Celeste to bed. She felt it, too.

After their first float-building session, Mac decided he would devote himself to proving to Rose that he was serious about her and Celeste — no matter how long it took.

That weekend, he volunteered to help with the cooking, since she'd done the majority since moving in. They worked well together, quickly finding a natural rhythm. One of them chopped while the other sautéed, one of them stirred while the other basted, one of them washed while the other dried. And, since Mac offered to help with the cooking, Rose offered to help with the outdoor chores. She said it was reciprocity, but he sensed (and hoped) it was because she wanted to spend time with him.

Sunday afternoon, Eleanor cut a bunch of flowers from her garden and arranged them into a bouquet, which she put in a vase on the kitchen table. She and Mac were cleaning up the cut stems when Rose came in, saw the bouquet, and gasped. "Eleanor! Are these all from your garden?"

Pride in her smile, Eleanor said, "Yes! My flowers are doing really well this year."

Rose leaned down to smell the bouquet. "They smell so good," she said. The look of pleasure on her face made Mac imagine all the ways he could bring her pleasure. *Think about cars.* He chastised himself. He should not be imagining sex with Rose when his mom was in the same room.

"What are these pink ones, here?" Rose wanted to know.

"Those are peonies," Eleanor said. "Aren't they pretty?"

"The prettiest. I don't think I've ever seen them before, but they are now officially my favorite flower."

Monday morning, Mac made a bouquet of peonies and left them in a small vase on Rose's desk at school. At the end of the day, she came up to his classroom. "I assume you are the thoughtful person who left those flowers on my desk."

"Guilty."

Leaning against the door jamb, Rose crossed her legs at the ankles and her arms over her chest. In her pencil skirt and floral blouse, with her hair in what could pass as a tidy bun, Rose looked every part the serious, studious woman who desperately needed to be undressed and loosened up. That thought made Mac smile, and he let his gaze roam from her face to her chest, where her breasts rested on her arms, to her waist, to her very unserious bubblegum-pink high heels. She cleared her throat, and he let his gaze reverse its course, traveling quite lazily back up to her face. He could tell from her scowl that she was trying to look mad, but her eyes were smiling. "Thank you. They're lovely."

"Do I get a thank-you kiss?" he asked.

Her arms dropped to her sides. "Mac! Not right now!"

"Does that mean I get one later? And does that mean you finished thinking about whether you want to keep kissing me?"

She shook her head. "I have been thinking about it, yes. I'm still thinking. Also, I really love the flowers. Thank you again."

She did an about-face and walked away, her stride is so sassy, he was certain she swayed her hips on purpose.

Tuesday, he ordered a coffee to be delivered to Rose in the school parking lot as soon as she pulled in. He would have brought it to her himself if he didn't have a zero-hour class. But the surprise, and the unusual means of getting it to her, paid off. Before she even went to her classroom that morning — he knew, because she still had her work bag slung over her shoulder and the coffee in her hand — she showed up at his classroom door again. "How did you know this is my favorite drink?" she asked him, holding the cup aloft.

She was so damn cute, in her black sweater with a pink silk scarf around her neck and her hair wild around her head and shoulders. When he said, "I have my ways," he had to grind his teeth together because he'd become so aroused at the vision of those curls tumbling around him as she straddled him in bed.

His methods weren't that mysterious. He'd solicited help from her friend, Jessie, who was more than eager to help stoke the flames of their romance.

Still leaning against the door jamb, Rose said, "It was Jessie, wasn't it? This is her favorite drink, too. And it's seasonal. Not everyone would know how much I love it."

Mac shrugged. "I'm afraid I can't reveal my source."

"Well, thank you. Very much. Hot coffee on this crisp morning was a pleasant and welcome surprise."

"I thought so. You're welcome." He raised his eyebrows at her, turned his head just a little, to indicate a question.

"No," she hissed. "We cannot kiss at school."

As he watched her walk away, hips swaying, he heard her laugh.

On Wednesday morning before they left for school, he presented Rose with a book for parents — the title contained the F word, and it was written like a nursery rhyme a person would read to children ... the tone syrupy sweet but the language crass as the narrator begged those children to go to sleep. Rose's eyes grew wide when she read the title and he said, "I heard some of the staff talking about this in the teachers lounge. It's hilarious. I thought you'd get a kick out of it."

Rose started reading, and by the end, she was cracking up. Hooting with laughter, she said, "This is great! I can't believe I haven't heard about this book. I'm getting this for all my parent friends!"

They were standing in the kitchen, then, so her we-can't-kiss-at-school argument didn't hold up. She closed the book, held it against her chest, and gave him a chaste kiss on the cheek. "I love it. Thank you so much. Do you think I should read it to Celeste?"

"No," he said, grinning at her. "Absolutely not. But if you get the hankering to read it to someone, you can read it to me."

"I might just do that."

Again, Mac envisioned the two of them in bed. In this vision, they sat side by side, backs against the headboard, while Rose read him the book. That scenario was cozy, for sure, but unusual for Mac. Sitting together in bed, reading, was so ... domestic. He filed that one away to think about later.

On Thursday, Mac stopped by the grocery store on the way home and picked up the ingredients to make spaghetti. When Rose and Celeste came through the door a while after he did, he announced that he and Celeste were in charge of dinner that night. He told Rose, "I'm cutting you loose. You're off the hook. Go do whatever you want to do. Read a book, take a bath, go for a walk. You have about an hour and fifteen minutes until dinner's ready."

He'd spent the few days before thinking about which tasks he could give Celeste, and he had her open cans of tomato sauce, season meat, and chop bell peppers while he browned the meat and stirred the sauce. Eleanor set the table, adding candles and fresh flowers. When Rose came into the kitchen, Mac could swear her eyes teared up.

"Did you make spaghetti? How did you know that's my favorite?"

"A little birdie might have told me," Mac said. He gave Celeste a "secret" high-five, but made sure Rose saw it — he wanted to be sure Celeste got the proper credit.

On Friday, Mac ordered lunch from Rita's, and sent his fourth-period teacher assistant to let Rose know she had a lunch date in

Johnny Mac's classroom. When the lunch bell rang, Mac watched the door from his desk until Rose came in.

"If I'd known I had a lunch date, I would have dressed up for it," she said.

Mac stood up. "You look beautiful." His fingers itched to touch her, but he couldn't say that or give in to the temptation — not at work, anyway.

"Gosh, I feel like it's my birthday week. You have really spoiled me."

"You deserve it," he said.

As they dug into their food, they talked about the week: homecoming prep, the fight that broke out at lunch on Tuesday, and the upcoming staff harvest party. They talked about home life, too: how Pinky had gotten her leg stuck in the fence, how Celeste was learning to steer the tractor and had found her first ripe pumpkin, and how they looked forward to making soup out of the butternut squash. As the conversation flowed, and the two of them laughed over the lunch, Mac realized he wanted this. He wanted lunches and conversations and laughter with Rose, forever. He could only hope she felt the same way he did.

Chapter Twenty-One

Rose awoke before Celeste Saturday morning, and lay in bed watching the first rays of the sun rise peek over the horizon. Most of the residual fear around dating Mac — or, the aftermath of dating Mac — had melted away over the past week. In fact, with all the time they spent together, she couldn't imagine *not* being with him. And if she had to rely on someone, why not rely on a thoughtful, considerate, and also very sexy man who wanted her to? Although Rose knew he was waiting for her answer, the idea of telling him sent butterflies fluttering in her chest. Next to her, Celeste stirred and opened her eyes. "Good morning, Mommy."

"Good morning. Are you going to help me make waffles for breakfast?"

Celeste stretched and nodded. "Yeah. Eleanor said we could pick some strawberries from the garden to put on them."

"That sounds delicious."

"And I'm going to check on the kittens when we go out there."

"Good thinking." Rose kissed her on the forehead.

"They're already so much cuter, Mama."

"I know. Babies grow up so fast."

The waffle iron heated and sausage frying in the pan a while later, Celeste and Rose stood at the kitchen counter. The morning sunlight streamed through the window, and Rose watched as Mac, shirtless, walked across the yard.

Her blood warmed as she imagined running her palms over the planes of his torso.

"Mommy! The waffle's done!"

Rose jumped and, noticing the abundance of steam coming from the waffle iron, hurried to remove the waffle as Mac came in through the kitchen door.

"Sure smells good in here," he said.

Celeste ran up to hug him, and while she did, he made a show of letting his gaze travel the length of Rose's body.

"I've got quite an appetite," he said, and Rose felt a rush of satisfaction — and arousal. In that moment, she wondered why she'd taken so long to decide she wanted to be with Mac. If she'd already told him, he would be walking up to her, planting a kiss on her cheek or her mouth, commenting on the shorts she'd worn just because she knew her legs looked good in them.

As it was, he was saying, "I'm going to go put on clean clothes. I'll be right back."

Yes, he looked like he wanted to kiss her. But he walked right by and Rose felt the absence of his touch as fully as if he'd touched her.

"Mommy. I think the sausage might be burning."

Eleanor came in then, a certain look in her eyes and a smile on her lips, and turned off the stove. "Good morning, ladies."

"Good morning," they said. Rose just knew Eleanor could tell she'd been lusting after Mac, and wondered what she thought of that.

As they all sat down at the breakfast table, Mac asked, "So, Celeste, have you thought about what you're going to be for Halloween?"

Mac's interest in Celeste made Rose want to hug him.

"I've thought about it," Celeste said. "Probably a dragon."

"A dragon sounds cool. How do you usually carry your candy?"

Celeste glanced at Rose, and Rose braced herself. "Usually I use a pillow case. But I want to get a bucket this year."

The pillowcase/candy bucket debate went on year round.

Celeste wanted a bucket, of course. Most of the kids had them. But Rose didn't want to store the thing for three hundred and sixty-four days of the year. At some point, Rose realized she didn't even care about storing the bucket, but felt like she had to stand her ground. So, the debate remained and Celeste still didn't own a bucket.

Mac cut a healthy slice off his waffle. "Buckets are cool, but I'm pretty sure a pillow case holds more candy."

Could he be any sweeter? It was as if he could read Rose's mind.

Eleanor, too, because she changed the subject. "Where do you you usually shop for your Halloween costumes?"

"Oh, everywhere," Celeste said. "It's actually really fun. Me and my mom go shopping with my Auntie Jessie and my Auntie Taylor every year. We like to go to the Halloween store, but we don't always find what we're looking for. We take a bunch of pictures in all the funny hats. And then we leave. Sometimes we go to Goodwill." She shrugged, shoved a piece of waffle into her mouth, and kept talking. "Sometimes we go to one of the other big stores. We just keep going until we find a cool costume."

"What about pumpkin carving?"

Celeste actually looked sad — Rose thought maybe she was playing it up. "Mommy says I'm not old enough."

Mac looked at Rose, and she smiled at Celeste. "Maybe you're finally old enough this year." To Mac, she said, "It's been forever since I carved a pumpkin. I used to love it as a kid. But I've waited with Celeste because I want her to be able to do most of it, herself."

"I loved it, too," Mac said before switching topics. "Who do you go trick-or-treating with?" he asked Celeste.

"Usually, just me and my mom go. Because, you know, Auntie Taylor and Auntie Jessie have to stay home and hand out candy. But now that Auntie Taylor moved in with Uncle Judd, she's not going to get any trick-or-treaters. I think she's going to be real bored on Halloween."

"You could invite her to trick-or-treat with you," Mac said.

Celeste wrinkled her nose. "Can I tell you something? I don't think she really wants to go trick-or-treating. I've invited her before, and even though she said she had to give out candy, I think she maybe just didn't want to go."

Rose laughed. "I didn't know you felt that way."

Celeste shrugged again, like it was no big deal. "I didn't want to hurt your feelings."

"I haven't been trick-or-treating in forever," Eleanor said. "You think I could join you this year?"

Celeste's eyes were so wide, Rose could see the whites all away around the irises. "Really? You'd want to?"

Palpable joy radiated from Celeste's little body, and it hit Rose in waves.

"Yeah," Eleanor said. "If that's okay. If you don't think an old lady would spoil your fun or slow you down."

Thoughtful, Celeste speared a sausage link with her fork. She took a bite off one end and chewed. "Nah, it's okay. I could slow down this year. I'm getting older, anyway."

"Well, thank you," Eleanor said, smiling at Rose. "I guess it's a plan."

Mac said, "If she's going, I'm going."

Celeste squealed.

For the first time in as long as she could remember, Rose felt herself looking forward to Halloween. What Celeste said was true — Taylor and Jessie usually declined trick-or-treating, and sometimes the activity felt a little lonely as a single parent. Was it possible for Rose to look forward to these traditions with a new little family? A tiny voice piped up in the back of her mind, telling her it might be too soon to consider Mac and Eleanor a family. She hushed it, deciding then and there that she'd enjoy this family while she had it.

That night, Rose made a point of waiting for Mac in the kitchen just as he had waited for her. He didn't see her at first, and when he did, the way his expression warmed confirmed Rose had made the right choice. She She lifted the glass of bourbon she poured for him, and he came and sat across from her.

"Thank you," he said. "You got Celeste to bed early."

"I wanted to talk to you."

Eyebrows raised, Mac lifted his glass to his lips. If Rose wasn't mistaken, she thought she saw a flash of nervousness in his eyes.

"I really like kissing you."

Laughter filled the kitchen, and Rose smiled.

"Is there a *but*, or an *and*?" Mac asked.

"An *and*. I really like kissing you. I'd like to do more of it. And you're right. Every time I thought about us being together — and I did think about it — I envisioned scenarios where things ended badly. But what you said is true. It doesn't have to be that way."

"I take it you've now envisioned a different outcome?"

Inexplicably nervous, Rose nodded. "I did. Or, not an outcome so much as a different perspective. Like you said, we're both adults. We enjoy each other. We enjoy kissing. Why not explore that? See where it goes without putting any expectations on either one of us?"

"I think that's a fantastic idea. I couldn't have said it better myself," Mac said. "So ... now what?" Mac asked.

Emboldened after the conversation, Rose stood and held out her hand. "Now, I think we kiss some more."

She was relieved when Mac took her hand, stood, and let her lead him outside.

Crickets chirped and frogs croaked under the wide open sky. Keeping a hold of Mac's hand, Rose headed across the yard. "One of the trickiest elements of this whole idea is my darling daughter and the lack of privacy she provides."

Mac chuckled, the sound deep and satisfied. "That is a consideration. Which, I assume, is why we are headed outside."

"Correct."

They'd reached Eleanor's garden shed, where a bench and table sat outside. Rose took Mac's glass from him and set both of their drinks on the table.

"I've been wanting to do this all week," she told him, wrapping her arms around his waist.

"You took the words right out of my mouth," he said.

Then he brought his mouth to hers. Rose felt her body relax into the contact. At the same time as the kiss was new, exciting, and exhilarating, it also felt like the place she'd been searching for, forever. Their bodies fit so well together. Rose had the sense they were made for each other, their souls fashioned for one another before being put into bodies.

One of Mac's hands came to her waist, and then up her ribcage to cup her breast. It had been so, *so* long since someone touched her that way, and Rose nearly came apart then and there. She let her hands roam down to his butt, which felt as muscular as his abs. He made a guttural sound and backed her up against the barn wall.

Unbuttoning her shirt, he continued to kiss her as if he were dying of thirst and she was the only source of water. She could feel his arousal against her belly, and then he was pulling down her bra, and his mouth was on her nipple, and she wanted him inside her more than she had ever wanted anything in her life. She reached for his belt, but couldn't quite unfasten it.

With a frustrated growl, Mac used one hand to yank his belt free, and that show of desire turned Rose on even more. Fortunately, unbuttoning and unzipping his jeans was no problem, and before she knew it, he filled her palm. As if that was the permission he needed, Max slipped his hand inside Rose's panties and began to stroke her, slow and gentle. She matched his rhythm with her hand, and he moved against her, increasing the intensity of his stroking, slipping his fingers inside her. Rose could feel her climax building, and when he brought his mouth back down on hers, they both found their release.

Chapter Twenty-Two

"I can't believe it's the last day of float building, Ms. Coffey," said Olivia. "They should give us at least another week."

"I agree," Rose said, "but we've got to work with what we've got."

"All we have left to do is paint, anyway," Mac said. "I think we can get that done today."

Olivia and Scarlett had arrived first, and they stood next to Eleanor's garden shed with Rose and Mac. Celeste had decided to collect eggs, and Rose could hear her in the coop, talking to the chickens. The weather was perfect for a fall day, Rose thought — a little crisp air cut through the warm sunshine.

A couple more cars pulled up, and a few more students climbed out. Looking over their progress so far, Rose figured *The Tempest* featuring a wrecked ship did them a favor. The mast stood at an angle, and the cabin roof sloped in the opposite direction. The junior class ship definitely wouldn't be seaworthy; in fact, it looked exactly like it had been through a real tempest.

"Let me guess," Mac said, coming to stand next to Rose. "You were thinking our ship is looking very ... ah, wrecked?"

Rose laughed. "Exactly. There are simply no words."

Mac put an arm around Rose's shoulders. "Fortunately, people sitting in the bleachers at the football game won't be able to see her imperfections."

"True." Rose leaned into his body. He kissed her on the temple, and she heard an, "Aww," from behind them.

"I knew it!" Olivia's long strides brought her over to stand in front of them. "I knew you guys were going to become a couple."

Mac dropped the arm he'd draped over Rose's shoulders, and each of them stepped away from the other.

"Oh, don't be shy about it," Olivia said. "You guys are so cute together! You're perfect for each other. You are my two favorite teachers!"

"So glad you approve," Mac said, his tone teasing.

"I do," Olivia said.

Celeste screamed and came running out of the coop, an egg clutched in each hand. "Henrietta pecked me! There's still more eggs, but she won't let me get them."

Shoving her chubby little hand at Rose while still clutching an egg, Celeste said, "See? See that mark?"

"I do," Rose said. She bent to kiss it.

"That Henrietta," Mac said. "She can be real grumpy sometimes. Here, let me help you. Let's go together." Before he walked off, he said to Olivia, "Hey, why haven't you started painting yet?"

Olivia shrugged. "You guys were distracting us."

Watching Mac walk off with Celeste, Rose smiled. "So sorry," she said to Olivia. "Get to painting. As you know, it's our last work session."

Mac and Celeste returned, her clutching the egg basket, which was filled to the brim with eggs.

"Mommy, I'm going to take these inside," she said. She started to bound away, but Rose stopped her, reminding her to walk carefully to avoid dropping eggs.

The kids moved their paint buckets and brushes closer to the float, and within a few minutes, there was a student painting every surface.

"See?" Mac said to Rose as the two of them watched. "It's coming together nicely. The paint covers up a lot of those imperfections."

Rose nodded. "You're right. It does."

For the next hour and a half, the students painted while Rose and Mac hung the tattered sails on the boom, made small repairs, and strengthened the float's joints. Just as they were finishing up, hammering the lids back on the paint cans, rinsing the brushes in the sink outside Eleanor's garden shed, and bundling up the drop cloths to be thrown away, a cracking, groaning sound cut through the air.

Everyone froze, and their heads swung toward the float. As they watched, the mast, under pressure from the newly hung sails, slowly tipped over. Deafening silence followed.

In a voice thick with despair, Henry said, "Oh, no."

More silence ... until Celeste's voice cut through the air. "The float is broken!"

This exclamation produced a round of laughter from the high schoolers.

"Don't worry!" Mac said, his voice confident. "This is totally fixable. Ms. Coffey and I will get this taken care of in no time! You guys can go on home and we will make it as good as new."

"Are you sure?" Celeste's voice remained at the highest possible volume level.

The students walked to their cars, their steps heavy, casting doubtful looks over their shoulders. The sunset started turning the sky a fiery orange.

"You really think we can fix this?" Rose asked. "I mean, the base of the mast tore a big chunk out of the top of the cabin."

"It's really messed up," Celeste said. "I'm going to check on the kittens, and then I'm going back inside."

Once she was gone, Mac grimaced at Rose, his expression so exaggerated, Rose knew he was joking. He said, "Of course we can fix it. I think we've proven we make a pretty good team."

"You're right."

"I love it when you say I'm right. How do you think we should start?"

Rose bumped her shoulder against his. "You're asking me? I thought you had an idea. You're the one who sounded so confident about fixing it."

"No." Mac laughed. "No idea. Let me think."

A lone bullfrog croaked. In a nearby tree, cicadas screamed.

"What if we use the reciprocating saw to cut a nice, clean square in the cabin roof?" Rose said. "And then create a new base for the mast? We can use two-by-fours to brace the base, and screw on the mast from underneath."

Mac nodded. "I knew if I waited, you'd come up with a great solution. You're so sexy when you talk about construction."

They agreed on a size for the new base, and while Rose cut a clean square around the damaged part of the cabin roof, Mac cut a new base out of plywood. The sun went down, and the automatic light on the side of Eleanor's garden shed came on. Crickets chirped and moths flitted around, bumping against the shed wall near the light. Rose and Mac worked together to remove the mast from the old base and screw it on to the new one. Then, they mounted the new base and mast onto the cabin roof. Afterwards, they stood back and admired their work.

"I'm really impressed," Mac said. "You are great with power tools. And did I mention sexy?"

"It's the only option when you're a single mom and you move around a lot," Rose said.

"Being sexy? Or using power tools?"

She swatted his arm. "Using power tools." She hoped it didn't sound like she was seeking pity, because she wasn't. She was proud of all the skills she'd earned. "It's been hands-on learning for the past five years."

Rose went over to where the kids had stacked the paint cans, and used a flat head screwdriver to open the brown paint. "I remember the first piece of furniture I assembled on my own. It was a dresser. I can't remember which big-box store it came from." She stirred the paint, and then stepped onto the float and started painting the new section of cabin roof. "You know how it is. That kind of furniture comes dismantled, all its pieces in a box."

Mac, who was re-hanging the tattered sails, said, "Yep. And you have to read terrible instructions, mostly in pictures, to put it together."

Rose nodded. "Exactly. I was determined to get that dresser put together, all by myself. The instructions said to assemble the drawers first. So that's what I did. By golly, I was going to get all those drawers is before Celeste woke up from her nap."

"Oh boy," Mac said. "I have a sense that your rushing is not going to pay off at the end of this story."

From her spot on the cabin roof, Rose smiled at him. "You're right. I did get the drawers done before Celeste woke up. Then, I was determined to assemble the body of the dresser that night, after she went to bed and before I did. I worked so hard on that thing. And I did it. All by myself. Then I went to put the drawers in, and realized I put the sides on backwards. The drawers were inside out."

Rose paused her painting to look look up at Mac, who smiled back at her. "I've done that before."

"That's not the only lesson I learned the hard way," Rose told him. "I've made finishing mistakes while refurbishing used furniture. I've made buying mistakes at garage sales. I once made a wiring mistake replacing a light switch. There were sparks. But, over time, I've become pretty self-sufficient. I can usually figure out where I went wrong, and fix it."

She'd finished painting the new base, and hammered the lid back on the paint can before hopping off the float to go rinse the brush.

"I hope you know how lucky Celeste is to have you," Mac said.

Rose nearly swooned. Although Taylor and Jessie often paid her compliments, Mac's words were unexpected.

"I tell her that all the time," Rose said, her tone light. "I tell her she's so lucky to have a mom who can fix things."

Mac finished hanging the sails, and carried the paint can over to the table.

Rose squeezed the water out of the paintbrush and set it next to the paint cans and other brushes to dry. Again, the two of them stood next to the float and surveyed their work.

"Hot damn." Mac lifted his hand for a high five. "We do make a good team. See? I told you it would look as good as new."

Chapter Twenty-Three

"I can't remember the last time I went to a football game with a girl." Mac grinned at Rose across his car's center console as they pulled into the parking lot at Prescott High School.

She smiled back from the passenger seat. "That's good, because I didn't want to have to live up to expectations you set in high school. I was a high schooler once. I know what girls do."

"You have absolutely nothing to worry about. I was never brave enough to ask a girl to a football game. I already know tonight will be the best yet."

Because it was homecoming, the stadium was packed, the energy level a frenzy. Mac could hear the horns and drums as the marching band played a fast, rousing song. Principal Vasquez had assigned each class a color, and the spectators sat in sections — blue, white, green, and black. Some kids held signs for their class, and some had painted their faces the appropriate colors. Many, many of them chanted and cheered.

"I kinda wish there was a section for staff." Rose had to yell so he could hear her over the noise. "The bleachers are packed. I don't know if I want to sit with all those kids."

Mac took her hand and tucked it into the crook of his arm.

"They *do* seem pretty rowdy. But at least we only have to sit with them for the first half. And then we get to drive the float."

"We're *driving the float?*" Rose said, her voice an adorable squeal. "You didn't tell me that!"

"Surprise!"

Mac hoped Rose didn't mind. The dad who owned the truck had offered to let the juniors use it as long as he didn't have to drive on the track around the football field during halftime.

Fortunately, Rose squeezed his arm and said, "That should be really fun. It'll be a first for me."

They climbed the bleacher steps until they found an empty spot about halfway to the top. Once they sat down, Mac realized he should have offered to buy them candy or snacks. He said as much to Rose, and she sat up straight, her smile wide. "I forgot about snacks! It's been forever since I came to a game, too. Let me get them. You save our seats. What do you want?"

"Popcorn and M&Ms."

She nodded, determined, and made her way over to the steps and down. He watched her go, her blonde curls sticking out from under her beanie, her petite figure adorable and her curves sexier than ever in jeans and a hoodie.

Just as she went out of sight on her quest for the snack bar, someone spoke close to Mac's ear. "So, you and Rose Coffey, huh?"

Uncertain of whether the voice held simple curiosity or the tiniest hint of venom, Mac looked over at the man who sat down in the spot Rose had just vacated. Mac didn't recognize him.

He made a point of keeping his expression neutral when he answered. "We're both advisors for the junior class. We helped build the float. So, we decided to come to the game together, see how the fruits of our labor turned out."

The other guy smiled and Mac thought he might detect a malevolent glint in his eye. "That's nice."

Then he was gone, and even though Rose was all smiles as she came back bearing the popcorn and M&Ms he'd requested, Mac couldn't shake the feeling that the guy was up to no good.

"Everything okay?" Rose asked as she handed over his goodies.

"Everything is great. Especially now that you've brought this bounty."

As he tore the corner off the package of M&Ms and dumped the chocolate candies into his bag of popcorn, Mac told himself to relax. The dude was probably just some jealous, immature jerk who had a crush on Rose. And, maybe Mac felt a little overprotective. He cared about Rose more than he'd cared about a woman in as long as he could remember. Ever, actually. Everything would be fine.

"You're mixing your chocolate and your popcorn?" Rose's incredulous voice pulled Mac back to the present moment.

"Oh, yeah. You should definitely try some."

When she raised one eyebrow, doubtful, Mac laughed. "I have a feeling you're going to like it."

"I'll try it. I trust you."

I wonder if that adventurous spirit applies in the bedroom.

"What did you get, anyway?" Mac asked.

"I got a Snickers. For Celeste. They're her favorite, and I feel a little guilty about not bringing her tonight. She loves football games."

She held up the Snickers, and then a package of peanut butter cups. "And I got these for me. Because they're *my* favorite. And the best way to fight mommy guilt is to eat chocolate and peanut butter."

Mac laughed out loud. "Good for you. I won't ask you to share, then. But I hereby assuage you of your mommy guilt. She's probably having a great time with my mom."

"I'm sure she is. She loves your mom. And besides, when we come to games, we always have to leave early, which she hates. Tonight, I don't have to deal with that ... unless you plan on throwing a tantrum and making me drag you out."

The first few notes of the marching band's traditional fight song floated through the air, and everyone in the crowd got to their feet. The song ended, a student sang the national anthem, and the game began.

The Prescott High School football team outplayed its rivals by two touchdowns in the first half. Mac loved football, but he found he enjoyed watching Rose love football even more. She cheered and hollered, did the wave and the traditional cheer, and by the time the first twenty-four minutes had passed, Mac felt tired, himself. The two of them walked down to the float staging area, and Mac didn't bother hiding the pleasure he felt when Rose not only accepted the arm he offered, but also smiled up at him like she couldn't believe the fun she was having.

About fifty members of the junior class gathered next to the shipwreck float. Mac recognized some of the kids who had come to his house, and a few of them were looking things over, adjusting the sails and adding extra staples to ensure the *Junior Class* sign would stay on. Esteban Lopez, the dad who owned the truck, approached Mac and Rose, holding up his keys. "They're all yours. The keys and all these kids."

"Thanks," Mac said, and Esteban smiled at his sarcasm. "Good luck."

"Should we do a quick walk around the float?" Mac asked. "Make sure everything is in order?"

"We should."

The sound of Principal Vasquez's cowbell brought the drivers and students to attention, and Ernie called, "One minute until departure. Everyone take your places!"

Mac ran around to open the passenger door for Rose, and before she got in, she gave him a quick kiss on the lips. They hadn't discussed whether they were making their relationship public, and Mac found himself glancing around to see if any of the kids had noticed.

She laughed and pulled her legs inside the cab. "Sorry if that was too forward. It just felt right."

Mac shrugged, kissed her again, and shut the door. Once he was inside, he started up the truck and the students who planned to walk next to the float cheered. Up ahead, Mac saw the freshman class float start moving forward, and then the sophomores'. As the truck crept forward, students gathered around.

Within a couple of minutes, they were on the track, making their way around the football field. Kids were chanting for their classes, and people in the bleachers were holding up signs, ringing cowbells, and blasting air horns.

Rose sat forward in the seat. "This is so exciting! Maybe even more fun than when I was in high school!"

Mac reached across the console and took her hand. "Too bad I'm driving, or we could partake in my favorite football game activity."

"Oh yeah? And what is that?"

"Making out under the bleachers, of course."

She shook her head and rolled her eyes, but the smile remained on her face. "I bet you didn't make out under the bleachers. You probably sat up at the very top of the bleachers, playing chess with your friends."

Mac laughed. "That's pretty close to the truth."

"How do we know who won for best float?" Mac asked as he put the truck in park once they'd reached the staging area.

"They'll announce it right after they announce the homecoming king and queen. Which I think happens next."

When Rose put her hand on the door handle Mac put his hand on her arm to stop her. "I'm pretty sure the seniors are going to win. Their Swiss Family Robinson treehouse is pretty awesome. And they have those giant dogs. Which means we could use this time to get in some more kissing."

She let go of the door handle, and that simple action made Mac aroused.

"I do like that idea," she said. "But I can't say I know of anywhere that's private, exactly, around here."

"I'm guessing you're not the kind of girl who hangs out under the bleachers."

Rose giggled. "Nope. In fact, my mama always told me nice girls don't hang out under the bleachers."

"I'm certain she was right. So why don't we find somewhere else to go?"

Mac stowed the keys on top of the drivers-side front tire, and Rose grabbed his hand and propelled him away from the truck. Her urgency turned him on even more, and he felt his jeans getting tighter as the two of them searched for a make-out location.

"I feel like a teenager again," he said.

"Me, too," she said, "although as a teenager I never would have made out with someone in public."

They'd made their way along the back of the football field and over to the snack shack.

"I haven't seen anywhere suitable, have you?" Rose said.

Mac shook his head. "No. I suppose going back home is out of the question?"

Rose sighed. "It does seem like the most convenient option. But I'm so afraid Celeste or your mom will walk in on us. I don't know if I'm ready to face either of those scenarios."

"What about one of those pay-by-the-hour motels? Too skeezy?"

At that, she wrinkled her nose. "Definitely too skeezy."

They stood there holding hands behind the snack bar. Mac could hear Principal Vasquez on the fifty-yard line, talking about the homecoming court. His arousal had turned into full on desperation, and seeing Rose under the bright stadium lights, looking fresh-faced and beautiful, he literally couldn't wait to get his hands on her.

She squeezed his hand. "I know! We can use your car."

Looking at her sideways, Mac said, "I don't know if you've noticed, but it's not exactly the most spacious."

Either Rose hadn't heard him, or she didn't mind the lack of space, because she was already towing him toward the parking lot. "I have an idea."

If Mac thought he was desperate before, at those four words, he was ready to break into a full-on sprint. That would be too obvious, and he didn't want anyone at the game to know just how much he wanted Rose Coffey. When they were a few yards from his car, he dug his key fob out of his pocket and unlocked the doors. Rose went right to the driver's door, opened it, and gestured for him to get in. "Sit."

"Ooh. I like your bossy side." He sat, and almost lost it when she climbed in, straddling him.

He managed to say, "This is a pretty good idea," just before she brought her mouth to his. One arm around her waist, Mac managed to use the other to pull the door closed. Rose's kisses seemed as desperate as Mac felt. He found himself wishing they could somehow be even closer. He ran his hands up her back and into her hair, then down to her waist. Their bodies were almost too close for him to cup her breasts, but he managed the feat and she groaned.

"Woman, I don't know how long I can last, with you being this damn sexy."

She barely paused. "Same."

Chapter Twenty-Four

Saturday morning at breakfast, Eleanor said, "I'd be happy to watch Celeste again tonight if the two of you want to go out on a proper date."

Rose immediately looked at Celeste, whose eyes went round before her face split into a grin. "A date? Mommy! You didn't tell me you and Mac were going to go out on a date. Is this like how Auntie Taylor went out on a date with Judd and she didn't tell you and Auntie Jessie right away?"

Caught. Rose glanced at Mac, who shrugged. "I told my mom you and I were considering dating. I just thought it would make things less awkward."

"And now that I have put my foot in my mouth, everything's out in the open," Eleanor said, hiding her smile.

Naturally, Celeste wanted to know what Eleanor meant by putting her foot in her mouth, and any awkwardness over the potential date dissolved.

While Eleanor explained the idiom, Mac said to Rose, "So what do you say? You and me? A date tomorrow?"

The decision proved easy. Rose watched Celeste and Eleanor for a moment ... they were both laughing as Celeste pantomimed putting her foot in her mouth. "That sounds lovely," she said to Mac. "Do you have any idea what you'd like to do?"

"Actually, I was thinking. The past few weeks have been kind of stressful, with mid-terms and homecoming. Why don't we do something fun? Bowling? Mini golf?"

Rose pitied Mac. He had no idea what he was getting into. "You're on. Mini golf it is. Although, I can't guarantee it won't be stressful for you."

He raised his eyebrows. "Oh, is that how you're going to play it? You just might be going down."

Rose shook her head. She wasn't going down.

"She's not going down," Celeste said, then, serious.

Mac pointed at Celeste and made a face as if to say, *How did she overhear that?*

Again, Rose laughed. "She hears it all."

She gave Mac a look, which he interpreted correctly. Rose knew because his cheeks turned pink and his gaze found the tabletop.

"What time do you two want to go out, then?" Eleanor asked.

Mac looked at Rose. "Six?"

Rose nodded. "Sounds great. I can make dinner for you and Celeste, Eleanor, so you don't have to worry about that."

Eleanor made a dismissive gesture. "Oh, go on and forget that idea. I'll order something in. You should be able to go out to dinner without having to cook dinner first."

That was settled.

The next evening, Rose felt a thrill as she and Mac got into his hot rod and he started it up with a rumble. She couldn't remember the last time she'd been on a real date.

"Wait," Rose said, putting a hand on his arm. "Before we go. Does the passenger get to play DJ in this car? I forgot to ask you when we went to the homecoming game last night. I was too busy thinking about the float." *And about kissing you under the bleachers.*

Giving her a side-eye, Mac said, "Usually, nobody plays DJ but me."

In mock surprise and outrage, Rose let her mouth dropped open. "Are you serious?"

Mac shook his head. "No. I'm totally kidding. Well, sort of. I don't generally drive people around, so I'm the only one who plays DJ. But Rose, I'd be honored if you would be DJ tonight."

"Yes," she said. "I feel like we've just hit a milestone."

He smiled as he put the car in reverse. "I can think of a couple other milestones I'd like to hit."

Amused, she said, "The only way for this to be effective it is for me to connect my phone to your car."

"By all means."

After a few seconds, Rose had connected her phone and decided on a station. She pressed the play button, and music came through the speakers. Mac covered his ears with his hands.

"You call this music?" he yelled.

Rose grabbed the steering wheel. "You call that driving?"

After putting his hands back on the steering wheel, Mac said, "Seriously. Is that what you like to listen to?"

Rose was laughing openly. "No, I was totally pulling your leg. Death metal is not my thing. I just wanted to see what you would say."

The only mini golf in town was at the Fun House, which also featured an arcade. Of course, the place was crawling with teenagers, and the air was thick with cheap cologne and perfume. Lights flashed and electronic sounds came from the machines.

"I'm glad the mini golf course is outside," Rose said, yelling so Mac could hear her over the din.

"What?!" he shouted back.

They got in line behind a group of boys and girls obviously dressed to impress one another.

"Hey, Ms. Coffey," said the teenager behind the counter when it was their turn.

"Hey, Manny. How are you tonight?"

"Busy," Manny said. "No Celeste tonight?" He gave Mac a look so obvious, Rose's cheeks burned.

"No Celeste!" Rose beamed. "This is Johnny Mac. I'm sure you heard of him. Science teacher at PHS? He's kind of a legend."

Manny's face lit up, his smile big and bright. "Oh, Johnny Mac!

I can't wait to have you for chemistry next year. Do you really light your hand on fire in class?"

Mac looked a little shellshocked, but recovered quickly. "I do. But only if my classes earn it. Nice to meet you, man."

They shook hands and Rose felt a rush of pleasure at seeing the two different parts of her life align so nicely. Manny handed them golf clubs and gestured at the ball rack on the counter.

"I take it you come here often?" Mac asked as they walked outside to the first hole.

"I do. I may or may not have a monthly membership, so Celeste and I can golf whenever we want."

"Uh oh. No wonder Celeste said I'm in trouble. You're going to be me, aren't you?"

Rose gave her her golf club a fancy twirl, like it was a baton. "I won't just beat you. I'll demolish you. Probably. But since it's our first time, I'll take it easy."

They watched the teens in front of them, who were still working on the first hole.

"I hope you're okay with my mom letting the cat out of the bag in front of Celeste," Mac said.

"To tell you the truth, I wasn't sure how to approach it with her. But I love the way your mom presented it. No-nonsense. And here we are, enjoying a lovely evening."

"Oh, good," Mac said. "I wouldn't want my mom to put the kibosh on our relationship before it even started."

"No." Rose shook her head. "If I can find a man who is as sweet to my daughter as you are, I'm not going to let a little thing like honesty get in the way."

The group in front of them moved on (once the last player used her foot to nudge her ball into the hole after eleven strokes).

"Ladies first." Mac made a gallant gesture with one arm. Rose put her ball on the mat and took her position.

Mac whistled. "Ooh, you already look like a professional."

He spoke just as she was taking her swing, and despite her giggling, her ball ended up balanced on the edge of the hole.

"That should have gone in," Rose said, and Mac laughed. "Getting a little huffy, are we?"

"Your turn."

Mac took his turn and sent his ball careening off the course and into the bushes.

Giggling, Rose called from her spot by the hole, "That's your Mulligan. Doesn't count. Take another turn!"

Mac hunted down his ball and once he found it, he held it up to show Rose. As he set it on the mat again, Rose said, "Don't hit it so hard this time. A gentle touch is all you need."

Before taking a swing, Mac raised an eyebrow at her. "I'll keep that in mind."

That time, his ball ended up a couple of feet from the hole. Rose cheered and clapped before hitting her own ball in.

"If you get yours in on this shot," she said, "We'll be tied."

"Only because you're giving me a handicap."

The way Mac lined up for his shot, adjusting his feet incrementally and eyeballing the path he wanted the ball to take, was adorable, Rose thought. So was the fist shaking he did when the ball missed the hole by about three inches.

"I swear that thing turned!" he said. "It went wide around the hole!"

"I know you're going to get it in this time."

Again, he gave her a look, obviously enjoying the innuendo.

While they waited their turn at the second hole, Mac wrapped an arm around Rose's waist and she rested her head on his shoulder. "I hope you're having a good time, despite how terrible I am at this game."

"I love winning, so, yeah. I'm having a good time." He chuckled, the sound deep and rumbly ... and arousing.

"Seriously, though," Rose said, "I barely get out of the house without my little sidekick. And when I do, it's usually for work. The last time I got out, just for fun, it didn't go well."

"How come?"

The question was simple enough, but thinking about the answer conjured up some of Rose's worst memories. "I don't want to get into all the details right now but suffice it to say, when Celeste was about a year old, I went on my traditional back-to-school shopping trip with Taylor and Jessie. Celeste was crying when I left. Celeste's dad couldn't get her calmed down, and when I got home, he was pissed. That one evening convinced him I was a horrible mother. And I left her for a few hours."

"A few hours?"

The group in front of them moved on to the third hole. Rose lifted her head off Mac's shoulder and stepped away from him, making a show of stretching her arms and cracking her neck in preparation for great play.

"A few hours," she said. "What made it really bad, according to Jared — Celeste's father — was that we stopped for lunch and happened to sit at the bar. We ran into some of our colleagues and someone snapped a few pictures, which they posted online. Jared acted like I was out drinking and partying, even though we had just made a pit stop for lunch. He didn't let me live it down for the rest of our relationship." Rose set her ball on the mat. "Which, by the way, wasn't much longer. Anyway, that topic of conversation is a real downer. Let's play."

After she hit her ball, Mac said, "I'm just glad you're not with him anymore. You deserve better than that. And, you deserve to spend a little fun time away from your daughter. Every parent does."

"Thanks," she said, doing her best to consciously shake off the icky feelings associated with Jared. Before she walked away, Mac swatted her on the ass. She yelped, and he laughed. "I can't believe you got a hole in one. You probably only missed last time because I distracted you."

Rose snickered. "Probably. But I did give you that handicap."

"You did. And it probably wasn't enough. Prepare yourself. That was your only distraction-free shot."

"Fair enough. I don't mind the distraction."

The rest of the game went much the same way, and despite the handicaps Rose gave Mac, she ended up winning, thirty-two to forty. After they returned to their clubs, Mac said, "I've worked up an appetite. Should we go to dinner?"

* * *

If parenting had taught Rose anything, it was that the child often dictated the timing. So when she and Celeste met Taylor and Jessie at the Halloween store that weekend, and Celeste broke the news ("Auntie Taylor! Auntie Jessie! My mom and Mac went on a date!"), Rose should not have been surprised.

Parenting had also taught her that children were (sometimes unbearably) honest. There was no use trying to discredit Celeste's claim.

"Did they, now?" Jessie said. "Tell us more, my little gossiping hen."

Jessie cackled, and Celeste giggled. "I don't know more," Celeste said. "All I know is they went mini golfing. And had dinner. And I got to stay home with Mac's mom, Eleanor. We ate dinner. And then we watched a movie and had popcorn."

Taylor beamed at Celeste. "I don't know who had more fun, you or your mom."

Jessie narrowed her eyes at Rose. "I can say with some certainty that Celeste's mom had a really great time."

Rose felt the heat of embarrassment crawl up her neck and into her cheeks.

Taylor whistled. "Ooh, she's blushing. This is unusual. Telling."

"Can we go inside?" Rose pretended to be exasperated. The reality was that she couldn't wait to share with her friends. It had been so long since she experienced romance. Or fun.

Inside the Halloween store, a werewolf greeted them with a growl, and a ghostly figure jumped out at them, screeching. Celeste screamed and grabbed onto Rose's leg.

Taylor reached for Celeste's hand. "Why don't we go over to the kids section? These things scare me."

While Celeste perused the kids costumes, paying particular attention to the variety of dragons, Rose told her friends about the date.

"So when you say you went mini golfing," Taylor said, "what you really mean is, you emasculated Mac with a golf club and a pink ball."

Rose smirked. "I did beat him. But our scores were close."

Jessie nodded. "I'll bet. How much of a handicap did you give him?"

Celeste came up to them and held out a dragon costume with shimmering golden wings, and matching horns, and wore a silver crown. "How about this one?"

"That one is cool!" Jessie said. "It looks like you might be able to make it breathe fire."

"Let's look at hats!" Celeste said.

"So then what?" Taylor asked as they headed for the hats. "What did you do after you beat him at mini golf?"

"We went to dinner. And I enjoyed two guilt-free hours of adult-only conversation."

"That sounds perfect," Taylor said.

"It was," Rose said, and Jessie said to Taylor, "Look at her. She is definitely smitten."

"Pick out a hat, guys," Celeste said. "We have to take our picture."

Each of them chose and put on an outrageous hat. Celeste beamed at them. "Those are perfect. Mommy, will you help me pick one?"

Rose found a tall, fuzzy, black hat, like she'd seen on the guards at Buckingham Palace.

"That thing is as tall as I am!" Celeste put it on and in keeping with tradition, Jessie took a few selfies. Celeste led them over to the accessories, where she started handing out weapons.

"So," Jessie said, brandishing a sword at Celeste. "Have the two of you discussed being exclusive?"

"What's exclusive?" Celeste wanted to know.

"It's kind of like boyfriend and girlfriend," Jessie said. "Like, your mom won't go on dates with anyone else, and neither will Mac."

Celeste nodded. "Of course they won't. That would be weird."

"Not yet," Rose said. "I mean, I'm living at his house. It's not like he's going to bring another date there, right?"

Jessie shrugged. "Right."

Rose hadn't even thought about that conversation. Maybe she should, though.

"Let's check out!" Celeste said then, and they followed her as she bounced off to the register.

As Rose pulled into the driveway at home a while later, she heard a text notification on her phone. In the backseat, Celeste was subdued, looking out the window with that end-of-a-fun day, glazed-over expression. Not knowing when she might have another chance to check her texts, Rose went ahead and looked at the message that had just come in.

It was from a local number she didn't recognize, and the notification bubble told her five images were attached. She smiled when she saw the first one. It showed Mac and her in the stands at the homecoming game, her hand in his bag of popcorn.

"We are so cute." Celeste didn't respond, which meant she was really tired. Rose should get her inside and fed so she could get to bed. She'd finish looking at the pictures first, she decided. The second photo showed Mac and her in the truck pulling the float. They held hands across the console. Rose looked at Mac, adoring, and he smiled, although his focus was straight ahead.

Rose wondered who had taken the picture. Probably someone from the junior class, she thought. Olivia, Scarlett, even Henry. The third picture showed the two of them leaving the stadium, hand in hand. Her body heated up at the memory of what where they had gone and what they had done.

She felt the smile fade from her face as she looked at the fourth picture. Obviously, someone had followed them to Mac's car, and there they were, in full color, enjoying a hot and steamy make-out session in the driver's seat. For a half-second, remembering that night sent a shot of heat down to Rose's lady parts. But fear quickly replaced arousal. Someone had followed them. Taken pictures. And then sent her those pictures. Looking at the first couple of pictures, the gesture seemed sweet.

But the voyeurism the photographer displayed set Rose's nerves on edge. Her hand shaking, she scrolled to the last picture. In keeping with the pattern, the fifth image was the most racy of all. It was taken in Mac's yard, in the moment the two of them had made out against the garden shed. She was wearing her dark jeans and pink hoodie, which meant someone had followed them home after their golf and dinner date. The idea that someone had come to their home and photographed them sent Rose into a frenzy. Her whole body vibrating with fear, she turned off her phone screen and shoved her phone into her purse.

When she said, "Ready to go inside, Celeste?" her voice sounded high and breathy. Celeste didn't seem to notice. "Yeah. What were you doing, anyway?"

Rose didn't answer right away. She took a moment to look in all three of her mirrors, to turn around and scan her surroundings. So far, it seemed like whoever sent her the pictures was interested only in her and Mac. But if they been at the house, they been close to Celeste, too. And that scared her more than anything.

She got out of the car and looked around again before opening Celeste's door.

"I said, what were you doing?"

Rose shrugged, as if her heart wasn't beating a million miles an hour against the inside of her rib cage. "Oh, nothing interesting. I was just reading a work email."

"Okay. I'm going to go in and show Mac my costume. Do you think he's going to like it?"

Rose reached in and grabbed the bag from the Halloween store. "I think he's going to love it."

Celeste went bounding into the house, and Rose considered what she was going to do. She could tell Mac, but she didn't want to risk scaring him. She could call the police, but really, all she had were a few photos and a phone number. No one had done anything illegal ... creepy, certainly. But not illegal. Maybe she would cross-check the phone number against her contact list, and see if that yielded any clues.

That evening, Rose told Mac and Eleanor she didn't feel well — "probably ate too much candy while we were Halloween shopping" — and put herself to bed at the same time as Celeste.

After such an exciting day, Celeste fell asleep within minutes, leaving Rose to contemplate the pictures and their sender once again. She hadn't had a spare moment to look at her phone a second time, but laying in bed, she took it out and opened the text conversation. She looked at each picture carefully, trying to remember who she'd seen at the homecoming game, hoping to make a list of potential suspects.

"Photographers," she corrected herself.

This time, when she scrolled to the fifth picture, she noticed a text bubble underneath it.

Looks like you're enjoying yourself these days. Having a lot of fun out on the town, without your daughter.

In that instant, Rose knew who sent her the pictures: Jared. That didn't mean he took them; having grown up in Prescott, he had plenty of friends there, and many of them were potential candidates for having attended the homecoming game. But none of them would have her number, which meant Jared had asked them to take pictures and send them to him.

Fury filled Rose's veins, and she realized her jaw muscles ached from clenching so hard. Throwing her phone across the room was tempting, but she didn't want to pay to replace it, and she didn't want to go without.

She'd been so stupid. Blocking Jared was one thing, but he'd obviously gotten a different number. And even if he wasn't watching her, someone else was. Rose felt sick to her stomach. Images from their last argument filled her mind.

Celeste was teething. The gums at the back of her mouth were angry and swollen, all four molars coming in at once. The poor baby whined and wailed for four days straight. Rose tried everything she could think of: teething tablets, frozen washcloths, baby Tylenol.

None of it worked. Desperate for answers at two in the morning, Rose went online. Of course, she knew the Internet wasn't always the best place to seek medical advice. But her baby was hurting, and she was looking at her fifth night of zero sleep.

She found an online moms' group, requested to join, and within minutes, received a notification an admin had approved her request. Within minutes, she was searching the group for all advice teething related. And boy, was there a lot of it. For every tip — rub clove oil on the gums twice a day, give your baby dried mango to chew on — there was someone for whom it hadn't worked, and someone for whom it had. Rose didn't have any clove oil or dried mango on hand, and she couldn't get any at two a.m.

One parent recommended bourbon, and although Rose didn't have any of that on hand, and Jared lived just around the corner from a twenty-four-hour liquor store. As bone tired as she was, Rose's pride would not stand in the way of her showing up there at two a.m. in her pajamas, wild hair and all.

Jared, of course, was sleeping (not like a baby, Rose thought darkly). She didn't want to risk his wrath if she woke him up, so she put Celeste in her car seat, stuffed a blanket in around her, and drove them both to the liquor store.

In hindsight, Rose thought, bringing Celeste with her probably wasn't the best idea. The place called with unsavory characters. But in that moment, all that mattered was getting Celeste some relief. She carried her, in the car seat, past the late-night customers in into the store. She debated what size bourbon bottle to buy. Surely, a tiny bottle would contain enough to rub on Celeste's gums. All the parents in that online group cautioned against using too much. But she could use a little bourbon, herself. The big bottles were really big, so she decided on a medium-sized bottle.

The cashier — Rose thought he also owned the place — looked at Rose with sympathy. "I take it you have a teething baby."

His compassion nearly brought Rose to tears. "I do. And I've tried everything else. Well, except clove oil. But I don't think the places that carry it are open at this hour."

The man shook his head. "Probably not. But bourbon will do the trick. Just a couple drops, is all. Take your time rubbing it in. Let it do its magic. I remember those nights. My wife and I, we have five kids."

Rose felt her eyebrows go into her hairline. "Five? I can hardly handle one."

He made a dismissive gesture. "You're doing just fine. Look at you here, at two in the morning. That's dedication. Good luck, all right?"

Rose cried all the way home, unsure if her tears were a result of feeling so understood, or of pure exhaustion.

Jared greeted them at the door, and his posture, tense and angry, and his facial expression, murderous, made Rose freeze on the front stoop. "Where were you?"

In an attempt at levity, Rose held up Celeste's car seat, where the bourbon was nestled between the baby's legs. She pointed at the bottle, in case he hadn't seen it. "Liquor store."

Jared sneered. "Liquor store?"

"I figured, we've tried everything else. I bought bourbon so we could rub a little on her gums."

"Bourbon?" The anger dripped from his voice.

"Another trick I saw was clove oil. But we don't have any, and the places that would aren't open at this hour."

"Why didn't you talk to me about this?"

"Because you were sleeping." *Idiot.*

"I *was*. But then, suddenly, things went quiet. I was worried about what you might have done to the baby."

Rose went from scared to angry in a millisecond.

"What I might have have done to the baby? I'm the one who has stayed awake with her all night for the past four nights. I'm the one who researched different things to try, to help her."

"And *you're* the one," he said, poking his pointer finger into her chest, "who is going to give bourbon to an infant."

Modern-day Rose shook herself out of that memory. Remembering it wouldn't do her any good. And, her five-year-old daughter was healthy as a horse.

But that night, when he poked her in the chest, grabbed her arm, hard, and pulled back his fist — Rose still didn't know if he planned to hit her, or was just threatening her — she left him.

A few years later, she heard through the grapevine that he'd moved to Reno. But if he was back, and angry about her relationship with Mac, she didn't want to think about what he might do.

Chapter Twenty-Five

"I know you said you plan on hanging around the house today," Mac said to Rose Sunday morning while they sat at the breakfast table. "But may I request your presence at a special activity at four p.m.?"

Her expression showed curiosity, and she was smiling when she said, "Of course. Is it a secret?"

"It is." He made a show of turning his attention to Celeste. "Celeste. Can you keep a secret?"

She giggled. "Course I can."

"In that case, can I borrow Celeste for little while this morning?"

Rose shrugged. "Sure. I was going to have her help me muck the stalls and clean the toilets, but I guess she can go with you."

Celeste giggled. "Mommy! You were not going to muck the stalls or clean the toilets. You said you were going to relax and read a book."

Standing up and kissing Celeste on the top of the head, Rose started to gather the breakfast dishes. "You're right. What time would you like to borrow her?"

"How about now?"

Celeste jumped up and ran for the door. Mac loved her enthusiasm. But he knew what Rose was going to say, and he wanted to beat her to it. "Hold up, hold up! You've got to help with breakfast cleanup."

"Oh yeah!" Celeste threw her head back. "Silly me!" She ran back to grab her plate, which clattered into the sink when she dropped it. Rose put a hand to her forehead, exasperated.

Mac walked over to where she stood at the counter and kissed her on the cheek. "At least the dish is in the sink."

"There's that."

Once they'd rinsed the dishes and loaded the dishwasher, Rose said, "Okay. I'll make myself scarce. I'll be in the bath or reading in bed if you need me."

Oh, Lord. He wished she'd stop saying things that made him imagine all the ways they could —

"Ready, Mac?" Celeste said. "What are we going to do?"

He made a show of looking around the kitchen to make sure Rose was out of earshot.

Celeste giggled. "She's gone. What's the surprise."

"We're going to go out to the garden and pick out pumpkins."

Her face lit up. "Like, for carving?"

"Yeah. For carving." She clapped and bounced. "I've never carved pumpkins before!"

"I know! It's going to be fun, right?"

"Right! And I think my mom is going to be excited!"

"I hope so. Come on. Let's go, before she comes out."

In the garden, the pair of pumpkin vines had yielded a decent crop — dozens of pumpkins. Some of them were still green, and others were plump and bright orange.

"Ohhh my gosh." Awe colored her voice. "There are so! Many! Pumpkins! I've got to get a better look!"

She ran to the retaining wall at one end of the garden, and started to climb the concrete blocks. Mac ran after her, grabbed her waist, and lifted her down. "Let's look from the ground." If he let her get injured the first time he did a project with her, Rose might never forgive him.

"Ma-ac," she whined, her little legs flailing until he set her on her feet.

"I know you're excited, but I don't want you to fall off the wall and hurt yourself."

"I won't." Her tone held a grumpy edge.

Hearing her talk like that, to him, amused him — and warmed his heart. She would talk that way only if she felt comfortable with him. Smiling, he said, "I know you probably won't, but if you did, your mom might never let me borrow you for a project again. And then we couldn't plan surprises for her."

Her lips still in a semi-pout, Celeste nodded. "Fine. But how am I gonna pick my pumpkin?"

Mac held out his arms. "Here. I'll lift you up, and you can point out the one you like."

That process took much longer than Mac expected, as Celeste had him set her down, lift a pumpkin, and turn it around so she could examine it from all angles ... over and over.

When she finally settled on a pumpkin for herself, Mac worried she'd insist on going through the same process to choose a pumpkin for Rose. He grabbed one for himself while saying, "Do you want to pick one for your mom?"

To his great relief, she shook her head. "You can pick it."

Celeste ran alongside him as he carried the pumpkins over to Eleanor's garden shed, one at a time, and hid them out of sight. After hiding the last one, Mac said, "I just remembered something. Whenever my dad and I did a project, just the two of us, we would go back inside and have a hot chocolate. Would you like to do that?"

Again with the face lighting up and the bouncing. *I could get used to this.*

Over hot chocolate, Mac thought about some of the time he'd spent with his dad on the farm. They worked together, of course, but his dad always mixed in a little fun. Hot chocolate, the tire swing, swimming in the creek. None of it was extravagant, but it was special. He hoped he'd have the chance to create some of those memories for Celeste.

"So, how are we going to surprise my mom with the pumpkins?" Celeste asked as Mac reminisced.

They made a plan, and Mac was surprised Celeste managed to

keep the secret all day. At precisely four p.m., Celeste led Rose to the kitchen table and had her sit down with her eyes closed. "Cover your eyes with your hands! We don't want you to peek."

Rose cast a quick glance at Mac before closing her eyes and putting her hands over them. He carried in the pumpkins and set them on the table. Celeste made a big deal of arranging them, and although Mac couldn't quite see her vision, he gave her a double thumbs up when she stopped moving them around.

She nodded. "Okay, Mommy. Open your eyes."

Rose did, and she gasped. "Pumpkins!"

"Did you know, Mommy?"

"No," Rose said. "You guy surprised me." Celeste hugged her, and Rose smiled at Mac over her head. "Thank you."

Her gratitude felt like a million little bubbles bursting against his skin.

"And now we get to carve them!" Celeste said. "This one is yours, Mommy. This one is Mac's. This one is mine."

"We put a lot of time into choosing the pumpkins," Mac said. "And, we got these fancy pumpkin carving sets."

He'd stashed them in his mom's china cabinet, and retrieved them and handed one to Rose, whose wide smile told Mac his pumpkin-carving idea was a good one.

Eleanor came into the kitchen then. "Am I hearing something about pumpkin carving?"

"You are," Celeste said. "It's my first time!" Suddenly, she looked sad. "But we didn't get you a pumpkin! Do you want one? You can share mine. I can carve one side and you can carve the other."

Eleanor put her hand on Celeste's head. "That's really sweet of you. But I have an idea. Why don't I be the official photographer while the three of you carve pumpkins?"

They put down some newspapers outside, and set to work designing their carvings. Rose went for the traditional jack-o'-lantern, and Mac sketched a vampire, uncertain of how it would turn out. Celeste wanted a unicorn, and the three of them spent some time perusing images on the Internet before settling on a design.

"I think we're ready to carve!" Mac said. Celeste squealed. Rose cut the lid for Celeste's pumpkin first, and handed her one of the scraping tools. Celeste plunged her hand into the pumpkin and squealed. "This is so slimy!"

An hour later, all three jack-o'-lanterns sat on the step just outside the kitchen door. Eleanor found some tea lights, and they lit up the pumpkins and stood back to look at them.

"Your unicorn is beautiful," Eleanor said to Celeste, who beamed. Mac couldn't tell it was a unicorn, but he knew better than to say so.

"This brings back so many wonderful memories," Eleanor said. Mac could see the wistfulness in his mom's eyes, and he put an arm around her shoulders. "It does for me, too."

Not for the first time, he was glad he'd left San Francisco ... the big city seemed so far away, and that felt like a good thing as he stood there with his arm around his mom and his eyes on a beautiful woman.

"I say we clean up and go out to dinner," Rose said. "My treat."

Celeste, of course, bounced in response. "Rita's! Can we go to Rita's?"

Mac loved the way an unexpected dinner out felt so exciting. Celeste and Eleanor headed for their shoes. Mac headed outside to throw away the newspapers they'd used, and when he came back in the kitchen, found Rose frozen in the same spot he'd left her.

"Everything okay?"

She came to life then, like she was one of those robots he'd seen on TV, and someone had flipped the switch. "Yes! Fine. Everything's fine." Something about her response seemed off.

"You know, we don't have to go out. I'm happy to cook tonight."

Rose closed her eyes, and Max could swear she was gathering herself. She opened her eyes again and said, "No, let's go. It's fine." She seemed to sense his concern because she rushed to explain herself. "I was just thinking for a moment how nice it would be to put on our sweats and t-shirts and cuddle on the couch. Maybe put on a movie. But we can do that when we get back."

Nodding, Mac put his hands on Rose's shoulders and looked into her eyes. "That sounds like a wonderful idea. I promise, when we get home, we can put on our sweats and t-shirts and cuddle up on the couch. I'm not too sure about the movie, though. Maybe we should wait until Celeste and my mom go to bed and cuddle alone, just the two of us."

Because his hands were on her shoulders, he could literally feel Rose relax. The smile she gave him then seemed genuine. "Sounds like a plan."

Rita made a beeline for their table as soon as they were seated, and Mac thought maybe he knew why Rose was reluctant to dine in. As she walked, popping her gum, Rita looked from Rose to Mac and back to Rose again. Once she reached their table, she said, "Well, well, well. Do we have another match made in heaven, right here at Rita's Diner?"

Out of the corner of his eye, Mac saw Rose look at him. Her expression said, *Help!*

Maybe that's why she had second thoughts about going out to eat.

He decided to act nonchalant. "We're here because we couldn't resist your charms, Rita."

Rita looked at Rose and pointed at Mac. "This one's a keeper."

Naturally, Celeste chose that moment to chime in. "Mac and my mommy went out on a date. Actually, they went out on *two* dates. They went to the football game, and they didn't take me. They said it's because of homecoming. But I think it's because they wanted to go on a date. And then they went mini golfing. Without me."

Rita handed Celeste a peppermint candy. "Aren't you just a fount of information?" Then she turned to her husband, who sat at the end of the bar up front. "Sal! Can you believe this? We have another pair of lovebirds coming in."

Sal lifted his fedora in salute.

"This is where the magic happens," she said to Rose, and Mac, before winking at Eleanor. "Go ahead and put that on the wedding invitations."

Chapter Twenty-Six

"If we were celebrities," Mac said to Rose as he drove them to the staff harvest party the Friday before Halloween, "we'd be making our first public appearance tonight."

Rose smiled, although she immediately thought about the text she'd received — and the person who'd sent it. "It's too bad our names don't combine very well for a couple's name."

Mac reached over and took her hand. "But you've thought about it."

"I have." They looked at each other, and Rose wished they could skip the party and go somewhere alone.

Mac stopped at a red light as they came into town. "Too bad neither of us is on social media. We could also go social media official."

The comment was harmless, but it made Rose's stomach churn with nerves. The light turned green. As they traveled along the city streets, she became hyper aware of passing under each streetlight. *Light, dark, light, dark.* She swallowed.

"Hey, you okay? I was just joking about going social media official."

Forcing a smile she hoped looked somewhat genuine, Rose said, "Everything's fine."

Her mind raced as she tried to come up with an explanation for why she hadn't responded to his joke. But anything she said would be a lie.

So, she changed the subject. "I have to say, I do love our costumes. If one of us doesn't at least place in the costume contest, I'm going to say it's rigged."

Mac put on his blinker and turned into the parking lot of the Hotel St. Michael, where the harvest party would take place.

"I agree. Your bookworm is very creative."

"And so is your atom."

The roiling in Rose's stomach increased in intensity as Mac parked. Sweat prickled in her armpits, and her hands shook as she thought about whether the person who'd taken those pictures would be at the party that night. Mac turned off the ignition, and in the sudden silence, he said, "Ready?"

She gave him another bright smile. "Yep."

He got out quickly, and she took her time, drawing out each step for as long as possible. Procrastinating was stupid. She would have to go in, eventually. Plus, her friends were waiting for her. Since she'd started working at the high school, she bemoaned the fact that she couldn't go to the staff harvest parties. The only people who really babysat Celeste — Taylor and Jessie — always went, too, which meant Rose stayed home. When she'd told them Eleanor had volunteered to watch Celeste so she could go, Taylor and Jessie had been beside themselves with excitement. And, Mac kept saying he couldn't wait for her to participate in all the traditions. He listed them off: pin the raven on the scarecrow, guess the number of pumpkin seeds in a pumpkin, drink the hotel's famous witches brew.

"As long as there's no bobbing for apples," she said, "I'll try everything once."

Hand on the door handle, Rose closed her eyes. The party had always sounded so fun. And now, there she was, able to go, and she was worried about some mysterious voyeur. Mac knocked on her window, and she jumped and opened the door. She accepted the hand he offered and he helped her up.

"I wasn't really thinking about the practicalities of this costume when I made it," she told him, hoping he would think that was the reason she hadn't gotten out of the car.

"Well, if anyone can pull off an impractical bookworm costume, it's you."

She shuffled away from the car and he shut the door. Before she made it two steps, he said, "You're forgetting the second half of your costume."

"Oh, my gosh. You're right."

They went to the trunk, and Mac pulled out the book cover Rose had made out of a giant cardboard box. He helped her put it on and then took her hands in his.

"Are you sure you're okay?"

Rose nodded. About ninety percent of the time, she appreciated how this man could read her. But at the moment, she wished he couldn't.

"Listen," he said. "No one has to know we're a couple. We can walk in separately if you want."

His words made Rose feel even sicker. The last thing she wanted was for him to think she was embarrassed of their relationship.

So, she put a hand on either side of his face and pulled his mouth to hers. Her stomach quieted. The tingling in her chest eased. And, as Mac put his hands on her waist and pulled her closer, a pleasant sensation took hold in her lady parts.

"I'm fine," Rose said when they ended the kiss. "I *am* a little nervous. It's been a while since I did anything social in a group setting like this." That, at least, was the truth. Not the whole truth, but some of it. "I'll be fine once I get in there. We'll head straight for the witches brew, okay?"

Mac nodded. "Okay. First mission: witches brew." His mouth set in determination, her took her hand and towed her into the hotel. When they reached the door of the Ponderosa Room, Mac said, "Ready?"

"Ready." Jessie and Taylor, dressed as a witch and a book fairy, rushed up to greet her.

"We're so glad you're here," Jessie said, and Taylor said, "You've got to come play the games."

Rose looked at Mac, and smiling, he said, "Go play games. I'll bring you witches brew." As he walked away, Taylor called, "Judd's at the bar. Look for the cowboy."

"That's not really a costume," Rose said as Mac saluted and walked off.

"I know," Taylor said. "But it's the most I could get him to do."

Taylor and Jessie each grabbed one of Rose's hands and led her along one side of the room. She quickly realized they were not heading for the games. Her friends pulled her into a secluded corner, where a tall cocktail table stood, four chairs around it.

"Dish," Jessie said, putting her elbows on the table and looking at Rose, intense. The party went on, costumed people talking and dancing.

"What?" Rose said.

"What's going on?" Taylor said. "You look like a deer in headlights."

"Nothing," Rose said, the word coming out in a rush. "I'm just a little nervous, that's all."

Taylor and Jessie looked at each other, then back at Rose.

"There's something she's not telling us." Taylor leaned closer to Jessie but her gaze remained on Rose's face.

"I agree."

"We don't have much time," Taylor said. "The guys will be coming back with drinks in a minute."

Jessie nodded. "Right. We've got to be at the games by then."

The silliness of the conversation struck Rose then, and she started to giggle. Taylor and Jessie looked alarmed and nervous, as if she was a bomb about to go off.

"This isn't good," Taylor said.

"You've got to tell us what's going on," Jessie said.

Making a split-second decision, Rose blurted out the real cause of her anxiety. She told them how she'd received that text with the pictures, and how she wasn't sure who'd sent them, but was certain Jared was involved.

Taylor's face went four shades of pink, and Jessie frowned.

"What the hell?" Jessie's volume rose.

"Yeah!" Taylor said. That's what I was going to say."

"And," Rose said, "because someone took those pictures at the homecoming game, I'm wondering if they're somehow related to the school."

"Which is why," Taylor said, and Jessie finished, "you're nervous about being here tonight."

"Right. And, Mac doesn't know."

Sharing her secret with her friends made Rose feel exponentially lighter. It also cleared her head. The girls promised to meet up with her over the weekend to discuss the pictures and their implications.

As they headed over to the games, Rose found herself able to think more clearly about why the message bothered her so much. *Someone is gathering evidence that I'm a bad mother who neglects her daughter.* Jared was preparing to take Celeste away. At that thought, Rose's hands started to shake again.

She, Taylor, and Jessie had reached the end of the line for Pin the Raven on the Scarecrow.

Rose took a deep breath, lifted her chin, and squared her shoulders. She saw Mac weaving through the crowd, carrying their drinks. She wouldn't let Jared threaten her. She was a great mom. She deserved to go out and have a nice time.

"One witches brew for the bookworm," Mac said, handing her a cup, which fizzed and steamed as if it were fresh from the cauldron. Rose took a sip.

"What happened?" Mac asked. "You look a lot more relaxed."

"I feel a lot more relaxed," Rose said. "I think it just took getting in here, seeing my friends, and watching this handsome stud of an atom walk back to me. Out of all the women in the room, this guy is with me."

He lifted his glass and she tapped hers against it. They sipped their drinks and moved forward in line.

"Hey, Mac," Jessie said. "Celeste told us you and Rose went mini golfing."

Rose knew what was coming.

"She did," Mac said. "Did Celeste also tell you her mother beat me soundly?"

Taylor laughed. "She did."

"But," Jessie said, holding up her pointer finger. "That's what I was going to say. Don't worry. Rose has way less practice at Pin the Raven on the Scarecrow than she does at mini golf. I am positive you will have the upper hand in this game."

The sounds of cheerful chatter, laughter dishes clinking, and cheering surrounded them, and although Rose felt better than she had when they first arrived at the party, she found herself looking around the room, trying to figure out who might have taken those pictures.

Elizabeth Tinsel, the musical theater teacher, stood on the stage across from where Rose stood in line. She wore an intricate witch costume, and had even put on long, fake, witchy fingernails and a few fake warts. Rose knew from teachers lounge conversation that Elizabeth was big on social media. She loved taking pictures at school events and sharing them with administrators, so they could post them online. But, she didn't seem the conniving type.

Although, Rose reasoned, if Jared had someone else roped in, he might have made it seem like the picture taking was all in good fun.

No, Rose thought. Anyone invading a couple's privacy the way the photographer had would know the stalking wasn't all fun and games.

The vampire running Pin the Raven on the Scarecrow was putting the blindfold on Taylor. Rose watched as he spun her around a couple of times, and then handed her a paper raven.

Rose looked at Craig Jansen, the physics teacher. Like Elizabeth, he enjoyed mixing it up, socially. He wasn't big on social media, but she often saw him with his phone out and in camera mode. But, she thought as Jessie took her turn with the blindfold and a paper raven, Craig was a nice guy. Hadn't he loaned Mac the welding mask?

"There's a lot of people watching to do, isn't there?" Mac said, his voice close to her ear making her shiver.

"Yes," Rose said. "I could sit in the corner all night and watch everyone."

"You're up," Jessie said to her then, handing her the blindfold.

The vampire – Rose recognized him up close as the janitor, Mr. Jim — plucked the blindfold from her fingers and tied it on.

"Want to give her a spin?" he said to Mac. Rose could hear the smile in Mac's voice when he said, "Boy, do I."

He put his hands on her shoulders and turned her around a few times. Someone placed a paper raven in her free hand, then took her shoulders and pointed her toward the scarecrow. Arm outstretched, she started walking. When Rose had watched the other staff members and her friends pin their ravens on the scarecrow, the process seemed to happen fast. But, Rose's turn seemed interminable. How long would it take her to reach the scarecrow? Unable to see anything — or anyone — terrified Rose. What if, at that very moment, someone was taking her picture? She could only imagine how foolish she looked, one arm outstretched, the other hand grasping a beverage, and a blindfold over her eyes. Her breathing became rapid and her heart hammered.

This was stupid.

She wanted to call out for Mac, to have him come take off the blindfold and get her out of this party, where she was suddenly certain someone lurked, watching her. She inhaled to call for him, and at that exact moment, her hand touched the wall. Unable to even think about where the scarecrow's shoulder was, Rose taped her raven to the wall and tore off the blindfold. She spun around to face the line, and Mac and her friends, and realized her heart was still racing. Her limbs felt weak and shaky as she walked to the ten feet back to the vampire and thrust the blindfold at him. Then, before she moved out of the way so Mac could take his turn, she put her glass to her lips and guzzled down her drink.

Chapter Twenty-Seven

With Halloween coming up, the high schoolers — not just Mac's students, but all of them — were squirrely and wound up. That meant a lot of discipline, and a long, exhausting week. To top it off, Mac thought as he pulled into the driveway Thursday evening, there was still another full day to get through.

Inside, the house smelled wonderful. Something savory was cooking on the stove. Mac could make out onion, garlic, maybe mushrooms. So, Rose was home, but the house was quiet. Typically, Celeste's squeals or shouting would greet him. But all he heard at the moment were the bubbling of the pot on the stove and the gentle ticking of his mom's cuckoo clock.

"Oh, hey, honey," Eleanor said, emerging from the hallway. "How was your day?"

He smiled at her, even while noticing how much older she looked these days. The lines around her eyes had grown deeper, and the bones in her hands and wrists stood out.

"Tiring. The school is a madhouse, as you can imagine, with Halloween coming up."

"Ah," Eleanor said. "I remember those days. You kids used to act like complete maniacs, anticipating all the candy and sweet treats you were going to get."

"Well, I don't remember acting like these kids act," Mac said. Although, come to think of it, he did remember his mom, exasperated, saying things like, "Will you just calm *down?*" Or, "Enough already!"

He walked over to the stove, lifted the lid off the pot, and inhaled the scent of what he now recognized as soup. "This smells delicious."

"I know," Eleanor opened the fridge and took out a sparkling water. "Rose made a chicken and rice soup."

"If you had said that to me before I smelled the soup, I would have thought it sounded boring," Mac said. "But I already know I'm going to have seconds."

Popping her can open, Eleanor walked around the counter and sat on a bar stool. A piece of mail there caught Mac's eye. The return address said *High Country Reverse Mortgage.* It could be junk mail, or ... "What's that?"

With his heart racing as fast as it was, Mac found it difficult to keep his voice tone light.

"Oh!" Eleanor said, as if she were seeing it for the first time. Mac knew she wasn't, because the envelope had obviously been opened. She picked it up, opened it, and pulled out the contents. It looked like a single sheet of paper, bearing the same logo as the envelope.

Unfolding it, Eleanor started to read.

"Dear Mrs. MacKinnon,

We received your inquiry about our reverse mortgage program. As you requested, we are writing with more information. Consider this letter and the enclosed brochure general information. If you would like a detailed proposal, we invite you to set up an appointment with one of our reverse mortgage consultants.

In general, a reverse mortgage enables you to live off the value of your house. You'll no longer have to pay a mortgage payment, and you pay back the loan when you sell your property.

Reverse mortgages can help you stay in your home throughout your retirement. That's why our program is popular among retirees. If you'd like to set up an appointment to meet with someone to discuss your options and obtain a detailed quote, please call the number below."

Eleanor cleared her throat and looked up at Mac. A burning sensation filled his torso. He felt like he could throw up. His vision went blurry at the edges.

"Are you thinking of getting a reverse mortgage?" he asked.

"I was considering it as an option, yes. Of course, that was before Rose and Celeste —"

"Mama," Mac said. "You can take out a reverse mortgage if you want to. This is your property."

Eleanor folded the letter and put it back in the envelope. "I know. But it's your property, too. After your dad died and you decided to stay, I think we both believed it was temporary. I don't know if you remember, but you were so anxious to get back to San Francisco. The big city. You hated it here."

Mac nodded. "You're right. I was. I did."

"After Rose moved in, I sensed that maybe things changed for you. You seem more ... settled."

Mac's heart had slowed down, but his voice still sounded breathy when he answered. "I *have* felt more settled. You know, I just realized this. It seems so obvious now, but hindsight, right?"

"Right." His mom smiled.

"When Dad died and I moved back home, it didn't feel quite the same. Yes, you're here," he rushed to add. "And I've loved spending time with you again. But dad being gone — it left a void."

Eleanor's eyes teared up, and Mac reached across the counter to take her hand. "I didn't mean to make you cry."

She sniffled. "No, you didn't. I felt the same way. It's been wonderful having you in the house again. But you're right. I can feel his absence. I can feel it in my very bones."

Her words made Mac unbearably sad. Not as much for himself as for her. She and his dad shared that once-in-a-lifetime love. *Rose.* The thought came to his mind unbidden. Was it possible he and Rose could have that, too?

Before he could explore that thought any further, his mom said,

"Honestly, I always thought you'd live here as an adult. But, after your dad died, I reconsidered. If you were feeling even a fraction of what I was — heartbreak every time I came in the door — maybe you'd want to find your own place."

Mac nodded. "I understand."

Tears streaming down her face, Rose placed a hand on her heart. "For so long, I felt an ache, here, every time I thought about him, which was at least once a minute." She laughed. "But then Rose and Celeste moved in. Even though no one will ever fill that space that represents your dad, something about the two of them being here makes it feel like home again."

Mac's throat felt tight. He nodded, swallowed. He hadn't even realized he felt that way until his mom put it into words.

. "Like I said," Eleanor went on, "I sent for that information several months ago. It was just an idea, and I never felt married to it."

Suddenly, Mac experienced a fierce knowing. Rose and Celeste belonged there, in the house, on the property, with him. *He* belonged there. A parade of images marched through his head. A sleeping Celeste, a laughing Rose, a diamond ring — yes, a diamond ring! Rose in a wedding dress, Celeste next to her as a flower girl or ring bearer. The three of them, sitting on the couch together, eating popcorn. Celeste tucked between them in bed, sleeping. He never pictured any of these scenes with another woman. But no other woman measured up to Rose.

"I can practically see your mind going a million miles an hour," Eleanor said, and Mac smiled.

"My mind *is* going a million miles an hour," he said. "You're right about everything. I can't believe you put into words so succinctly what I've been feeling for the past several weeks. I'm in love with Rose Coffey, and I'm going to show her that she loves me, too."

Eleanor stood up and drained her sparkling water. "That's my boy."

She picked up the reverse mortgage letter, and started to tear it in half.

Mac put a hand on both of hers, to still her motions. "Hold on. Don't tear that up just yet. We have to make sure Rose realizes she's in love with me before we discard any options."

Eleanor laughed and put the paper down on the counter.

"I'm pretty sure you'll have no trouble convincing her. But we don't want to jinx it, do we?"

Chapter Twenty-Eight

Rose had always loved Halloween. During the weeks leading up to the holiday, she took note of the crisp, cool, evening air, the changing leaves, the spooky spiderweb and skeleton decorations, and of course, the costumes, caramel apples, and candy all around.

On Halloween itself, Rose started the day by baking pumpkin cookies. Celeste helped by rolling the dough into balls, a skill at which she'd improved. At five, she finally seemed old enough for them both to really enjoy the holiday. She was much less likely to run out in the street, Rose thought as she watched her set each ball on the cookie sheet, and Rose wouldn't feel as rushed to get home for bedtime. Plus, Halloween fell on a Saturday, so they had all day to prepare and could sleep in on Sunday.

After Rose put the cookies into the oven, Mac poked his head into the kitchen from the hallway and asked Celeste if she could go outside and gather the eggs. Once she was gone, he said to Rose, "Is it all right if I give Celeste a candy bucket? I know how much she wants one, and I just happened to see them at the store that goes perfectly with her dragon costume. I already bought it, but if you really don't want her to have it, just say so."

Glancing behind her to make sure Celeste hadn't come back,

Rose kissed Mac long and hard. "I'm sure she'd love it. Yes, you can give it to her. Thank you."

"Geez, if I'd known buying inexpensive gifts for your daughter would get me that kind of thank-you, I'd have started buying them weeks ago."

Rose gave him a playful swat on the shoulder, and Celeste came back in with the eggs. They spent most of the day outside on the property, weeding the garden, harvesting produce, and raking leaves into piles (which Celeste then jumped in or ran through). Rose made an early dinner of homemade pizza so they could trick-or-treat on full stomachs. After eating a few bites of her tomato-and-basil pizza, Celeste pushed away her plate and said, "I'm full. Let's go trick-or-treating."

Rose pushed the plate close to her again. "You've got to eat a little more, or you're going to be hungry."

"If I get hungry, I'll just eat candy."

Eleanor covered her smile with her hand, and Mac looked down at his own plate, suddenly very interested in the pepperoni and bell peppers on his pie.

"I like your thinking," Rose said. "But if you eat candy instead of dinner, you won't feel well, and we'll have to come home early, and you won't get as much candy."

Celeste pursed her lips, considering for a few seconds. "I guess you make a good point."

She picked up her pizza and took another bite. Mouth full, she said, "It's just that I'm really excited to go trick-or-treating."

Before Rose could remind Celeste about speaking with her mouth full, Mac reached across the table and touched Celeste's hand, then made a pinching motion with his fingers. Celeste nodded, chewed with her mouth closed, swallowed, and repeated, "I'm just really excited to go trick-or-treating."

Mac winked at Rose, who winked back before telling Celeste, "I know. But consider this pizza your fuel for an energized trick-or-treating experience."

Celeste eventually finished her pizza. The four of them did a quick cleanup, and then Rose helped Celeste put on her dragon costume.

"Wait! Before we go, Celeste, I have a surprise for you." Mac came out of his bedroom holding something behind his back. When he revealed the candy bucket, she squealed, screamed, and threw herself at him, wrapping her arms around his legs.

"Thank you, Mac! Thank you so much. I've wanted one of these *forever*."

"Forever, huh?"

"Forever!"

Rose's heart did a little pitter patter at that interaction, and it stayed with her as they loaded the car. They'd decided to trick-or-treat in downtown Prescott, where a few of the older neighborhoods were renowned for a great Halloween experience. Even though it was still early, trick-or-treaters swarmed the streets. Rose parked a couple of blocks from the neighborhood they planned to visit. Celeste took the lead, bouncing along in front of them, and Eleanor quickly caught up to her. Rose and Mac walked behind them, and Rose found herself brimming with joy. Not the superficial kind of joy she might experience if she got a new puppy or an amazing Christmas gift, but a profound, quiet joy that fed contentment.

Just as she experienced that realization, Mac took her hand in his. "This is really nice."

She looked up at him, smiling. "You're right. It *is* really nice."

The trick-or-treating neighborhood did not disappoint. Residents had strung Halloween lights, and their yards were delightfully spooky. Rose saw costumes of every type — cute puppies, creepy goblins, funny sumo wrestlers.

"Mommy! Look! Another dragon!"

"How many dragons do you think we'll see?" Mac asked.

"No telling," Rose said. "But at least she's excited about it. The year she dressed up as a unicorn, she got angry every time we saw another unicorn."

The three adults took turns walking Celeste up to front doors. Each time she received a piece of candy, she identified it out loud as she came back down the walkway.

When she announced she'd gotten a Snickers bar, Mac whispered to Rose, "Think we can steal that and split it after she falls asleep?"

And when she got a pack of M&Ms Rose said to Mac, "I'll grab those, and we can put them in some popcorn while we watch a movie."

When Celeste reported she'd received peanut butter cups, Eleanor said to Rose, "I think I'm taking those."

Rose was having so much fun, she almost couldn't believe it when the sky became dark.

"Let's see how full your bucket is," Rose said, and Celeste held it up. Rose gasped, genuinely surprised at how much candy Celeste had. "I think our work here is done," she said, and Celeste said, "not yet! We still haven't made it to the end of this street."

"Tell you what," Rose said. "We can go to the end of the street. If you promise to share some of your candy with your three chaperone."

She didn't even hesitate. "Course I will." They were off again, and as they walked, both Eleanor and Mac reminded Celeste to stay close, hold hands as they walked across driveways and side streets, watch for cars, and to say thank you. That sense of joyful contentment stuck with Rose. By the time they reached the end of the street, Rose didn't think it was possible for Celeste to fit anymore candy in her bucket.

"We made it!" Rose said. "Now we're going to head straight back to the car, without stopping."

Celeste nodded, and, whether the excitement came from knowing how much sugar she had in her possession, or from the atmosphere, Celeste couldn't help but skip instead of walk. After one or two strides, candy started dropping from her bucket. She heard one of the bars hit the sidewalk, and when she looked down, she tripped over her own feet, sending what looked like her entire load flying.

That, of course, resulted in immediate panic, with screaming and everything. Of course, people nearby turned to see what was going on. Rose took a step toward Celeste, but Mac held up a hand. "I'll get it."

And then, that wonderful man was at her daughter's side, talking in a quiet voice, saying something that made Celeste stop screaming and start laughing within a matter of seconds. Rose couldn't believe it.

"Is he some kind of magician?" she said to Eleanor, who chuckled. "I don't know if he's a magician, or if he just understands how upset she is. As a little boy, Mac was a bit tightly wound."

Candy picked up, bucket full, and smiles on their faces, Celeste and Mac stood up

"Ready to go?" Celeste grinned as if she hadn't been in meltdown mode a few minutes before. Eleanor took Celeste's hand and Rose and Mac fell into step behind them.

"Thank you," she said to Mac. "You just saved the evening from turning into disaster."

Again, he took her hand and interlaced their fingers.

"You're welcome. I saw the look on your face — '*oh no*' — and I knew I had to act fast."

"I appreciate it. Look how much fun she's having."

In front of them, Celeste chatted away to Eleanor, talking nonstop about all her candy and the order in which she planned to eat it.

"I think everyone's having fun tonight," Mac said.

"I think so too. And even though it's almost bedtime, I think I'm going to have to put on a movie, just to get Celeste calmed down."

Back at home, Rose gave Celeste a quick bath and had her put on pajamas. Mac queued up *It's the Great Pumpkin, Charlie Brown*. He went to make popcorn while Rose and Celeste settled onto the couch and Eleanor sat in the recliner. When Mac came back into the living room, a bowl of popcorn in his hands, Celeste patted the spot on the couch next to her. "You sit here, Mac."

He did, and draped his arm over the back of the couch so he could rest his hand on Rose's shoulder. Celeste ate a few handfuls of popcorn as the movie started to play, and was asleep within a few minutes.

When she started snoring, Eleanor said, "Well, I guess it's officially bedtime."

An urgent desire hit Rose. She wanted nothing more than to be alone with Mac.

"Will you wait up for me while I put her in bed?"

Her body throbbed with anticipation as she waited for his answer. He stroked the back of her neck with his thumb, sending chills over her skin. "I will."

Rose stood and stretched and Mac did the same.

"I'll get her," he said.

Rose didn't argue. Watching the way he cared for Celeste made her all warm and fuzzy inside. He lifted Celeste's limp body off the couch and she settled onto his shoulder like she'd been doing it her whole life. Rose followed Mac into the bedroom she shared with Celeste. She watched as he laid her daughter in her little bed, pulled the covers over her, and brushed the hair out of her face.

As Mac stepped aside to let Rose kiss Celeste good night, he gave her arm a gentle squeeze and let his hand trail down over her butt.

"I'll be in the living room."

Rose knelt and kissed Celeste on the temple, then straightened the blanket again, even though Mac had done a perfectly fine job of tucking her in. She went back out the living room where Mac was waiting, a glass of wine in a glass of bourbon on the coffee table in front of him.

She picked up the wine and sat down. "Thank you." She snuggled up to Mac's side, again pleased at how well their bodies fit together. He leaned into the contact and pressed a kiss to her cheek.

"Finally, some alone time," Rose said. Mac responded with his deep chuckle. "I was thinking the same thing, but I didn't want you to think I didn't enjoy the evening with Celeste. I did. But I've been very much looking forward to getting you alone."

"No one understands that better than I do."

Rose turned her head, and Mac brought his lips to hers. When their tongues met, he moaned, the sound soft and arousing. So arousing, in fact, that Rose found herself stretching out along the couch, pulling Mac down to lay next to her. He slipped a hand under her T-shirt and let it rest on her waist.

She brought her hands to his face, her kisses becoming greedy and urgent, her hips moving against her his. His hand traveled up her rib cage and when he found her breast bare, he groaned. His palm felt rough and calloused against her skin, and her nipple perked up at the contact. He kissed her neck, and she whispered his name, her lower half grinding with even more urgency. She felt like she might actually die if he didn't get inside her. Soon. Lifting her shirt, he brought his mouth to her breasts, and his hand between her legs. She was slick and ready.

"It's taking literally all of my self-control not to take you here and now," he said.

He nipped her nipple, she gasped.

"We should take this into the bedroom," she said.

She felt him nod. "Please."

That single word undid her. She stood up and pulled him to standing. He led her past her bedroom, tiptoeing, and into his, where he shut the door quietly and locked it. Just inside the door, he pulled her T-shirt over her head, and yanked her pants down.

She stepped out of them and he motioned with his pointer finger for her to turn around. "Let me look at you."

Suddenly shy, her gaze dropped to the floor as she began a slow revolution. As she turned, she could feel his gaze roam over every inch of her skin.

"God, you're beautiful," he said as she turned to face him again. She saw his erection pulse, and she imagined him sliding it between her legs. Her gaze remained on the floor.

"Look at me," he commanded.

She did, and when she saw the fire in his eyes, she felt herself smiling a slow, knowing smile. He closed the distance between them and put his hands on her hips and his forehead on hers.

"You're so beautiful."

"Let me look at you," she said, her voice certain.

Much as he'd done, she pulled off his shirt, pulled down his pants and stood back to look at him. Her once-over paused just below his waist and she emitted an appreciative growl before reaching out for him and giving him a few long strokes. Then they were tumbling onto the bed in a rush of kisses and touches and pleasure-filled sounds.

"Please," she said again.

Mac positioned himself above her, and when their eyes met, he drove himself into her. She gasped, and they began to move together, the rhythm and intensity building. Just before she went over the edge, Rose thought, there will never be anyone else. She cried out in release, and he poured himself into her.

Chapter Twenty-Nine

S unday morning, Mac woke up energized and craving Rose's body ... and alone. They'd agreed the night before to sleep in their own beds so Celeste wouldn't wake up to find Rose unexpectedly gone.

Remembering the previous evening, Mac became aroused all over, and immediately thought about when he might be able to make love to Rose again. In desperate need of cooling off, he got up and took a cold shower. The frigid water shocked his system, and he was finally able to think clearly when he got out and dried off.

While he did, he considered what he could say or do to convince Rose the two of them were meant to be together. From what she'd said about Celeste's father, he knew she wasn't looking to rush into any sort of long-term commitment.

But. Everything he and Rose experienced together showed him they were meant to be. He pulled on jeans and a T-shirt and headed into the kitchen. Rose wasn't up yet.

You tired her out, you scoundrel. He smiled as he poured coffee. It was early enough that he could make breakfast before doing the chores, and he set to work on a frittata. As he chopped and stirred and salted and peppered, he considered the various ways he could illustrate just how much he cared for — no, *loved* — Rose and Celeste.

He could take Rose on a romantic getaway; pamper her and shower her with affection. Right away, he discarded that idea. Whatever he did had to include Celeste. They would be a family, and he wanted his plan to symbolize that. He got out a pan and turned on the stove to heat it. After a few minutes, steam rose from its surface, and Mac poured in the frittata mixture.

"Good morning." Rose's voice came from the kitchen entrance.

She leaned against the wall, wearing her fuzzy socks, tiny sleep shorts, and oversized shirt. The craving he'd experienced that morning intensified. He actually had to adjust his jeans.

"Good morning to you." He Crossed the kitchen in a couple of strides and kissed her. As soon as their lips met, his hand found her breast, and she groaned, before she sMaced his hand away, giggling. "Not that I don't like it, but what if your mom walks in?"

Feeling randy and playful, Mac reached around and grabbed her butt. "I'm pretty sure she knows what happens between two adults who are attracted to each other," he said.

"But still." Rose walked over to the stove. "Seeing it is a whole different matter." She leaned over the pan, smelled the frittata. "This looks and smells delicious. Did you use the last of the yellow squashes from Friday?"

"I did. Is that okay?"

"That's fine. I was hoping you did, actually. I didn't want them to go bad."

How such a mundane conversation — about squash, for goodness' sake — could ignite such a powerful feeling in Mac's body, he didn't know. But he wasn't going to fight it. Even though Rose had just swatted him away, he came up behind her at the stove and put his arms around her waist. He cupped her breasts and could feel his erection pressing against her but. She arched her back, just enough to add to the pressure, and gently removed his hands from her breasts.

His lips on her neck, said, "Are you hungry?"

She rubbed against him some more, and said, "Famished."

"Me, too."

The sound of bare feet on the floor came from the hallway, and Mac stepped away from Rose.

"Good morning, guys," Celeste said.

Rose turned around and smiled. "Good morning, my little dragon. Did you sleep well?"

Celeste made a show of stretching. "I slept great."

Eleanor came in the kitchen door then, and Mac served everyone breakfast. As they all sat around the table, eating eggs from their chickens and vegetables from their garden and discussing the high points of Halloween the night before, Mac knew: this was what he wanted. He wanted holidays with his mom, Rose, and Celeste. He wanted to make new memories with them, enjoy long, leisurely weekend breakfasts at the kitchen table. He wanted it forever. He looked at his mom and realized was watching him. Not for the first time, he got the sense she knew what he was thinking. She looked just about as happy as he felt.

Over the course of the next few days, Mac's idea took shape. He wasn't one for grand gestures. He always believed that the smaller moments, gathered up over time, mattered more than anything else. As he went through his typical routines, he settled on a plan that stripped down all the extraneous stuff to leave just himself, Rose, and Celeste. On Wednesday afternoon, as the three of them got home after school and gathered in the kitchen for snacks, he said to Rose and Celeste, "What do you ladies think about a quick camping trip this weekend?"

"Camping? Like, in a tent?" Celeste's excitement level rose with the pitch of her voice.

God, I love that kid.

"Yeah. In a tent. With a camp fire and s'mores."

Bouncing, Celeste said, "Yes! My first camping trip! Let's do it!"

Rose, on the other hand, looked somewhat dubious. "It sounds fun, but I'm not sure how much help I would be. I haven't been camping since I was a kid."

"Does it really sound fun," Mac asked, "or are you just hoping not to disappoint Celeste and me?"

He kept his tone light, but the truth was, he'd be disappointed if she didn't want to go. Never mind, he told himself. If she didn't want to go, he could come up with a better plan. But Rose was smiling, her expression more certain. "The more I think about it, the more fun it sounds. And I might be a rookie, but you can just tell me what to do."

"I'd love to tell you what to do," he said, shooting a devilish grin across the room at her.

She shook her head. Rolled her eyes. Smiled.

God, I love that woman.

"What about the animals, though?" she wanted to know. "Will they be okay if we're gone for one or two nights?"

"They will," Mac said. "We can set them up with extra food and water. And it's probably wise to go for just one night, since it'll be Celeste's first camping trip."

"This actually sounds really fun," Rose said. "Should we go Saturday night?"

"Yeah. Let's plan on that."

Suddenly, right there in the kitchen, Mac found himself thinking about sharing a tent with Rose overnight. Not for their upcoming trip, since Celeste would be there. But the idea of being in a quiet, secluded outdoor setting with Rose made Mac want to plan a subsequent camping trip right then and there.

"Be right back," he said.

As he walked toward his bedroom to wait for his arousal to settle down, he thought he could probably use another cold shower. Instead, he'd have to make do with thinking about being *this* close to Rose, and unable to do anything about it. She was driving him crazy, and he liked it.

* * *

Mac woke early Saturday morning to take care of the chores, leaving extra food for the animals, and checking to make sure the automatic waterers were working. He went through what he'd loaded into the back of Rose's car the night before. While taking his inventory, he thought back to the previous afternoon when he and Rose had discussed which car to take. He had his trunk open, and was measuring to determine how much he'd have to stuff into the backseat with Celeste.

Rose came up and leaned against him, wrapping an arm around his waist and putting her head on his shoulder. "I'm sorry to say, despite your great taste in cars, this might not be the most practical choice for camping. Why don't we take mine?"

He'd agreed, and as soon as she opened the liftgate on her SUV, his inexact measuring system told him their gear and food would definitely fit. Although she hadn't said, "I told you so," the twitching of her lips and her single raised eyebrow said it for her.

That interaction was so simple, so everyday, and yet so impactful. Being with Rose just felt right. Thinking about it made Mac sigh like a lovesick teenager.

Mac realized he'd packed everything on his list except a headlamp. He grabbed two of those from the garage and put them in his backpack, then found Rose in the kitchen, packing the cooler.

"I think we're just about ready," she said. "Good idea to start out with just one night. There's a lot to pack."

He nodded. "It *is* a lot to pack. And it's a lot to unpack. But it's worth it."

She closed the cooler, straightened up, and kissed him, and the yearning hit him again. Holding onto her hips, he said, "What do you say to a camping trip, just the two of us, next time?"

Smiling, she said, "A romantic night under the stars? Yes, please."

An hour later, they arrived at their spot, on the edge of a cove on Watson Lake. As Mac slowed to a stop, Celeste said, "Wow," and Rose said, "This is beautiful."

Granite boulders surrounded the lake, their reflections crystal clear in the water. Cattails grew along the edge, and lily pads floated on the surface.

"I knew you'd like it," he said. "This is where we used to camp when I was a kid."

"Where can we set up our tent?" Celeste ran around, looking.

"Let's explore." Mac walked along the boulders that enclosed the beach area. "We'll find a good flat spot."

It didn't take long to find a spot, and then it only about thirty minutes to unpack the car, set up the tent, inflate their air mattresses, and set up their camping chairs.

Celeste was anxious to move on to the next activity. "Can we go for a boat ride?"

They piled into Mac's two-person kayak, Celeste perched on the bow. A few other kayaks, canoes, and dinghies dotted the lake.

"I feel like we're part of a painting, or a picture," Rose said. "This is just so perfect. We couldn't have asked for better weather."

"Or better company," Mac said.

Rose turned around and smiled at him. "I agree."

"Can we go around the whole lake?" Celeste asked.

"Yes we can, Captain!" Mac and Rose paddled the kayak to the edge and then started the loop.

After about fifteen minutes, Mac's shoulder muscles ached. "Good thing this is a small lake. I'm not sure I could paddle all the way around a bigger one."

"I'm sure you could," Celeste said. "I've seen your muscles."

"Thank you," Mac said.

In front of him, Rose's shoulders shook with laughter. A fish jumped out of the water at the kayak's bow, and Celeste squealed and jumped, nearly falling off her spot. Rose grabbed the front of her life jacket, and all three of them dissolved into laughter.

"It was just a fish," Mac said, and Celeste said, "I know! But it scared me!"

Rose pulled Celeste off the bow and settled her between her legs. "I hate to think what would happen if we saw a shark."

"A shark?"

"I was just kidding," Rose said. "There are no sharks here."

Celeste relaxed, her elbows on Rose's knees. After they paddled the rest of the way around the lake, they docked the kayak on the shore and had lunch in their camping chairs.

"What are we gonna do next?"

Mac and Rose exchanged a look. Mac gestured at the giant boulders piled around them. "We could go rock climbing."

Celeste stood up, setting her half-eaten sandwich on her chair. "Let's go!"

Rose simply pointed at the remaining half of the sandwich and Celeste sighed before sitting down to finish it.

"*Now* can we go rock climbing?"

Watching that little girl scramble up the rock faces, fearless, ignited an unexpected pride in Mac. Each time she reached the top of a boulder, she said, "I want to go higher!" Rose and Mac followed her up each time.

"I think we're all going to sleep well tonight," Rose said, and Mac said, "Yep," even though he felt certain he wouldn't sleep a wink while lying next to Rose and being unable to touch her.

After dinner and s'mores, Celeste climbed into Rose's lap and curled up. Within a few minutes, Mac could see her eyelids getting heavy.

"I think it might be bedtime for at least one of us." Mac's gaze met Rose's over Celeste's nodding head.

Rose smiled back at him, and in the firelight, he thought, *that's exactly what an angel looks like.*

"Come on, Celeste. Let's get you tucked in."

"But I'm not tired," Celeste said, her voice slurred with sleepiness.

Cradling Celeste in her arms, Rose stood up. She said to Mac, "If you have the energy for a little more time around the fire, I'll come back out as soon as she's asleep."

"I'll be right here."

The flames danced, reds, yellows, oranges, and even a few blues. The wood popped and crackled as Mac listened to Rose put Celeste to bed. After telling her a short bedtime story, she granted Celeste's request to scratch her back for a few minutes. Then, after a short period of silence, Mac heard the unzipping of the tent, and Rose crawled through. She scooted her camping chair closer to his, so the arms touched.

When she sat down, she held his hand and leaned her head on

his shoulder. "This camping trip has been magical. Thank you so much."

"You're welcome."

They sat without speaking for a few minutes, both of them focused on the fire. Mac had never experienced a more perfect moment.

"Rose?"

"Yeah?"

"This trip has been magical for me, too. It's been magical because I love you. I love Celeste, and I love you. I can't think of a more perfect way to spend the day, or two people I'd rather spend it with."

Breath bated, he waited for her response. Although he wanted to hear it, he also knew, deep down to his bones, that she felt the same way. He could feel it, could sense it, every time they were together.

Still, when she snuggled even closer against him and said, "I love you too, Johnny MacKinnon," he almost came undone.

Chapter Thirty

Throughout the day Monday, Rose felt like she was dancing among the clouds. Buoyant and effervescent, she practically sparkled with the feeling of being in love. She was in love with Johnny Mac. And he was in love with her.

At lunch, she met Taylor and Jessie at the picnic table outside the library. They were already seated, and when she walked up, Jessie looked her up and down and then said to Taylor, "Well, she is definitely glowing."

Taylor nodded. "She's a veritable ray of sunshine."

Rose sat down and unzipped her lunch box. A little bouquet of flowers was the first thing she saw when she opened the lid.

"Now I know why you're glowing," Jessie said. "You are dating the most romantic man in Prescott."

Rose smiled involuntarily. "I guess I am."

"So what's got you all aglow?" Taylor wanted to know. "What happened this weekend?"

Rose told her friends about the camping trip, about how Mac had planned every detail to make sure she and Celeste had a nice time. About how he bought Celeste a life jacket to wear on the kayak, and how he brought s'mores sticks and magic powder to make the fire change colors.

"I think *I'm* in love," Jessie said.

They spent the rest of the lunch discussing Taylor's plans for her new business, Sugar Pine Barn, and Jessie's plans to prep some meals for her neighbor, Alvin.

When Rose got back to her classroom, she found a sticky note stuck to her desk. *Hope you're having a good day.*

XO Mac

P.S. Do you have 11 protons? Because you're sodium fine.

Smiling, Rose peeled the sticky note off her desk and stuck it on the side of her computer monitor.

"You look happy this afternoon," said a voice from behind her.

Rose turned to see one of her students, Olivia, walking in.

"I am," Rose said.

"I don't usually see teachers this happy on a Monday," Olivia said. "You must have had a really good weekend."

"I did," Rose said. Her face felt warm.

Olivia sat down at her desk, glanced at the clock, and apparently deciding she had a few more minutes before class started, she got out her phone. Rose straightened the piles of handouts she'd copied for the next period, and reviewed the notes she'd made for that day's lesson. She checked her phone one last time before stowing it for the class period.

Her heart lurched into her throat when she saw the text.

This time, the photos came from a different phone number. There, in bright colors that perfectly represented reality at the lake during their weekend camping trip, was an image of Celeste in the split second she had almost fallen off the kayak. Her wide-eyed, open-mouthed expression conveyed fear. Although she had been afraid — of the fish and, possibly, of falling out of the kayak, she'd never been in any real danger. Rose had grabbed her right away, and anyway, she knew how to swim and was wearing a life vest. She'd never been outside of arm's reach.

The text under the photo read, *Your daughter could have died.*

Rose's rational side knew Celeste was nowhere close to dying that day. But someone could make the claim that by letting her sit out on the bow, instead of in a real seat, the third passenger on a kayak meant for two, Rose had put her in danger. Her heart pumped fast and hard, and she heard whooshing noises in her ears. She literally saw red.

"Are you okay, Ms. Coffey?" Olivia said.

"Yeah," Henry said. "You look sick all of a sudden."

"Yeah," said another student from somewhere in the back of the classroom. "And the bell rang, and you haven't reminded us to get out our notebooks."

Rose closed her eyes. She pushed the button to darken the screen on her phone and set it face down on her desk. She took the deepest breath she could, filling her lungs, waiting, and then exhaling.

Finally, she opened her eyes and pasted on a smile. "I'm fine," she lied. "Go ahead and get out your paper. The bell work is on the whiteboard."

"Um, Ms. Coffey?" Olivia said. "Everyone already got out their paper. I think we've all done the bell work."

Her students murmured in agreement. Rose looked around. Sure enough, almost everyone had notebooks out and paragraphs written.

Rose brought her hands together in a single clap. "Great. Let's get started."

She moved through her next two classes as though she were swimming in molasses. Her limbs felt slow and heavy, and she worried that at any moment, she might drown, suffocating in the thick, sticky substance.

She told herself she'd block the latest number as soon as the final bell rang. When it did and she picked up her phone, she saw she'd received a voicemail. The students in the hallway outside her room hollered and laughed as usual, making it too loud for her to try to listen. She tapped over to read the transcription.

Hello Rose, this is Miriam Bellevue from the Department of Child Safety. We've received a report about your daughter, Celeste, and you are required to meet with one of our social workers. Your response to this message is required by law. Please return this phone call within twenty-four hours. If you do not return the phone call, the Department of Child Safety will take legal action.

Rose's entire body vibrated with pure, unfiltered fear. The Department of Child Safety? That was the organization that took people's children away and put them in foster care.

"Jared." Her voice came out in a whisper. He'd done it. He'd found a way to get Celeste taken from her. Just as she finally got on her feet, found a stable living situation, and ... fell in love. Jared had found a way to ruin her life, just like he promised all those years ago. Rose retched, nearly throwing up her lunch.

She stuffed her phone into her purse and zoomed around the classroom gathering her things. Without locking her classroom door, she ran to the car and then drove to Celeste's preschool. Her whole body unfolded in relief when she heard Celeste's voice as she got out of the car. "I bet I got more candy than you! I had a whole bucket full!"

Definitely her daughter. Talking in a bratty voice, but still. She was there, safe and sound. Still tense from head to toe, Rose took several deep breaths as she walked to the entrance of the daycare. She pasted on the best smile she could as she opened the door. When she signed Celeste out on the sign-out book, a realization struck: the sign-out book was a months-long record of their precise schedule. She glanced at the columns for drop-off and pickup and realized the times in each column were within minutes of each other. If someone wanted to take Celeste, all they had to do is get their hands on the sign-out book and they'd know, within two or three minutes, when Rose dropped her off and picked her up. Rose tore out Celeste's page, folded it in half as many times as she could, and stuffed it in her pocket. She made sure to shut the book. Then she walked into the backyard, where she heard Celeste's shrill voice. Her daughter saw her right away and came running. "Mommy! Juan said he got more candy than me, but he didn't! I got the most."

Settling an argument over candy was the absolute last thing Rose wanted to do. But she didn't want to let on that she was frazzled. "It doesn't really matter, right?" she said to the kids, both of whom looked up at her with round eyes, waiting. "As long as you both got some candy, that's what matters."

"But she —" Juan started, pointing an accusatory finger at Celeste, his eyebrows drawn, his mouth in a frown.

Rose held up both hands. "You guys like each other too much to argue."

Until she had Celeste buckled into the car, Rose felt like she couldn't quite draw a breath. Then she laid her head on the steering wheel and took several gulps of air.

"Are we going to go?" Celeste sounded uncertain.

Rose sat up. "Yep! We are going to go."

Go where, Rose didn't know. Although she felt safe at Mac's house, Jared knew they'd been staying there. Come to think of it, if he knew where they'd been staying, he probably knew their routine. He could be lurking at that very moment, waiting for her drive away.

She checked her mirrors, her head moving rapidly from the side-view mirror to the rearview, to the other sideview, and then looking left and right. Then she sighed and adjusted her grip on the steering wheel.

You are being an idiot. Even if someone was watching her, he wouldn't be standing out in plain sight. He'd be hiding, probably slouched in his car. Several years had passed since Rose saw Jared, and even if he still looked the same, chances were good he drove a different vehicle. She didn't even know what she was looking for.

"Mommy?"

"We're going."

Pulling away from the curb, Rose kept her eyes on the mirrors. So far, no one followed them. What was she going to do?

Home. Home with Mac was the only place she felt safe. She would get them home and then she would decide what to do. Meanwhile, she couldn't let anyone find out what was going on.

Chapter Thirty-One

"I'm going to ask Rose to marry me," Mac said to his mom Monday when he got home from school. They stood in the kitchen, Eleanor trimming flowers to put in a vase and Mac leaning against the counter, a cold iced tea in his hand.

The scissors stilled in Eleanor's hand as she looked up at him, half hopeful and half disbelieving. "Did I hear you correctly?"

Mac felt his mouth tugging upward into a wide grin. "You heard me right. I'm going to ask Rose to marry me. I'm in love with her."

Eleanor resumed her flower trimming. Matt recognized her nonresponse as a practiced to reaction to big news. Whenever he told her about something major as a kid or teenager, she acted like it was no big deal. He'd always thought it was because she didn't want to discourage him from providing more details. It worked, too.

Into the space her silence provided, he found himself telling his mom all the details of their weekend camping trip.

Celeste had filled her in, from her perspective, the night before as they sat around the table eating enchiladas. As he shared with her about the conversation he and Rose had after Celeste went to bed, she stopped cutting again and put a hand on her chest. Looking at him, she said, "This is wonderful. I have to tell you, I wondered if you'd ever settle down."

Mac inhaled, about to defend himself.

Eleanor held up a hand. "Now, now, it's not because I thought you were a wild child or anything. It's just because you've dated a nice variety of young women, and you've never seemed serious about a one of them. Until now."

"Until now," he echoed.

"So when are you going to ask her?"

Eleanor pointed at the cabinet above the refrigerator and Mac got down a vase and handed it to her. She went to the sink to fill it.

"I don't know," he said. "I was trying to think of a special occasion."

"You don't have to wait for a special occasion, honey. When you find the right person, that once-in-a-lifetime love, you make your special occasions."

Inspired by that idea, Mac nodded. "You're right. I'm going to make my own special occasion. I'll let you know what I come up with."

Rose wasn't home by the time Mac finished the chores, so he went ahead and started dinner. Twenty minutes later, when Rose and Celeste blew through the door, coming in from the blustery fall evening, they went straight to their bedroom. That was unusual, but for Mac, alarm didn't set in until he saw Rose's face ten minutes later. When she came into the kitchen, she looked stricken, as if she'd just watch someone run over her puppy.

"Rose," he said.

Wanting nothing more than to comfort her, he walked toward her, arms open. When she practically fell against him, he wrapped his arms around her and started to experience panic mode, himself. He was about to ask whether something had happened with Celeste, but she bounded into the kitchen just then, her curly hair a halo, and her singsongy voice a balm to his worry.

"Is everything —" he started, and Rose cut him off. "Not right now. She stood up straight, creating a couple of inches of distance between them. Gripping his biceps, she said, "We'll talk later. Thank you."

And then she sank into him again. For the first time, she felt fragile to him, but he reminded himself she wasn't. She was strong, resilient. And although something was certainly wrong, she would get through it. Seeing her in that state though, obviously upset and shaken, shook Mac, too. Holding her, all he could think to do was take away her pain.

"I'm here for you. You know that."

He felt her nod against his chest. He kissed the top of her head and she stepped away again, grabbed his hand, looked into his eyes, and took a deep, steadying breath.

"It will be fine," she told him. "I don't want you to worry."

"No promises."

"Smells good in here. Thank you for starting dinner."

"You're welcome. Let me know if there's anything else I can do."

Rose squared her shoulders. "I will."

By some miracle, Celeste had seated herself at the kitchen table and was working on a worksheet. Squinting, Mac could just make out rows of shapes she traced.

The way Rose sat down in the chair next to Celeste, she looked like she was collapsing from weakness. He wanted to get her alone, so he could find out what was going on and help her through it. But he knew the timing wasn't right. For now, he told himself he would just have to wait.

That evening, Mac waited in the kitchen as had become routine. He sat in the empty kitchen, a drink for each of them on the table. Thirty minutes after he heard her say good night to Celeste, he took a sip of his drink. Five minutes later, he realized Rose wasn't coming. He took a healthy gulp of bourbon, then put his elbows on the table and twirled the glass while brainstorming about Rose's strange behavior.

Was it possible their camping trip had scared her? Melting, the ice shifted in his glass. He didn't know the details of her past relationships, but he got the sense Celeste's dad was a jerk, and things didn't end well between him and Rose. If she'd been hurt before, she might be reluctant to get serious again.

Mac felt the first effects of the alcohol: the loosening of his limbs, a slight relaxation. Taking another sip of his drink, he told himself patience was key. Rose was obviously scared — he'd seen the fear in her expression when she came home.

Although he could rationalize Rose's behavior, it also hurt that she felt like she couldn't tell him what was going on.

He briefly considered leaving her wine glass, full, on the table, so she would wake up and realize he'd waited for her. But he dismissed that idea right away. Passive aggression wasn't really his style, and anyway, there was no point in guilting her when she was obviously in distress. Plus, if Celeste was the first up and found a full wine glass, who knew what she would do.

He stood, drained his own glass, then dumped the ice and Rose's wine into the kitchen sink. He put his own glass in the dishwasher and washed hers by hand before going to bed.

He barely slept that night, unable to stop thinking about what could have possibly bothered Rose.

At three in the morning, the deepest part of the night when all problems seem the biggest, Mac convinced himself *he* was the problem. Lying in his dark bedroom, listening to the sound of his mom's clock ticking, reminding him of the passage of time, he panicked. Pushing her wasn't going to help. But it wouldn't hurt to do a little investigating, just to be sure.

If he didn't figure out what was wrong, he could lose Rose. And at the moment, losing her meant losing everything.

Chapter Thirty-Two

Rose woke with a start in the middle of the night. Darkness cloaked the bedroom and Rose could hear Celeste's breathing, deep and even. Her daughter was safe for the moment. The alarm clock read 3:01 a.m. Rubbing her eyes with the heels of her hands, Rose fought off another round of tears. She'd last looked at the clock at 2:16. She couldn't remember the last time a night had passed so slowly.

Waiting for business hours to roll around so she could call Miriam from the Department of Child Safety was the exact opposite of waiting for Christmas morning. Instead of excitement, Rose felt dread. The kind of dread that felt like she was wearing an iron corset, and someone had a key to tighten it every sixty seconds. She could barely breathe.

Tell Mac. You can trust him.

"No," she whispered into the darkness.

After everything he done for them, she couldn't tell him. Not yet, anyway. She didn't want him to think Celeste was at risk because of him or something he'd done. The whole terrible situation had begun when the two of them started dating.

Mac cared about her. He cared about Celeste. She didn't want him to blame himself for the texts and phone call. And she didn't want him to have to carry around stress related to the terrible situation.

Not that she didn't want to tell him. He knew she was upset. He'd want to support her, and even if he didn't know what to do, figuring that out would be so much easier with help.

She had to go back to sleep. Not only because she was tired, but also — primarily — because she needed morning to come. She rolled onto her side, plumped her pillow, and closed her eyes. Opened her eyes to look at the clock. 3:11. She started to groan, but silenced herself right away. The only thing worse than lying awake, herself, was waking Celeste and dealing with the aftermath of that when it came time to get ready for school. She must have drifted off, because her alarm startled her awake at 5:30. She went ahead and gave into the luxury of groaning, then. Celeste had to get up anyway.

Mac.

She didn't want to face him. Not yet. Not until after she made that phone call. She got out of bed and cracked the blinds so she could look into the backyard.

"Good," she whispered when she saw him walking across the yard to the barn. He'd just started the chores, which meant she could throw something together for breakfast and then get in the shower. By the time she went back into the kitchen, Celeste would be there too, and she and Mac wouldn't be able to discuss anything serious.

The plan worked, and although she had to endure Mac's worried looks from across the kitchen table, she didn't have to explain why she'd been so upset the day before. Having overcome that hurdle, the next thing Rose had to do was find someone to sit with her class at 8:00 a.m. so she could return the phone call and make her case.

Before school, Rose ducked into the teachers lounge, hoping to find an aide who could spare a few minutes at that time. The microwave beeped as Rose walked in, and Elizabeth Tinsel opened it, removed a cup of hot water, and set it on the counter before turning around.

"Rose! Is everything all right? You look a bit frazzled." Rose

blinked, and Elizabeth said, "That's not to say you don't look beautiful,, as always. The height of fashion. I just love your sense of style.
So unique. Anyway, honey. Are you all right?"

Rose shook her head again, more to sort out an answer than to
signify she wasn't, in fact, okay. Elizabeth said, "I'm so sorry." She
tittered, and Rose felt one corner of her mouth lifting in a half-smile.
Elizabeth put both hands on her chest. "You know me. Always
talking a mile a minute. My mother used to say, 'For Elizabeth, life is
a performance,' and I guess that holds true today."

Rose blinked again, and Elizabeth said, "You don't look quite
well, honey. Is there anything I can help you with?"

Rose remembered then that Elizabeth had first-hour prep.
Which meant, barring any unusual circumstances, she should be
able to sit with Rose's class.

"Actually," Rose said. "There is something you can help me
with." Just thinking about making that phone call caused Rose to
hyperventilate.

"Yes? Anything."

"I need to make a phone call today during business hours," Rose
said. "I'd like to make it right at eight o'clock. I'm anxious to get it
over with." She grimaced. "Do you have time to come sit with my
class for, say, ten minutes or so?"

Elizabeth beamed at her. "You're in luck. I decided to make my
tea first thing this morning. Usually I make it at the beginning of first
period and I would have missed you. You've got it. I'll be in your
classroom at seven fifty-eight sharp."

Rose couldn't believe she'd ever suspected Elizabeth of taking
the pictures of Mac and her.

Body sagging with relief, Rose said, "That would be wonderful.
Thank you so much. I have an activity planned, so the kids should
be busy. All you have to do is make sure no one does anything
crazy."

Elizabeth tore open the packaging on her tea bag, pulled it out,
and dunked it into the hot water. "Sure thing. See you then."

True to her word, Elizabeth rapped on the doorjamb at 7:58 and
walked into the classroom with a bright smile. Rose grabbed her

phone, thanked Elizabeth again, and hurried out outside. She'd already decided to make the call from her car. She didn't want any of her fellow staff members, including Mac, to overhear. Once she was safely in her car, doors locked and windows up (she remembered reading that cars could reach deadly temperatures within a matter of minutes), she dialed the number Miriam from the Department of Child Safety had left on the message. Someone picked up before Rose even heard a full ring. "Miriam Bellevue."

To instill some confidence in herself, Rose lifted her chin and straightened her spine. Although she experienced a multitude of stress responses — rapid heart rate, shaking hands, shallow breathing — she cleared her throat and spoke with as much certainty as she could muster. "This is Rose Coffey. I'm returning your call from yesterday."

Rose heard the sound of rustling papers, and Miriam said, "Ah, yes. Ms. Coffey. As I said in my message, I called because we received reports indicating your daughter, Celeste, isn't it? Might not be safe. I'd like to schedule a time to come do a home visit."

"Right. I'll just need to check my calendar."

If a sound could illustrate a person's feelings, Miriam's loud sigh painted the clearest mental picture of a frustrated woman tired of dealing with disorganized parents. "I'm afraid we need to schedule this home visit right away," Miriam said. "Unfortunately, this can't wait."

Rose hoped Miriam could read the frustration in her own sigh. "Fine. It'll have to be outside my normal work hours."

Again, Rose heard the rustling of papers and wondered if Miriam was looking through a planner or a calendar. Rose panicked. She'd hoped that by saying she had to look at her calendar, she could buy herself a little time. If it was the relationship with Mac Jared was after, maybe Rose could pretend she lived somewhere else. With Jessie or Taylor, maybe. Or, she could go back to the hotel.

No, a hotel was too temporary.

"Let's see, today is Tuesday," Miriam said. "Why don't we meet, say, Thursday? You're a teacher, right? So would meeting at four p.m. give you enough time?"

"That should be fine," Rose said, purposely keeping her intonation flat, hoping Miriam Bellevue would sense her irritation.

"Great. Let's see, I don't have your address on file. Will you please email it to me?" She rattled off an email address, and Rose scrambled to find a pen and something to write on. All she came up with was a page torn from a coloring book. Ironically, it was a picture of a villain from one of Celeste's cartoons, and Rose couldn't believe how quickly her mind superimposed Jared's face onto the drawing.

Rose made the trip back to her classroom in record time. Her students worked quietly, and Elizabeth sat at a table at the back of the room. When she saw Rose, she stood, a question in her expression. Rose smiled and gave her a thumbs up, like everything had gone swimmingly. Elizabeth returned the thumbs up, and on the way out, she paused to give Rose a reassuring rub on the back.

Miraculously, Rose survived the day. As she drove from the school to Celeste's daycare, she found herself glancing in her mirrors every chance she got, checking to see if anyone was following her. As usual, she could hear children playing outside when she got out of her car after parking down the block from the daycare. She let herself in and went straight to the backyard.

Typically, she could pick out Celeste in a nanosecond. She always figured a mother's instinct connected her to her offspring when they shared the same space. But that day, Celeste was nowhere to be found. Rose's body went into panic mode before she had a chance to rationalize. All of a sudden, she felt like she was having an out-of-body experience. She could almost see herself looking around wildly, eyes wide. "Celeste!"

Sometimes Celeste liked to play cashier at the little store around the corner. Her stride strong and fast, Rose rushed around the side of the building. The play store stood empty. No shoppers, no employees, no cashiers. The world started to tilt. "Celeste!"

Rose couldn't believe this was happening. Someone had come and taken her daughter from daycare. The teachers should know no one other than Rose ever picked up Celeste. Taylor and Jessie were the only approved adults on the list. Why would they let some random guy pick her up?

The daycare's outdoor area was too small for an adult to run in, but Rose ran nevertheless, checking every corner, every nook and cranny. She felt a tug on her pants. "Celeste's mom?"

Chest still heaving, Celeste looked down. Juan, the little boy Celeste had argued with over candy, stared up at her, his brown eyes concerned. "Celeste is in the bathroom. She had to go potty."

Rose nearly wept with relief. When the back door slammed, and Celeste came out, singing the hand-washing song, Rose actually did weep.

"Your mom is sad," Juan informed Celeste.

Chapter Thirty-Three

Mac considered he might be overstepping some boundary, crossing some line. But he loved Rose and he would do anything to make sure she was safe. At home Tuesday morning, he acted like everything was normal, like he wasn't worried about Rose and Celeste, like thoughts about them weren't occupying ninety percent of his mental capacity.

During the longer passing period between second and third hours, Mac ducked over to the library. He didn't know the librarian, Taylor, very well, but the way Rose and Celeste talked about her, he knew she did. And he was certain she would help him.

She heard him come in, and she set the book she was reading on the counter in front of her. "Johnny Mac," she said, smiling. "To what do I owe the pleasure?"

Before he could answer, she gasped. "Wait! Don't tell me! You're here because you're going to propose! You want help picking out a ring! Wait! Don't say anything. Jessie should be part of this."

Flabbergasted, Mac held up a hand. "You're a step ahead of me," he said, and he couldn't help but chuckle. "Actually, you stole my thunder. I do plan to propose, but that's not the urgent matter at hand."

The smile faded from her face as quickly as it had come. "What could be more urgent than that? Is everything okay?"

Matt took a deep breath. "I'm worried I might be violating Rose's privacy in some way. But from what I can tell, you, Jessie, and Rose are thick as thieves."

Taylor nodded, serious. "The thickest."

"Something happened yesterday. Rose came home and she seemed ... I don't know, scared. Freaked out. Like a deer in headlights. Or worse, like a rabbit that just realized it's been spotted by a snake."

Taylor's face went pale. Which scared Mac.

"Do you know what it is?" Mac demanded, his tone stronger than he intended. "Sorry," he said, rubbing his forehead. "I'm coming on a little strong. I'm just worried."

Taylor nodded. "I have a pretty good idea. I don't know for sure, because she didn't say anything to me yesterday. Let me do some investigating, and I'll get back to you."

Mac turned to leave, but Taylor's voice stopped him. "For what it's worth," she said, "she told me she's in love with you. I've never heard her say that about anyone else."

The words should have soothed Mac, calmed him down. But they only made him worry more. If she loved him, but still felt like she had to keep a secret from him, then it must be bad. Really, really bad.

During fourth period, Rose texted Mac saying she had to work through lunch. He figured it was a lie, or a stretch of the truth at best. He wrote back with a thumbs-up emoji and, *I'll miss you, but I hope you get a lot done.* She responded with a heart emoji, and Mac decided he would go on a second fact-finding mission while she was occupied.

As he expected, Taylor and Jessie sat at the picnic table outside the library at the start of lunch. They were deep in conversation when he walked up, and they both pressed their lips together, going silent before greeting him with over-bright smiles and overenthusiastic waves. If he hadn't been so worried, he would have laughed.

Mac sat down on the same side as Taylor so he could look at

Jessie. "I'm sure Taylor told you I came to talk with her this morning," he said.

She nodded, waited. He went on, "Have you heard anything new from Rose? I don't want to be too nosy, but I get the sense that she's really scared. And that sense — my Spidey sense, or whatever you want to call it — is hardly ever wrong."

"Taylor and I were just talking about this," Jessie said. "We have a feeling we know what's going on, but we want to talk to Rose before we give you the scoop."

"Only," Taylor said. "She's kind of avoiding us."

"Me, too," Mac said.

He didn't know where to take the conversation from there. They obviously weren't going to give him any information yet, and he didn't know where else to look for it without committing an extreme violation of privacy.

"I've thought about searching her bedroom," he blurted out. "But that feels like taking things a step too far."

Jessie laughed. "I like you. Don't go searching her bedroom just yet. We'll get to the bottom of this."

"I just hope we get to the bottom of it before it's too late."

Rose's friends looked at each other, and the sick feeling in Mac's stomach threatened to boil over.

"I guess I'll go back to my classroom then. I'll wait to hear from you."

At the end of the school day, Rose texted that she was going to pick up Celeste, hit the grocery store, and come home. She asked if he needed anything. He wanted to write back, *Put answers on your list.*

Just as he set down his phone (after typing, *No, thanks*), Jessie came into his classroom, looking over her shoulder before shutting the door. She motioned to the corner, where they could stand without anyone seeing them through the window in the door. Her sneaky behavior seemed a little over the top, but he followed her silent instructions anyway. She knew Rose better than he did, and if she was worried about Rose seeing them, he was worried, too.

Once they were safely in the corner, Jessie glanced at the door again and said, "We got some information for you."

"What did you find out?"

Wringing her hands, Jessie said, "How much has Rose told you about Jared, Celeste's dad?"

Butterflies knocked against the inside of Mac's stomach. He shook his head. "Not much. But from what she has said, he doesn't seem like the nicest guy."

"There isn't enough time in the day, any day, to explain what a jerk he is. Suffice it to say, he was very controlling. And by the time Rose finally decided to leave him, it was because she was afraid he was going to get violent."

A little flame of rage ignited in Mac's consciousness.

"You might want to take a deep breath. Unclench your jaw. If I can already tell you're getting pissed off, we're not going to be able to reason through this."

Mac nodded again, and inhaled through his nose, unclenched his jaw, and exhaled. While he did those things, she rolled her shoulders and shook out her hands.

"Good," she said when they were both done. "Here's what we know. Right after the homecoming game, someone sent her some pictures of the two of you, along with a text saying something like, 'It looks like you're enjoying yourself and having a lot of fun out on the town, without your daughter.'"

When Mac inhaled, clenching his jaw again, Jessie held up a finger. "Wait. Stay calm."

"Right," Mac said, even though his calm was sliding out the door at that very moment.

"That's why she was acting so strange at the staff harvest party," Jessie said. "She was worried whoever took the pictures at the homecoming game might also be at the party."

Thinking back to their drive to the party, Mac remembered how nervous Rose seemed. She said she was anxious about socializing in a group setting and he believed her. But now, knowing she'd had a much bigger reason for feeling stressed, his heart ached for her. He'd taken her words at face value. He should have dug deeper.

As if she could read his thoughts, Jessie said, "You couldn't have known. When you went to get the drinks, Taylor and I cornered her, and she admitted she was stressed. We should have known one text wouldn't be the end of it." She shook her head. "Anyway, right after your camping trip, someone sent another picture and text. The picture made it look like Celeste nearly fell off the end of the kayak."

Mac swore.

"I know. Rose explained what happened. She said Celeste was never in any danger. Which I could have told you. Nevertheless, Monday afternoon, Rose had a voicemail from someone from the Department of Child Safety."

Mac's fists clenched, involuntarily.

"I know," Jessie said again. "The person from the DCS said Rose has to schedule a home visit with a social worker. As soon as possible, apparently."

Why didn't she tell me?

Again, Jessie demonstrated an uncanny ability to read his thoughts.

"She didn't tell you because she didn't want you to worry. She didn't want you to blame yourself, since the first set of photos were all taken of the two of you."

"Of course I would be worried," Mac said. "But I'd also help her. Don't you think she knows that?"

Jessie sighed, and for the first time, she looked forlorn. "Rationally? Yes. I'm sure she knows that. But I wish you could see what Jared did to her. Does to her. Somehow, that scumbag excuse for a human makes Rose question herself. At this very moment, she probably feels like she really did put Celeste's life in danger. Like her relationship with you could be detrimental because it's taking attention away from Celeste."

But I love Celeste.

"I know," Jessie said. "It's so stupid. Anyone with half a brain can tell that little girl has always been in a stable home, and that she's getting more love and attention now than she ever has. I'm sure whoever does the home study will see that. If only Rose didn't have to go through the stress."

"This Jared guy is a first-class asshole," Mac said.

"Top of the class," Jessie agreed. "But listen. You can't say anything to Rose, okay? Let her come to you. Taylor and I don't want her to know we shared any of this with you. We didn't want to leave you in the dark, but we also don't want to betray her trust. She's still trying to figure out what to do."

"What do you mean?"

Suddenly, *Jessie* looked like the rabbit who'd just realized a snake spotted her.

"Oh. Well, she isn't sure which address to give the DCS lady for the home study."

The words sent a sharp pain through Mac's torso. Which address? Why wouldn't she give the lady their address? The address where she and Celeste were living? Where they'd started to make new memories, to form a new family?

"Where else would she go?"

Jessie looked at her feet. "My house."

Mac couldn't speak.

"Please don't be upset with her," Jessie said, the words tumbling out of her mouth. "She's afraid Jared is going to argue that your relationship is distracting her from parenting. That was his M.O. the one or two times she went out with us when Celeste was a baby. He made her feel like a bad parent for spending a little time out on the town."

"I'm not upset with her," Mac said.

He was hurt, but not angry — not at Rose, anyway. He knew exactly where to direct his anger, and he was going to start working on that right away.

* * *

At home, Mac once again made a point of starting dinner as soon as he finished the chores. He hoped to ease Rose's mental burden but when she and Celeste came through the door, he realized he wasn't going to be able to do that.

Her shoulders were tense and her mouth was set in a grim line as she carried in grocery bags and set them on the kitchen counter.

"Can I help?" he asked.

"I think we got everything." She didn't even make eye contact before digging cream cheese and butter out of one of the bags and starting for the fridge.

"That's not what I meant," he said, blocking her path.

When she looked at him, he saw sadness in her eyes, and it nearly broke his heart.

"I know." He stepped out of the way and she ducked past.

With her usual perfect timing, Celeste announced that she had to go to the bathroom, and Mac took advantage of her absence to say to Rose, "I'm worried about you. Do you want to share what's going on so I can help you?"

She opened the fridge, put away the cream cheese and butter, and shut the fridge. But she didn't turn around to face him.

When she spoke, he could tell she was on the verge of tears. "I don't think you can."

With her usual terrible timing, Celeste returned to the kitchen, announcing she was done in the bathroom.

Rose resumed putting away groceries, and Mac joined her. Celeste danced around their legs, singing the theme song to one of her cartoons, oblivious to Rose's emotional state.

Once the groceries were put away, Rose said, "Thank you for making dinner." Then she disappeared into the bedroom, coming out only to eat before saying she didn't feel well and was going to sleep.

When the door shut behind her, Eleanor whispered to Mac, "Did something happen between you two?"

She stood with her back against the sink, a glass of water in her hand.

For what felt like the millionth time that day, Mac sighed. "Something happened. Not between us, but with Rose. She won't say what it is, though, and I don't want to push her."

"Just give her time, honey. She'll come around."

I don't know if we have time to give her.

"I hope so."

"Look," she said, setting down her glass on the counter next to her. "Whatever's going on, I know you two have something special. From what I can tell, she's used to doing things on her own. She probably doesn't know how to depend on people. Yes, she has her friends, but she also has an independent streak a mile wide."

She was right. Mac couldn't expect her to change the way she'd been operating in this world just because he wanted to care for her, wanted her to depend on him. If her ever got his hands on the asshole scumbag who'd made her feel she had to be that independent, he'd wring his scrawny neck.

Eleanor went to bed then, leaving Mac alone with his thoughts. He decided to pour himself a double glass of bourbon to keep him company, and carried it and his laptop into his bedroom, where he locked the door.

Back against the headboard, legs outstretched in front of him, bourbon on the table next to him, and his laptop on his lap, Mac went to work. Rose might be scared of Jared, but he wasn't. And he'd make sure that punk never hurt her again ... and never threatened to take Celeste away.

They were his family now, and he'd protect them, no matter what it took.

Chapter Thirty-Four

Rose called in sick Wednesday and returned to the house after dropping Celeste off at daycare. Eleanor was waiting in the kitchen when she walked in and Rose tried to duck straight through to her bedroom. It didn't work.

"Hey, honey," Eleanor said just as Rose put her hand on the doorknob. "What's the matter? I could make you some tea."

Nearly weeping at the woman's kindness — she'd become like a second mother in the short time Rose had lived there — Rose shook her head. "Thank you. It's my stomach. I'm not sure I can keep anything down. I'm just going to lay in bed."

"You should have let me take Celeste to school," Eleanor said. "I wouldn't mind. In fact, I would have enjoyed seeing where she goes every day. Checking out this Juan character, who's always arguing with her."

That, at least, brought a smile to Rose's face. "I should have," she admitted. "I'm just so used to doing things on my own. I'll take you up on it next time."

Eleanor smiled, and Rose could swear she understood the depths of her stress. "You're going to have to get used to accepting help," she said, her tone gentle. "It took me years to figure that out, but when I did, it made a world of difference. I learned that receiving help takes strength."

Rose nodded. "You're right. In that case, I'll take that tea."

At that, Eleanor beamed. "Coming right up. I'll bring it to you."

Leaving the bedroom door open, Rose took off her shoes and slid between the cool sheets. She wanted to lay down, go back to sleep, ignore all the stress of the home visit and the secrets she was keeping. But she needed to make a plan. So she sat up, back against her headboard, and thought.

First, there was the issue of where to have Miriam Bellevue from the Department of Child Safety come for a home visit. Bringing her to the farm meant telling Mac everything. Which was tempting. She could finally get it all off her chest: the texts, the photos, the phone call, the home visit. But what if she told him and he realized Jared was right, that she was a terrible mother?

And, she thought, pulling the covers up just a bit higher, as if they could protect her from this horrible situation, now that she was looking at things from Jared's perspective, the farm could be a dangerous place.

Celeste ran around the yard all the time. They lived in Arizona, home to thirteen species of rattlesnakes. She could be bitten at any moment. And although the cow was gentle, it could accidentally step on Celeste's foot and crush the bones. Yes, a garden shed seemed harmless enough, but those gardening shears were sharp. One false move and Celeste could cut off a finger, or even a hand.

A knock sounded at the door, halting the runaway train in Rose's mind. Eleanor came in, a cup of steaming tea in her hand.

"Here you go, honey," she said, setting the mug on Rose's nightstand. "It's still hot. This tea has ginger in it, which should settle your stomach."

"Thank you," Rose said, deciding not to tell Eleanor her stomach upset resulted from nerves rather than illness.

"You're welcome. Want me to make you something to eat? Some toast, maybe?"

Rose shook her head. "Not right now, but maybe later, if you're not busy."

"Girl," Eleanor said, "I keep myself busy but I'd love nothing more than to dote on someone, since I don't get to do that anymore."

The thought of Celeste growing up, leaving Rose without someone to dote on, caused another lump to form in her throat.

"You can dote on me anytime," Rose said, forcing a smile.

Eleanor returned her smile, put a hand on her shoulder for just a second, and left the room.

Alone again, Rose thought about the perils a social worker might see on the farm. The snakes, the cow, and the gardening shears aside, Celeste could fall off the tire swing and break an arm. She could get into the goat pen, and a goat could butt her. Pinky *seemed* sweet, but what if she was just waiting to get Celeste alone when the adults weren't around? And then there were the chickens. Rose and Mac reminded Celeste to wash her hands every time she went near the coop (every time she went back inside after being outdoors, really), but what if she didn't, and she got one of those gross germs like salmonella? Come to think of it, couldn't she get E. coli from the cow?

Rose groaned.

She picked up the tea and inhaled its steam. The ginger smelled wonderfully spicy, and she detected hints of peach, too.

Not to mention Mac. The social worker might consider Rose's fascination with Mac a threat to Celeste's well-being. She might consider Mac a threat.

God.

Going to Jessie's house would be better, Rose told herself as she took the first sip of tea. It was hot, but it was also soothing. She took another sip. Jessie's cute little bungalow was the perfect family home. No cows, no goats, no gardening shears, no Mac.

It also wasn't set up for a child. The social worker would know she and Celeste were in yet another temporary living situation, however cow-free it was.

Eleanor passed by the bedroom door and peeked in. "Oh, good. You're drinking the tea. How is it?"

Despite having drank about half the tea, Roses's stomach was still in knots. But Eleanor didn't need to know that. "It's delicious," she said. "Thank you again."

"Anytime." To Rose's dismay, Eleanor pushed open the door, came into the bedroom, and sat on the edge of the bed. "I hope I'm not butting in too much," she said. "But I want you to know that Mac really cares about you. I get the sense that something is going on with you ... something more than an upset stomach."

Rose froze. She didn't move or speak or even breathe.

"You don't have to tell me," Eleanor said. "But whatever it is, no matter what, I know Mac will support you. I know you're used to operating on your own. In my book, being a mother is the biggest responsibilities on the planet — and being a single mom? Even more so. But that doesn't mean we have to go it alone."

Staring into her tea, Rose warred with herself again. What harm would it do to tell Eleanor what was going on? *No.* She couldn't. She couldn't let Eleanor and Mac get wrapped up in this nonsense with Jared. Mac being involved would only fuel the fire. And end up breaking his heart and Eleanor's.

"Thank you for saying that," she said, finally lifting her head and meeting Eleanor's gaze. "I appreciate it. I appreciate you. And you're right. Something *is* going on. I just hate to get you and Mac involved in it."

Eleanor's smile looked said. "You may not realize it yet, but we *are* involved. And we'll be here when you're ready to let us in."

Once again, tears threatened. "Thank you," Rose whispered.

The older woman nodded, patted Rose's leg, and stood up. "That offer to make you something to eat is still on the table."

Rose nodded. Eleanor left, closing the door behind her. As soon as she was alone, Rose burst into tears. Silent sobs wracked her body. The whole situation felt so unfair. She'd thought that leaving Jared meant she and Celeste would be free from his controlling nature, from his abuse. But apparently, leaving him only stoked the flames of his jealousy. Him discovering her relationship with Mac had fanned those flames. Now, he wanted to burn down everything Rose had built without him.

She couldn't let that happen. From the beginning, Mac and

Eleanor had been nothing but wonderful, generous, and kind. They deserved nothing but those things in return.

When her sobs finally calmed, slowing to hiccups, she made a decision: she'd take Celeste to Jessie's for the time being, and decide what to do after the home study, depending on how it went. She would end things with Mac, saving him and Eleanor from any more heartache. And she would go back to being on her own. It was the only way she could keep her daughter safe.

The tea had cooled, and Rose finished it off before getting out of bed, locking the bedroom door, and packing hers and Celeste's belongings into a single suitcase. Then, she texted Jessie: *I'm finally taking up on the offer to stay at your place. We'll be there this afternoon, for a few days, if that's okay.*

Without waiting for a response, she changed out of her sweatpants and into jeans. When she saw Eleanor walking out to the garden shed, she snuck out the front door. Once she got in the car, she realized her first mistake: it was only ten a.m. which meant she wouldn't pick up Celeste for another five hours. Still, she had to get away from Mac and Eleanor's house — from the place that made her think it might be possible to have the stability she'd always craved.

And the love she always dreamed about.

Fifteen minutes later, she parked in the public library's lot. There, she reasoned, she could hang out for a few hours without notice.

Before she got out of the car, though, she sent Mac a text: *I'm so sorry. I had to leave. I'll explain later.*

It wasn't nearly what she wanted to say. It wasn't nearly enough. But it would have to do.

Inside the library, Rose grabbed a novel off the shelf before heading for the upstairs study room, which was almost never in use. She was in luck: it was empty. Settling down into one of the squishy armchairs, she cracked open the novel. Although her eyes read the words, her brain didn't capture a thing.

All she could think about was Mac.

No, she hadn't broken things off — yet — but she missed him, already. Probably because she knew she wouldn't see him that afternoon after school, or that evening during dinner or after putting Celeste to bed.

The sound of her fingers on the paper as she turned the page was loud in the silent study room.

A couple of hours later, Rose woke with a start and looked at her watch, heart racing with fear that she'd overslept Celeste's pickup. But no, it was only half past noon. Time passed at a snail's pace until finally, *finally*, she could leave the library to pick up Celeste. She wondered if any of the daycare staff had noticed that she'd removed Celeste's sign-in/sign-out sheet from the binder. No one said anything about it when she got there, so she snagged Celeste, buckled her in, and drove away as quickly as possible, checking her mirrors to make sure no one followed them.

"I have a surprise for you," she said to Celeste.

"Really?" In the rearview mirror, Rose could see Celeste's eyebrows raised in anticipation.

"Really!" She infused her voice with as much cheer as she could.

"What is it?"

"We're going to Auntie Jessie's!"

Silence, then, "Oh. That's the surprise?"

"Yes!" More forced cheer.

"Hm. Okay."

That was not the reaction Rose had expected. Typically, Celeste loved going to Auntie Jessie's, which was, she said, "the coolest house," thanks to its rooftop deck.

"I admit, I thought you'd be a little more excited."

Another glance in the rearview mirror, and Celeste made — and then broke — eye contact. "It's just that I like being at home. With Mac and Eleanor."

Rose's throat constricted. She swallowed. "I do, too. This is just for a few days, okay?"

"Okay."

Jessie was there to greet Rose with a giant hug when she climbed out of the driver's seat. She put her hands on Rose's shoulders and looked into her eyes. "You okay?"

Swallowing again, Rose said, "I hope so."

"Auntie Jessie!" Celeste yelled from the backseat.

Jessie rushed to let her out of the car, and the two of them hugged like they hadn't seen each other in weeks.

"I'm so glad to see you," Jessie said, and Celeste said, "I'm glad to see you, too, but we're going home soon."

Hugging Celeste, Jessie looked at Rose. "I know."

Inside, Jessie handed Celeste a little bag containing the tea set she'd bought for her. "Here. Take this up to the deck and organize our tea party. Your mom can help me make the tea. We'll be right up."

Celeste bounced off, leaving Rose and Jessie alone.

"What's going on, Rosie?" Jessie grabbed the tea kettle off the stove and brought it to the sink to fill it.

"You know how that DCS social worker wanted to schedule a home study?" Rose paced the kitchen behind Jessie. When Jessie nodded, she went on. "Well, I haven't given her an address yet. I couldn't decide where to have her come. Of course, right now, Mac's farm feels like home. But the more I thought about it —"

"Let me guess: the more you thought about it at three in the morning." Jessie put the lid on the tea kettle and brought it back to the stove, which she turned on with a click and a *whoosh*.

"Right," Rose said, finally settling in a chair at the kitchen table. "The more I thought about it at three in the morning, the more I realized. The farm is dangerous for a little girl. There are rattlesnakes and a cow and a goat and gardening shears. There are so many ways she could get hurt."

Jessie's eyes were round. "Rose. Celeste could jump off the deck at this very moment."

Panic set in, fast and hard. Rose leapt into motion, heading for the stairs on the other side of the kitchen. Jessie grabbed her arm. "Stop. She's fine. The point I'm trying to make is that *anywhere* could conceivably be unsafe for a child. The farm is a wonderful place for her. She loves it. You guys have taught her about staying safe there, right?"

"Right," Rose said. "But there's something else."

"I thought so."

"What is that supposed to mean?"

Jessie shrugged. Pursed her lips. "Sit." Rose sat, and Jessie sat, too. "It's just — I didn't think that was the only reason you'd come here. I feel like there's something else."

"It's Mac," Rose said.

"Mac, who absolutely adores the both of you and has done nothing other than prove that, time and again?"

A bark of laughter escaped from Rose. "Yes. See? That's the thing. I haven't seen or spoken to Jared in year, and, right when I start dating Mac, he resurfaces. Right?"

"Right," Jessie said, drawing out the word.

"And he's focused on me ... me and Mac. That first set of pictures? Me and Mac. The second set? Celeste in danger ... with me and Mac."

"So? Jared doesn't even know Mac. Surely, this social worker, whoever she is, will meet Mac and realize Jared is full of it."

Rose shook her head. "I can't risk it. What if he's told her lies, and they take Celeste away?"

The tea kettle whistled, mirroring Rose's stress level.

"Honestly?" Jessie said as she stood and turned off the stove. "I think that's impossible. Anyone with half a brain will be able to see he's a good guy. Jared is messing with your mind."

Leaving the kettle on the stovetop, she tore open a few teabags and put them into the tea pot that went with Celeste's set. She poured the hot water over them, and then used a pot holder to lift the teapot. "Grab those cookies and let's go on up. We have a tea party to attend."

Celeste's tea set had always had dishes for four, but she'd never set up a fourth spot at the table for someone who wasn't there — until now.

"This is Mac's spot," she told Rose and Jessie as they came to the top of the stairs. The sunlight felt almost blinding, and the fall breeze felt cold, even though Rose's car had told her the temperature was a nice seventy-two degrees. Rose shivered.

"That was nice of you," Jessie said. "Do you think he'll mind drinking out of a pink cup?"

"Nah," Celeste said, smiling up at Jessie. "He says real men don't care what color they get."

"Jared hated pink, as I recall," Jessie whispered to Rose. "I'll pour the tea."

He did hate pink, and the fact that Mac didn't made Rose ache for him. She opened the package of cookies and set them out on the platter. Jessie had finished pouring the tea, and Celeste picked up her cup, pinky finger extended.

"I wish things could be different," Rose said as she picked up her own cup and took a sip.

"What do you mean?"

"I mean, I wish I could be with Mac."

Jessie froze, her cup halfway to her lips. "Well, that's the silliest thing I've heard you say in a long time."

"What do you mean?" Conscious of Celeste listening to their every word, Rose said, "Let's talk about this later."

"I think we should talk about it now," Jessie said. "Why can't you be with him?"

Rose glanced at Celeste, hoping Jessie would pick up what she was putting down, but Jessie plowed ahead. "I mean, you *love* him, Rosie. He loves you."

"Mac loves you?" Celeste said.

"Yes," Jessie said. "He loves her. And I that's special. When you find that once-in-a-lifetime person, you stop at nothing to be with him."

Celeste nodded, her expression sage. "You stop at nothing, Mommy."

"Can we just drink our tea?" Rose said.

"Sure," Celeste said. She took another drink.

"Sure," Jessie said. "But I'd love for you to think about why this conversation makes you so uncomfortable."

A hot blush crept up Rose's neck and onto her cheeks. She nodded, sipped her tea, and did as Jessie asked. Why *did* the conversation make her uncomfortable? If she were being honest with herself, it wasn't solely Celeste's presence. The conversation made her uncomfortable because she *did* love Mac and that scared her. She'd thought she loved Jared too, and he'd turned out to be a first-rate jerk.

Celeste offered her a cookie and she took it.

But hadn't Mac proven again and again that he cared for her and Celeste? Hadn't he demonstrated thoughtfulness and dependability? And wasn't their love-making out of this world? Didn't she love him? And his mom? And his property?

"I'm an idiot," Rose said.

Jessie shrugged. "I still love you."

"Me too," Celeste said.

"Thanks," Rose said. She turned to Celeste. "As soon as we finish this tea party, we're going home."

Chapter Thirty-Five

F inding Rose's scumbag of an ex-boyfriend online didn't take Mac long. Fortunately (and not surprisingly), his social media profiles were wide open — no privacy settings whatsoever.

From what Mac could tell, Jared had moved to Reno, Nevada, shortly after Rose left him. He'd stayed there for a few years, returning to Prescott about a month before Mac and Rose became an item. And, from what Mac could tell, he'd employed someone to dig up the dirt on the two of them ... he recognized the guy who'd come up to him at the homecoming game in several of Jared's pictures.

Tuesday night, he went to bed with a plan in place and Wednesday morning, he woke ready to put it into action.

He called in sick to work, but got up and dressed like normal. Since Rose had taken to avoiding him anyway, he figured she wouldn't notice he wasn't at school.

He drove to McDonald's where he bought a large coffee and sat down in a corner booth. He called Taylor to ask for Judd's phone number; he was the School Resource Officer but could probably access police systems.

"I realize this is probably not above board," Mac said to Judd when he picked up, "but I'm calling for a favor."

Judd's response after he explained the situation filled him with gratitude: "Let me see what I can do."

For the next hour, Mac sat in the booth, sipping his coffee and continuing his search for anything incriminating on Jared. The guy was controlling and abusive, Mac thought. Certainly, he'd done *something* bad enough for Mac to use as leverage.

The night before, Mac had made a few discoveries. The guy was good looking, Mac supposed. He had that All-American-boy smile — big, straight, white teeth, strong eyebrows, and hair out of a salon catalog. If that was all there was to a person, he could see why Rose fell for him.

But, based on what he chose to post on social media — and it was a lot — he was an immature, judgmental idiot. He shared his strongly worded opinion on just about everything, from current events and politics to celebrity fashion to the weather. And in every picture of him, he stuck out his tongue and he made some kind of hand gesture.

Mac knew he needed more than a bunch of dumb social media posts for true leverage, but he hit dead end after dead end. Finally, his phone rang. Judd's number came up on the screen.

"Hey, man. Get anything?"

"I did," Judd said. "And I think you're going to like it. Just remember, we never had this conversation."

"Got it."

"Good. And Mac?"

"Yeah?"

"Be careful, okay? We don't know what this guy is capable of, or willing to do."

"Right. But I know what *I'm* capable of, and what *I'm* willing to do."

"I hear you," Judd said. "Just call me if you need me, okay?"

"I will."

A few minutes later, armed with what he needed, Mac left McDonald's. According to Judd, Jared's last known address was in a trailer park in the trees near Willow Lake. The trailer's roof slanted (not by design, Mac thought, wondering how long until the whole building fell over). The occupants had hung blankets in the windows and front porch sagged.

Serves the guy right.

A couple of cars squatted in the driveway, each missing at least one wheel. Next to them stood a pick-up truck, its back window cracked all the way across.

Up until that very moment Mac, infused with indignation and anger, had felt fairly confident about confronting Jared. Just then, sitting outside the trashy house, imagining walking up the front porch and knocking on that door, he suddenly felt nervous. Someone like Jared could be capable of anything.

But Rose and Celeste were worth the risk.

Mac threw off his seatbelt and strode to the front porch. The steps creaked under his weight, and he wondered if the porch would kill him before he got his hands on Jared. The wood gave under him, but didn't crack. The grimy front door fit improperly in its frame, and Mac could see light between the door's edge and the door jamb. Someone had obviously kicked the door at some point; there was a large dent in the middle.

Bravado had kept Mac company until that moment. Staring at the door, nerves set in. He knocked anyway, three hard pounds.

"What the hell?" someone yelled inside.

"Guess they're not expecting visitors." Mac took a step away from the door.

Loud, fast footsteps thundered toward him and again, Mac pictured the whole house falling down. Maybe that would get him before Jared did. He realized he'd clenched his fists and relaxed them. Coming on too strong, too aggressive, wouldn't do.

The doorknob twisted and the door opened fast. To Mac's surprise, it wasn't Jared who stood on the other side. It was the guy from the football game.

"What are you doing here?" he demanded.

What a greeting. "I'm looking for Jared. He here?"

"Maybe. Depends. What do you want?"

Mac shifted his weight, worked his jaw. His parents had taught him manners, and this guy didn't have any. Bad manners rubbed him the wrong way.

"Who is it?" someone else called from farther inside the house.

"That guy, Johnny Mac," said the door answerer.

More footsteps, and Jared appeared beside the first man. He was just as handsome in person as he was on social media — and his eyes were just as cold. He wore baggy jeans and a plain white t-shirt with stains on the chest.

"What do you want?" He sneered. His stance, feet set apart, arms crossed, and his demeanor, aggressive, fueled Mac's anger.

"What do you think I want?"

"I don't know, man. Never seen you in my life."

Infuriated beyond self-control, Mac took one big step forward and grabbed Jared's collar, yanking him close so their faces were within inches of each other. "Haven't you?"

Jared's arms flailed, knocking him off balance. He tried to step back, but Mac's hold on his collar kept his upper body immobile. His friend or roommate or whatever he was stood frozen, eyes round in his round, stupid face.

"What are you talking about?" Jared said.

"The pictures," Mac ground out. "Even if you didn't take them, I'm positive you saw them. Tell me I'm wrong."

Acknowledgement flashed in Jared's eyes. "You're not wrong, man. But I — I'm just trying to keep my daughter safe."

"Safe from *what*?" Mac asked, twisting his fist so Jared's collar tightened around his neck.

Immediately, he noticed the irony of the question, as close to choking this man as he was. That thought caused him to smile, looking right into Jared's eyes. The friend sprang into action. He grabbed Mac's wrist and tried to pull his hand off Jared's shirt. Mac let his grip loose and as soon as his friend let go of his wrist, he grabbed Jared's throat, instead.

To the friend, he said, "Don't even think about touching me. You reach for me, I squeeze harder."

The friend nodded, gulped.

"The only thing your daughter needs protection from is you," Mac spat. "Tell me how you got those pictures."

"Why should I?" His face was turning purple, which Mac found satisfying.

"Because you don't want me to beat the ever-loving shit out of you, I guess."

"Beat the shit out of me, and you'll go to jail," Jared managed. "Then I'll have even more ammo to keep Celeste out of your house."

Mac saw red, but Jared didn't know who he was dealing with. He kept talking.

"Rose doesn't deserve Celeste. That's why I called DCS. She's a terrible mother. She's making out with you in a car while Celeste is probably with some second-rate teenaged babysitter who spends all night on her phone."

He released Jared's throat, grabbed his shoulders, and kneed him between the legs, hard. Jared doubled over.

"Rose is an excellent mother. The best," Mac said. He gave Jared a solid upper cut to the jaw. While he was reeling from that, Mac said, "And for your information, Celeste was with my mother. Who has a flip phone." He punched him in the stomach.

The friend was talking, muttering something about calling the police, but Mac didn't care. Jared's shock was apparently wearing off, and he'd gathered his bearings and started swinging at Mac.

Mac caught his right fist. "Never insult Rose or my mother again." He twisted, causing Jared to cry out. If he twisted any harder he'd put his shoulder out of socket, and as satisfying as that would be, Mac couldn't bring himself to take things quite that far.

Instead, he used the heel of his palm to strike Jared's nose — not hard enough to break it, but hard enough that blood started gushing. *This is addicting.*

"Now tell me what you told DCS. I'm sure all of it was lies."

Even while Mac continued to pummel the lowlife asshole, a tiny voice in the back of his mind told him he'd be facing some consequences. But those consequences were worth it.

He realized then that Jared was saying something. He'd gotten so carried away, he hadn't been able to hear anything other than the gratifying sound of his fists on Jared's flesh.

"Okay, okay. Stop, man. I'll tell you whatever you want to know."

"Better start talking." He shoved Jared to the floor and put a knee on his stomach.

"Get off me." He was panting, and Mac half hoped he'd pass out.

"Tell me what you told DCS," Mac could taste blood, and had no idea where it came from.

"I didn't tell them anything."

Mac wrapped his hand around Jared's throat again. "That's a lie."

Jared licked his lips. "It's not. I swear."

"Then why did Rose get a call from DCS?"

He was coughing now. Mac figured it was for dramatic effect, but he released his grip on his throat.

"It was fake."

"What?" Mac gripped his throat again. The fear Rose experienced was anything but fake. The pain Mac experienced, seeing her feel that fear, was so, so real. He could kill this guy.

"It was fake."

"I heard you. Elaborate." *If you even know what that means.*

"A girl I know. She owed me a favor. I asked her to call Rose, pretend to be a DCS social worker, and set up a home study."

"Why?"

"I told you, man. I just wanted to keep my daughter safe."

"How would a *fake* home visit keep her safe?" Mac demanded, squeezing harder. He didn't realize Jared couldn't breathe or answer until his face turned purple again. He let go, and Jared had to catch his breath before answering.

"She was going to tell Rose that she was going to recommend that Rose and Celeste move away from your property. For Celeste's safety. I know Rose. She's a coward. She wouldn't go against that recommendation. She'd leave the farm, no questions asked."

And go back to a life of instability and stress.

"This isn't about Celeste's safety, is it? This is about you. You want Rose back. You went to Reno, got into some trouble there, and had to come back. You thought you'd waltz right back into Rose's life and the three of you would be all cute and cozy together. But then you found out Rose was seeing someone. Me." He stuck his thumb into the soft spot just above Jared's collarbone. Jared sucked air through his teeth. Mac said, "You sent someone to take pictures to make Rose look like a neglectful mom — a pattern of yours, I've heard — and you saw that she and I have something special. She and I actually love each other. And you know what? I love that little girl, too. And I will stop at nothing, absolutely nothing, to keep them both safe from you. That includes telling everyone in this town exactly what you did in Reno. You'll be exorcised here, and you know it."

Jared licked his lips again. Good. Mac was getting to him.

"Listen. You contact Rose or Celeste again and I will end you. You hear me? You come near them, I will end you. I don't care if I have to go to prison for life. I. Will. Kill. You. And it will be slow and painful. Do you understand, scumbag?"

The longer he spoke, the more infuriated he became, and he pulled back his arm to give Jared another good punch in the mouth.

"Prescott Police!" several pairs of footsteps thundered over the creaky front porch, and Mac leapt away from Jared as one of the police officers shouted, "Get away from him!"

Consequences.

But, looking down at Jared's bloodied face, his eyes swollen and his nose and lower lip bleeding, Mac didn't care.

"Sir, can I ask you to step outside, please?" The officer gestured to the front door. Mac nodded, and after taking a couple of steps that direction, he turned and said to Jared, "See where good manners get you?"

He could swear the cop rolled his eyes, but he didn't speak until they were outside.

"Want to tell me what happened?" he said, voice calm.

Mac nodded. "I sure do."

Forty-five minutes later, the cop booked Mac into the Yavapai County Jail. His knuckles were sore and bleeding, his shirt was torn, and he had a smile on his face.

Chapter Thirty-Six

Driving from Jessie's house back to the farm, Rose felt lighter than she had in days.

"I am a good mom," she said, not realizing she'd spoken aloud until Celeste piped up from the backseat. "You are a *great* mom."

"Thanks."

She'd never let Jared or anyone else make her question herself again, she decided. And when she saw Mac, she was going to tell him she loved him and wanted to be with him for the rest of their lives. The changing leaves and fall sunlight only lifted Rose's spirits more. She couldn't believe her fortune, to have met a man like Mac. And to think it had all started when he found her camping out in the teachers lounge at work.

Her momentum slowed a bit when she pulled into the driveway and didn't see his car there. Well, she could wait. She'd wait as long as it took.

Inside, Eleanor stood at the kitchen counter, mixing something in a bowl. She turned when Rose and Celeste came through the front door, and smiled so warmly, Rose felt it in her body.

"I thought you'd taken off," she said. She opened her arms and wrapped Rose in a hug.

Celeste clung to her leg. "No, we were just having a tea party with my Aunt Jessie."

"That's good to hear," Eleanor said, rubbing Rose's back. "Real good."

"What are you making?" Celeste wanted to know.

"Pumpkin cookies," Eleanor said. She released Rose, still smiling. "I thought Mac and I were going to have to eat all of them ourselves."

"We'll help you," Celeste said.

"I'm sure you will," Eleanor said. "Want to help me put them on the baking sheets?"

Celeste dragged a chair over to the counter and Rose settled in at the bar, her heart soaring with love for Eleanor and Celeste and the relationship they shared. Why had she ever thought running away from this was a good idea?

Eleanor asked Celeste about her day, and Celeste chattered away. Just as Eleanor went to put the last ball of dough on the cookie sheet, her phone rang.

"Will you see who that is? I still have cookie dough on my hands."

Rose glanced at the screen. A fluttering took hold in Rose's torso when she saw the Caller ID. "It's the Yavapai County Jail."

Eleanor's head whipped around. "The jail, you said?"

The phone kept ringing.

"Yes. The jail."

Eleanor sighed. "Would you mind answering it, honey? I'll take it as soon as I get these in the oven and get my hands clean."

Rose tapped the screen and put the phone to her ear. "Hello?"

A recorded voice said, "An inmate is calling you from the Yavapai County Jail." Rose gasped, and whispered to Eleanor, "It's an inmate."

Surely they'd dialed the wrong number. Eleanor froze, her hand still on the oven handle.

Mac's voice came through the earpiece: "Johnny Mac," and the recorded voice finished, "would like to speak to you. Press one to accept this call. Hang up to decline it."

Rose pressed the one and hissed to Eleanor, "It's Mac."

Eleanor's eyes went round, but she didn't move. Rose waited through a series of clicks. Then she heard Mac say, "Mom?"

The sound of a sharp intake of breath startled Rose, and then the realized it had come from her. "Mac. It's Rose."

"Rose? But — I called my mom, didn't I?"

"You did. But her hands are covered in cookie dough." Why wasn't he cutting to the chase? "Are you in *jail*?"

A strange gasping noise came through the earpiece, and Rose worried he might be crying. But then he made a hooting sound, and she realized he was laughing. Hysterically maybe, but he was definitely laughing.

She waved to Eleanor, who still hadn't moved. But then she jumped, like Rose had broken her out of a trance. Rose pointed to the sink, and Eleanor rushed over to wash her hands.

Celeste stood in the middle of the kitchen, her head swinging back and forth between Rose and Eleanor.

"What is going on?" Rose said.

"You wouldn't believe it," he said. "It's the funniest thing."

"Is it?"

He hooted again, and Rose wondered if he'd gone crazy. "Rose, I love you," he said.

"I love you, too."

"Damn," he said, then, obviously switching gears. "That was satisfying."

Rose heard a voice in the background: "Sir, you have one more minute."

Eleanor had finished washing and drying her hands, and stood in front of Rose.

"Mac," Rose said. "You'd better talk to your mother."

She handed over the phone, and Eleanor's eyes closed as Mac spoke. Rose couldn't hear what he said, but Eleanor's pursed lips belied exasperation. Celeste stood facing her, hands fisted on her hips, eyebrows drawn in concentration as she watched Eleanor's face.

Finally, Eleanor spoke: "While I'm tempted to let you stay

overnight, I'll send Rose with the money to bail you out." She held the phone away from her ear, and Rose could hear Mac saying, "No, Mom, please —"

"Your time's up, sir," said the woman in the background.

Eleanor tapped the screen to end the call.

The two women stood there, looking at each other.

Rose spoke first. "So?"

"Apparently, my idiot of a son, in some misguided idea of chivalry, hunted down your ex, went to his house, and beat the tar out of him. The roommate called the police, who arrested my son, and now, here we are."

Hunted down my ex?

"What in the world?" Rose said.

Eleanor shook her head. "Your guess is as good as mine. Did you know about any of this?"

"Not a thing. But I'm starting to put the pieces together."

Eleanor put a hand to her forehead, and Celeste rushed forward and put a hand on her thigh. "Are you okay?"

"I'm okay," Eleanor said. "You get your child to adulthood without one run-in with the law, and then he gets arrested for beating up some lowlife." Celeste nodded, her sage expression making Rose's lips twitch. Eleanor looked at Rose, and said as an aside, "Sorry. No offense to your ex."

"Oh, he's a lowlife," Rose said. "No offense taken."

"I'd go get Mac," Eleanor said, "but I'm going to pull the old-age card. Plus, it sounds like he has some news for you."

Rose's stomach swirled with a fresh wave of nerves. "Does he?"

"I'm certain it's good news," Eleanor said. "Now, let's check those cookies."

* * *

Rose had never been inside the jail building, much less bailed someone out. She didn't even know where to park and ended up choosing the spot farthest from the entrance. Inside, the receptionist sat behind a glass partition, wearing thick-rimmed glasses and a frown.

"I'm here to bail someone out of jail," Rose said, thinking as she spoke that those were some of the most ridiculous words she'd ever strung together.

"Name?"

"Rose Coffey."

The woman tapped her keyboard, looked at her computer screen, frowned even deeper. "I don't see any inmates here by that name."

"Oh," Rose felt the heat burning her face. "The inmate's name is Johnny MacKinnon. Sorry."

Rolling her eyes, the receptionist typed again, scanned her screen, and nodded. "Payment?"

"Right." Rose dug into her purse for the cash Eleanor had given her. She slid the envelope through the opening beneath the glass partition. "Here you go."

With another sigh, the woman took the money out of the envelope and counted it, slowly, setting every bill on her desk. When she was done, she put the cash in a box she pulled out like a drawer, and then pointed at the chairs behind Rose. "You can wait there."

"Um, okay."

Rose sat, wishing she knew what would happen next and how long it would take. All she could do at that point was agonize over being reunited with Mac. It was entirely possible he was upset with her; she'd told him she was leaving. But, if he'd really beat up on Jared, then maybe he wasn't too upset. And, if he'd beat up on Jared, he probably bore some marks, too ... and that wouldn't look good during the home visit.

"Rose Coffey," the receptionist said in the same bored voice. "Your inmate is ready. Exit through that door." She pointed at the door Rose had come in.

Your inmate. Rose could feel a giggle bubbling up, but she held it in as she stood and opened the door. And there he was, shirt untucked, lip bloodied and swollen, and a big smile on his face. All her worries about him being upset with her flew right out the window.

"Hey," she said.

"Hey," he said.

"Fancy meeting you here," she said.

"Same."

She walked up to him and wrapped her arms around his waist. He wrapped his around her shoulders.

"I would offer you a kiss," she said, "but it looks like that might not be in the cards for a few days."

His chest against her cheek, she could feel him laughing.

"You're going to have to tell me what you find so funny about all this," she said.

"I will." His voice sounded so weepy, Rose had to laugh, too.

"Let's get out of here."

Mac spoke once they were safely inside Rose's car. "Can I tell you everything once we get home? I don't want to have to say it all twice, and you'd better believe my mom is going to want the details after she had to spend a thousand bucks bailing me out."

Sure enough, after giving her son a big hug, Eleanor made sure to give him a long, stern look. "You're going to pay me back for every cent of that bail money."

"I will, Mom," Mac said. "I promise."

"Bail money. I never thought I'd be saying I bailed my son out of jail."

"I know," Mac said. "It's a real bucket-list item."

"What's a bucket list?" Celeste asked. She'd spent the moments since Mac's arrival staring at his bloodied lip, cringing every few seconds.

"Stuff you want to do at least once in a lifetime," Rose said, and Celeste's eyebrows came together in a frown.

"You *wanted* to go to jail?" she asked.

"I was joking," he said. "I didn't want to go to jail."

She shook her head, looking as exasperated as Eleanor.

Smiling, Mac said to Rose, "Am I going to have to get used to the three women in my life looking at me like that all the time?"

"I'm afraid so," she said, and Celeste said, "Want a cookie?"

Rose sent Celeste outside to gather vegetables and eggs so the adults could have some time to talk. She filled three glasses with water, and Mac said, "I think we're all going to need something stronger."

Shaking her head, she got out three tumblers, dropped a few ice cubes into each, and poured the bourbon over them. They all sat at the table and the women looked at Mac, waiting.

"It all started at homecoming," Mac told them.

Rose and Eleanor exchanged a glance.

"Remember when you went to get us snacks?" he said to Rose and Eleanor said, "You let her go get the snacks? Where are your manners?"

"I insisted!" Rose hoped to stave off any lectures that would delay Mac's telling his story.

"Fine," Eleanor said. "Carry on."

"This guy came up to me and said something like, 'you and Rose Coffey, huh?'"

"Why didn't you say anything?" Rose demanded, realizing her mistake too late.

Mac smiled. "Probably for the same reason you didn't say anything about the text you received after homecoming."

Like a deer in headlights, Rose froze, her glass halfway to her lips.

"What text?" Eleanor asked.

Rose tipped back her glass. "Someone took some, ah — pictures of Mac and me. During the float parade and, ah — after." She cleared her throat. "In the car."

"In the car?" Eleanor raised an eyebrow and directed her glare first and Rose and then at Mac.

Mac cleared his throat, looked down at the bourbon in his glass. "In the car."

"Young man, haven't I taught you anything? You don't take a young lady to a car!"

"At least it wasn't under the bleachers." Mac smirked.

"Let's fast forward," Rose suggested, her tone over-helpful.

"Good idea," Mac said, and although Eleanor looked at him with heavy-lidded exasperation, he went on, "I didn't know at the time that you'd received those texts. So I thought that guy who'd come up to me on the bleachers was just an old flame of yours, or had a crush on you. But then you started acting weird."

Eleanor's glare jumped back to Rose, who shrugged and said, "I did."

"You acted weird at the party, and you acted weird a few days later when, apparently, you got another text."

Eleanor's mouth dropped open and she drained her glass. "Tell me it wasn't another set of photos of you in a car."

"No!" Rose said. "They were photos of our camping trip."

"Your camping trip? With your *daughter*?"

Rose nodded. "You can see why I was freaked out."

"But you didn't tell Mac," Eleanor said.

Shame rising from her toes to her eyebrows, Rose nodded. "Right. I didn't want him to worry, or to blame himself."

"But I could have helped you," Mac said, and Rose sighed. "I know. I wasn't thinking clearly."

"I went behind your back," Mac said then, his grimace showing guilt.

"What do you mean?" Rose asked.

Eleanor's head swung between them like she was watching a tennis match.

"You were acting strange. I was worried. I enlisted help from Taylor and Jessie."

"I don't know whether to be grateful or angry," Rose admitted.

"Maybe both," Eleanor supplied.

Rose nodded.

"They told me about your second text, and about the woman calling from DCS."

"DCS?!" Eleanor said, her voice rising.

"Yeah," Mac said. "Lady said she was a social worker, and insisted Rose schedule a home study."

Rose nodded. "It's tomorrow. Because the text messages along with the photos implied my relationship with Mac was causing me to neglect Celeste —"

"Psh," Eleanor said, making a dismissive gesture with her hand.

"I know," Rose said. "But for a second, I believed it. That's what Jared does — *did* — to me. I panicked. I looked around the farm and saw danger everywhere. So I planned to have the home study at Jessie's, even though it would have seemed like a temporary situation."

"What an asshole," Eleanor said, surprising Rose, who laughed.

"I know," Rose said. "Why do you think I left him?"

"He *is* an asshole," Mac said. "I spent yesterday evening researching, and called in sick today—"

"I called in sick today, too," Rose admitted.

"You did?"

"I did."

"I made her tea," Eleanor said.

Mac smiled. "I called in sick today to do a little more research and take a little field trip. You should have seen that bastard's face when I got to his house. He was terrified."

Rose felt a flicker of pleasure at the fact that Mac had gone off on a journey to defend her. He was *this* close to being a knight, armor or no.

"Anyway. His roommate — the guy from the football game — answered the door. I confronted Jared, and he admitted calling in a favor and asking a friend to pretend to be a social worker. That's who called you."

"Wait," Rose said.

Mac nodded.

"It was all fake. DCS hasn't received any reports about your parenting. There is no home study. Jared admitted he orchestrated the whole thing to scare you into leaving me and going back to him."

"Over my dead body," Eleanor said. "Give me his address. I'm going to kick his ass myself."

"No need," Mac said. "I've taken care of it."

Relief flooded Rose's body first. No one had actually questioned her parenting. DCS was not going to come after her and take away her daughter. Tears threatened. She couldn't believe it. They were safe. And, they could stay at the farm.

Then, outrage set in. How *dare* he? How dare Jared try to scare her away from this lovely, loving place she now thought of as home, and from these lovely, loving people she considered family? If she could wring his neck, she would. But, Mac had taken care of that.

"How badly did you hurt him?" she asked.

Mac shrugged and stretched his arms, then cracked his knuckles (apparently having forgotten they were cut and bruised, because he winced). "Badly enough."

He smiled, his expression so deadly satisfied, Rose knew Jared would think twice before crossing her again.

"Thank you," she said, her voice thick with emotion.

"Any time," he said.

Eleanor held up a hand, pointer finger extended. "I'm not saying I'm not glad you gave that jerk what he deserved. But the fact remains, you were arrested. Which means you're going to have a trial, right?"

"I'm not sure. But the cop who drove me to the jail said they were going to charge me with a class three assault, which will probably end up being fines only."

Eleanor shook her head. "I can't believe my son was arrested for assault."

"Believe it," Mac said. He reached across the table and took Rose's hand. "And I'd do it all over again."

Chapter Thirty-Seven

Going to jail wasn't truly on Mac's bucket list, but he'd definitely added kicking the shit out of Rose's ex-boyfriend and seeing the relief she experienced when he told her there was no DCS case.

The evening Rose came and bailed him out of jail, they agreed to call in an order from Rita's. Rose and Celeste went to pick it up. Mac and Eleanor stayed home, sitting at the kitchen table with another pair of bourbons.

"I cannot believe my son was in jail this morning," Eleanor said. "There's something about the fact that you were tossed in a cell before noon on a Wednesday. I almost would have preferred a week-end-night barfight."

Mac winced when he smiled and felt the cut split on his lip. "Sorry, Mom. I couldn't stand by and let him treat Rose that way."

"I'm proud of you, son. Not for acting like a caveman, but for standing up for Rose and Celeste."

"Ha. Very funny. Thanks. It was a no-brainer."

"Let's just hope you don't have to do actual jail time."

Rose and Celeste came back a few minutes later and despite the pain in his lip and knuckles, Mac experienced a whole new level of fulfillment as they all unpacked the food and sat around the table.

He passed out napkins and threw away the plastic bags, then watched as his mom helped Celeste with her takeout container while Rose handed out silverware.

"Do you have plans for Thanksgiving, Rose?" Eleanor asked once they all settled in and tucked into their food.

Rose shook her head. "I could go to my parents' in Florida, but with just a few days off, it's not really worth the stress of traveling. They came here last year, but they just got a new puppy and don't want to leave her."

"Oh, good," Eleanor said. "I hope we can all spend the day together."

"Course we can," Celeste said.

And just like that, Mac thought, his plan clicked into place.

That evening, Mac waited in the kitchen while Rose put Celeste to bed, just as he had on so many other evenings.

"I have to tell you," he said when she walked into the kitchen, "when I saw you waiting for me at the jail, I thought you were the most beautiful thing I'd ever laid eyes on."

Smiling, she sat down and picked up the glass of wine he'd poured her. "That's a nice thing to say."

"It's true. And not just because I was in a moment of desperation. That place was awful, even for as short of a time as I was in there. It's because I thought you'd left, Rose." Admitting his feelings of despair made his throat tight, and he took a sip of bourbon. "I saw your text and thought you'd decided to give up on me. On us. And that broke my heart. But when I realized you'd come to the jail, I thought, maybe she hasn't given up on us."

"I hadn't," Rose said, reaching across the table to take his hand. "I wouldn't." She smiled, conspiratorial. "I *did*. For a couple of hours, I let Jared get inside my head again, just like I used to. For a short, short window of time, I believed that maybe he was right — maybe me being in a relationship was detrimental to Celeste."

Thinking about Rose, who he knew only as a strong, independent woman, questioning her own choices, second-guessing whether she deserved a healthy, loving relationship, made Mac's heart ache.

247

"Don't worry," she said, seeing the look on his face. "I realized the error of my ways after a certain friend set me straight."

"It was Jessie, wasn't it?" he said.

"It was."

"She's a pistol."

"Yes, she is," Rose said. "And apparently has no problems sharing my secrets."

Mac knew they'd have to address this — his going behind Rose's back to figure out how to help her — eventually.

"I'm sorry," he told her, rubbing her knuckles with his thumb. "I went to your friends. I told them I knew something was wrong, and I wanted to help. Helping didn't turn out exactly as I'd anticipated, but ... all's well that ends well?"

She smiled, and he felt a little relief creep in. "To tell you the truth, I'm glad you didn't leave me to my own devices. I've always wanted so much to be independent. Jared used to tell me I was incapable of parenting without him, and I'd started to believe him. Recently, I realized everything I did was to prove to Jared that I *am* capable. Which is so stupid. I know I'm capable. I don't need to continue seeking his validation."

"You are capable. More than capable. And part of being capable is building a strong support network," Mac said. "We all need help, once in a while. Accepting it is more a sign of strength than a sign of weakness."

"Sounds like you've been talking to your mom," Rose said, smiling.

"She's a pretty smart lady," Mac said.

"She is. And she's sleeping. How would you feel about taking me to bed?"

"I'd love to," Mac said, his body already responding to the idea. "Just as long as you're gentle with me. I'm a little sore."

Rose giggled. "I don't want to keep talking about Jared, but I wish I'd seen the look on his face when you showed up on his doorstep."

"I'll tell you," Mac said, "he wasn't as terrified as I thought he should be — at least, in my rage-fueled observations. He didn't look terrified until after I grabbed his throat."

Rose stood up, pulling Mac up with her. Right there in the kitchen, she wrapped her arms around his waist and kissed him — gently, so as not to reopen the cut on his lip.

"I love you, Johnny MacKinnon," she said.

"I love you, too, Rose Coffey," he said.

"Now, take me to bed."

"Yes, ma'am."

Hand in hand, they walked down the hallway to his bedroom. Mac shut the door and locked it before pulling Rose over to the bed. They lay down, facing each other.

"When I thought you'd left," Mac whispered, "I was devastated. I couldn't bear it. I always thought I wanted to go back to San Francisco after my mom passed. But then I met you and I realized, no matter where I am, you're what I want. We could live at the North Pole for all I care."

She brought her forehead to his. "When I believed I had no choice but to leave you, I was devastated. I was stupid. I'm so sorry that's what it took for me to start overcoming the damage my relationship with Jared did."

"You're here now," Mac said. He brought his mouth to hers and ran a hand from her hip to her shoulder and back down again. "Will you stay?"

"I will."

They kissed again, and Rose grabbed the hem of his shirt to pull it over his head. He unbuttoned her shirt and removed it before using his hands to explore every square centimeter of her skin. When his palms cupped her breasts, she arched against him, moaning softly. He slipped his hands under her pants and slid them down, and then took off his own. She ran her hands over his stomach. Her fingertips brushed the waistband of his boxer shorts, and his erection throbbed, begging for her touch. Pulling down the lacy edge of her bra, Mac teased her nipple with his tongue. One hand on the back of his head so she could press herself against him, Rose used the other hand to stroke him.

Ravenous, he whispered, "Harder."

She increased the pressure, but said, "I thought you wanted me to be gentle."

"I did," he said as he continued to tease her nipple. "But you feel so good."

"Let's get naked."

A laugh rumbled up his torso and out of his mouth, and in the dimly lit bedroom, he could see her smiling at him. He unhooked her bra and nearly came undone when her breasts came free. She tugged off his underwear, and he followed suit.

"Since you're so tired after defending my honor, why don't you let me be on top?" she said, and he almost lost it as he rolled onto his back and she climbed on top of him.

"Ready?" she said.

Groaning, he grabbed her hips and pulled her down onto him. "So ready."

Then they were moving in perfect rhythm. Rose leaned forward and looked into his eyes as she rode him, harder and faster. She cried out when she came, and he pulled her mouth to his to quiet her. When their lips met, he went over the edge and poured himself into her.

For a long moment, they lay still while their breathing slowed.

Once he could finally speak, Mac said, "Can I make a confession?"

"Sure," Rose said, her voice drowsy.

"Since I first laid eyes on you at work, I've been imagining you in my bed."

"You have?" She sounded incredulous.

"I have. And in my shower."

"Well, we've crossed one of those off the list. Should we take care of the other?"

If it were even possible, Mac's erection throbbed again—like it was saying, "Let's go."

"We *should* take care of the other," he said. "Come on."

A few minutes later, Rose stood behind Mac and used a washcloth to clean his body while the hot water ran over both of them. "Can I make a confession?" she said.

"Sure," Mac said. "Please do."

"Since I first laid eyes on you at work, I've been imagining you in my bed."

"You have?" He was incredulous.

"I have. And in my shower. So I could do this." She wrapped one arm around his waist and used her other hand to stroke him. Slowly at first, and then faster and faster until he lost control.

He felt her forehead against his back and could hear the smile in her voice when she said, "Yep. That was as satisfying as I imagined."

"Then we've got to do one more thing," Mac told her. "Sit." He pointed at the shower bench, and when she sat, he knelt in front of her. She tasted just as good as he'd thought she would. She thrust her fingers into his hair and gripped the back of his head, grinding against him, and he used his mouth on her until her shuddering release. He sat up, wiped his mouth with the back of his hand, and grinned at her.

"Yep. That was as satisfying as I imagined."

They rinsed off, got dressed, and climbed into bed. Since Rose had moved in and Mac had known they'd eventually sleep together, he'd thought he'd stay awake all night, just to soak it in.

But as Rose pressed her body against his, Mac found himself so content — and so exhausted — that he couldn't help but fall asleep. Just before he did, he thought, *this is it.*

Chapter Thirty-Eight

W aking up next to Mac felt like waking up in a fairy tale. He was still asleep, and Rose took her time admiring his profile in the light cast by the first rays of the sunrise. She couldn't believe she was laying in his bed in the morning, after a full night of love making. And that shower. Placing a hand low on his stomach, she whispered, "Good morning, Johnny Mac."

He wrapped his arms around her before opening his eyes. "Good morning, Rose Coffey."

"I'd better get back to my own bedroom before Celeste wakes up."

"Do you have to?"

She giggled, curling her body against his. "I do have to. Plus, we have chores to do and work to get to."

"Right," he said. "I thought I'd started living in a fantasy world."

"So did I," she said. "I mean, we're still here, together. And we can do this again tonight. That's pretty much a fantasy for me."

"If only we didn't have to go to work," he said.

"Right. But we do." She gave him a long, lingering kiss while cupping his butt in her hand.

Groaning, he got out of bed. She could see his arousal under his boxer shorts and wished she could feed it at that very moment. She knew what she'd be thinking about all day. He grabbed her hands and pulled her to standing, then wrapped his arms around her shoulders. "I can't wait for tonight."

"Me, neither," she said. She gave him one more kiss and said, "I'll go start breakfast."

When she parked in the school parking lot, Taylor and Jessie were waiting for her.

"This is an apology coffee," Jessie said, handing Rose a paper cup as she walked up to them.

"What are you apologizing for?" Rose wanted to know.

"For butting in and telling Mac your business," Taylor said. "We didn't know what else to do. But we're sorry."

Overwhelmed with gratitude, Rose felt like she could cry. "I love you guys." She opened her arms for a hug, careful not to spill her coffee as she embraced her friends. "No apologies necessary. You probably saved my relationship — and my future. I'd let Jared get inside my head and I didn't realize it until yesterday afternoon, Jessie, when Celeste and I were there."

The women ended their embrace and stepped back, standing in their customary morning circle.

"But, from what I heard through the grapevine," Taylor said, "Mac beat up on Jared pretty good."

"He did," Rose said, "although he didn't escape without a few scratches, himself."

Jessie smirked. "I'm sure it was worth it."

"Mac says it was," Rose said.

"How romantic is he?" Taylor said. "Judd said that when Mac called to ask how he could find Jared's address, Judd warned him that he could go to jail if things got physical. Mac said he didn't care. He said he'd do anything for you, even if it meant going to jail. He said he wanted Jared to get real justice for what he'd done."

"Aww," Jessie said, an exaggerated sigh making her chest rise and fall. "That is romantic."

"It will be slightly less so if he ends up in jail," Rose said.

"Judd doesn't think he will," Taylor said. "Apparently, Mac

found out Jared has some priors, and hiring that lady to pretend to be a DCS social worker could land *him* in jail. Since it's Mac's first offense, he'll probably get a misdemeanor charge — community service and a fine, most likely."

"Let's hope so," Jessie said. "Come on, let's walk."

When she got to her classroom, Rose found a vase of peonies on her desk and her heart melted. With everything Mac had been through in the past twenty-four hours, he'd still thought to bring her flowers.

She texted him: *Thank you for the flowers. And for last night.*

He responded right away: *You're welcome. See you at home for a repeat.*

A rush of heat hit her lady parts, and certain her arousal was obvious, she glanced around to make sure none of her students noticed. No one seemed to, so she quickly sent back a smiling devil emoji, then slipped her phone into her purse.

Throughout the rest of the day, Rose experienced a deep sense of peace, gratitude, and calm. Her body felt relaxed for the first time in weeks, and her mind felt quiet. She enjoyed every minute of her day, and looked forward to going back to the house and spending the afternoon with Celeste, Mac, and Eleanor.

Finally, she had exactly what she'd always wanted: a loving partner and a beautiful home and a sense of belonging so deep, she knew it could sustain her through anything.

And yes, she thought as she packed up at the end of the day to head home, Mac was a big part of it. But more than anything, her relationship with him had helped her find the strength she'd always had. And that was something truly remarkable.

Chapter Thirty-Nine

Just more than a week had passed since Mac's arrest and short stay in jail. During that week, he'd carefully considered his next steps.

Saturday morning, he asked Rose if he could borrow Celeste for the afternoon. Their first stop: Rita's Diner, where they sat at the bar and he bought her a hot chocolate.

"So what're we doing today, anyway?" she asked, wiping the whipped cream off her lip.

"Well, I wanted to talk to you," Mac said, suddenly nervous.

"Go ahead," Celeste said, cutting him absolutely no slack.

He figured if Celeste could be as straightforward as she was, she'd probably appreciate him doing the same. "I'd like to ask your mom to marry me."

Her eyes went round, and before he knew what was happening, she'd jumped down off her stool and was bouncing across the restaurant. "Yes!" she shouted, her arms raised above her head. "I knew it!"

Laughing, Mac said, "Come back here! There's more!"

Celeste giggled wildly as she bounced back and hopped onto her stool. "What else?"

He cleared his throat. "You may have just answered my question, but I wanted to make sure you liked the idea of your mom and I getting married."

"I love it!"

"Whew." Mac pretended to wipe sweat off his forehead. "I'm relieved."

She smiled and took a drink of her hot chocolate. "Good. What else?"

"How do you feel about living on the farm?"

"We do live on the farm. I love it."

"Right. But, I mean, how do you feel about living there, like, for a long time?"

"I love it!" she said again. "Imagine all the things we can do there. We can swing and swim and pick vegetables and milk the cow. And I already thought about where we can put our Christmas tree."

"You did?"

"Course I did. Halloween already happened. It's just Thanksgiving and then Christmas."

At that moment, Mac could see why people considered Christmas magical.

"Right. Okay, so where are we going to put it?"

"Right next to the fireplace in the living room. That way, Santa will see it when he comes down the chimney."

"Sounds good," Mac said. "Now, there's one other thing."

"What is it?"

"I need your help choosing a ring for your mom. I can't ask her to marry me without a ring, can I?"

"You definitely can't. When are we going shopping?"

This kid. "How about right now? Or, right after we finish our hot chocolate?"

"Sounds great." She drained her mug and set it on the counter with a *thunk.* "Let's go."

"Did I hear something about shopping for a ring?" Rita approached the table, hand on her hip.

"Yep. Mac and I are going right now. He's gonna ask my mom to marry him. But he had to talk to me, first."

Rita looked at Mac, and he swore he could see cartoon hearts coming out of her eyes and floating above her head. "Is that right?"

"Yep," Celeste said.

"In that case, the hot chocolate's on me. Get out of here, you two."

As Mac and Celeste made their way out of the diner, Celeste reached up and held his hand. Mac heard Rita saying, "Sal, you hear that? Another successful match made right here at Rita's Diner. I can't believe it. Get me a Kleenex, will you?"

* * *

During the walk between Rita's and the jewelry shop, Mac thought back to choosing pumpkins with Celeste and hoped he hadn't made a mistake inviting her to help him choose the ring. Watching her skip along next to him, feeling her hand jump in his as she did, he thought, never mind. It was an experience they'd both remember forever.

Rows of glass cases filled the jewelry shop's main floor and Mac led Celeste to the back of the shop, where the engagement rings had their own case. The diamonds glittered up at them.

"Wowww," Celeste breathed. "Those are beautiful."

"I know," Mac said. "Let's pick a beautiful ring for your beautiful mom."

Celeste nodded, obviously overcome with the weight of this important duty. "I think she'd like one of the round ones. She's kind of old-fashioned, you know."

Mac nodded. He'd been thinking the same. "I agree. Which one do you like best?"

Celeste put her pointer finger on her chin. "Will you lift me up, so I can see from the top?"

He hoisted her onto his hip, and they both perused the round stones in silence for a few minutes.

A salesman came out from the back of the store. "Can I help you guys?"

"We're looking for a ring for my mommy," Celeste informed

him. "We like the round ones. Could we please touch that one?" She pointed at the ring she liked, and the salesman unrolled a length of black velvet on top of the glass case before setting the ring on top of it.

"Can I pick it up?" she asked.

"Sure," the salesman said.

Celeste did, and turned it this way and that under the lights. "This one's pretty nice, Mac," she said. "But I think we should also look at the one with the colored stones on the side. It says, 'I'm not like everybody else.'"

That last part, Celeste said in her fancy voice, and Mac and the salesman laughed.

"It does," Mac said to her. To the salesman he said, "Can we see that one, as well?"

"Of course," the salesman said.

Celeste examined the second ring just as she had the first, and after a thorough inspection she said, "Yes. This is the one."

"Agreed," Mac said. "We'll take it."

He set down Celeste, and said, "They have a bunch of really cool costume jewelry over there. Why don't you go look at it while I pay?"

She bounced over to the case Mac had pointed out. He and the salesman ironed out the details and a few minutes later, Mac and Celeste headed for the car.

"Remember," he told her as he helped her unbuckle her booster seat a while later. "This is a surprise for your mom, so don't tell her about the ring, just yet. I want to ask her when the timing's right."

Serious, Celeste nodded. "Got it." She held out her pinky finger. "I won't tell. Pinky swear."

He entwined his pinky with hers. "Thank you." He winked and started to walk inside.

"Mac." Celeste grabbed his hand to stop him. He looked down at her and she said, "Thank you for taking me today. And not just to hot chocolate."

He grinned, his heart melting. "You're welcome."

Chapter Forty

T hanksgiving. Rose couldn't think of a more perfect holiday to represent how she'd been feeling for the past few weeks since Jared's arrest.

Just as Judd had told Mac, because of Jared's previous criminal activity, his hiring a friend to act like a DCS worker (and threaten Rose) meant jail time for him. And, because beating up Jared was Mac's first offense, he was off the hook with a fine.

And there they were, Rose thought, gathered in the living room Thanksgiving morning, eating cinnamon rolls and watching the Macy's Thanksgiving Day Parade on TV.

"Mommy," Celeste said from her spot on the floor, "when are we going to make the pie?"

Her feet in Mac's lap, Rose stretched. Mac ran a hand up her leg to her inner thigh and winked at her. Remembering the night before, when they'd made love in near silence so as not to wake Celeste, she shivered.

"I guess we'd better make it now," she said. "That'll give it time to cool before we eat it."

Celeste stood and came over to the couch. She grabbed Rose's hand and pulled on it, trying to get Rose to stand up. "I'm just so comfy," Rose said.

Celeste, who'd recently been five going on fifteen, rolled her eyes. "Come on. This pie's not gonna make itself."

"Yeah," Mac said. "Get up, woman."

Rose stood and Mac swatted her butt. Rose yelped.

From the other couch, Eleanor groaned. "Stop swatting that woman's butt in front of your mother."

Despite her complaints, Rose saw that her eyes twinkled with amusement.

In the kitchen, Rose and Celeste got out all the ingredients for the pumpkin pie.

"Good thing we baked this pumpkin last night," Celeste said. "Otherwise, the pie would never be done before bedtime."

They set to work scraping the flesh out of the pumpkin, each of them working on a half. Mac came over and slid onto a barstool at the counter, watching them. He looked so thoughtful, Rose asked, "What are you thinking about?"

He smiled and winked at Celeste, who winked back. "Oh, nothing."

"Doesn't seem like nothing," Rose said.

Mac shrugged and walked back into the living room.

"What was that all about?" Rose asked Celeste.

"Oh, nothing," Celeste said.

"Hmph," Rose said.

Celeste laughed, but didn't say anything else.

That little interaction tugged at Rose's mind throughout the day but she didn't put too much thought into it. They passed the time cooking, snacking, and napping, and she and Eleanor set an extravagant table with a tablecloth, candles in silver holders, mini pumpkins, and a vase of orange mums. Just before dinner, Eleanor lit the candles. They all carried in the various serving dishes: turkey, rolls, green bean casserole, sweet potato casserole, and salad.

"I should have warned you guys," Mac said, looking at Rose and then Celeste. "My mom is going to make us do the thing where we go around the table and everyone says what they're grateful for."

Pretending to be huffy, Eleanor said, "Well, it *is* Thanksgiving."

"I love this idea," Rose said. "I'll go first. I'm grateful for this, right here. I thought I was doing great on my own — and I *was* doing pretty great — but I didn't realize how much I was missing out on a whole family. I'm so grateful that you found me sleeping in the teachers lounge." Mac and Eleanor chuckled. Rose continued, "I'm so grateful to you for inviting us to stay here, and that we've all enjoyed it so much."

"Hear, hear," Eleanor said. She lifted her glass and everyone else followed suit.

"Can I go next?" Celeste asked.

The adults said, "Sure," and Celeste beamed. "I'm grateful for this, too, like my mommy said. I'm also grateful that Mac is not in jail. I'm grateful for Eleanor. It's like having a brand-new grandma. And, I'm grateful for Mac." She winked at him, the movement so exaggerated, Rose had to laugh even while she wondered what they were up to.

"You go next," Celeste said, pointing at Eleanor.

"I would love to," Eleanor said. "I, too, am grateful for the way all of this has transpired. When the two of you first came to live with us, I never would have imagined everything would turn out the way it has. And seeing my boy —" teary-eyed, she reached out and put a hand on Mac's shoulder before continuing. "Seeing my boy fall in love, well, let's just say it makes this old heart happy. I only wish your dad was here to see it, too."

Eleanor's emotional speech made Rose a little misty-eyed, herself.

"Your turn, Mac!" Celeste said. She pointed her fork at him, and Rose gently pushed her hand back down to the table.

Mac cleared his throat. His eyes darted from Eleanor to Celeste to Rose and back to Eleanor. He licked his lips. His nervous behavior stood in direct contrast to his attitude about this activity before it started. *That's interesting.* "I guess I'm going to echo what everyone else has said. I'm so grateful for the way this arrangement has worked out. His gaze settled on Rose. "It's better than I could possibly have imagined. It's been life-changing, and not just because it landed me in jail."

Celeste whooped with laughter.

Mac cleared his throat again. "I know I've said this before, and it bears repeating. I'm in love with you, Rose." He directed his focus to Celeste. "I love you, too, Celeste. When I first moved back to Prescott, I couldn't wait to get out of here and back to San Francisco, where I thought I belonged. But almost from the moment the two of you moved in, I realized that *with you* is where I belong."

Celeste gasped, her mouth remaining open and both eyebrows raised as she looked from Mac to Rose and back again. Although Rose saw her out of the corner of her eye, her attention was on Mac. Celeste jumped off her chair and ran around the table to climb into Eleanor's lap.

"I would love for the two of you to stay here, on the farm, with the two of us. But if you'd like for us to go somewhere else, I understand. All I care about is that we are together."

Mac stood up and walked into the kitchen. Rose could tell from his purposeful movements that he was on some kind of a mission. She waited, barely breathing, to see what he did next. He opened the tiny cabinet above the refrigerator and reached way, way back. He retrieved something small enough to put in his pocket, which is what he did before walking back to the table. Then he knelt down next to Rose's chair. Was he about to — she couldn't even think the word. Of its own accord, her body turned toward him. He took both of her hands in his. "Rose, the first time I laid eyes on you, I thought, now there is a beautiful woman. I also thought you'd want nothing to do with me. There you were, so colorful and fun and free. And there I was, so ... khaki."

Rose laughed. "I saw you as more than khaki," she said, unable to resist.

He smiled at her. "I always wanted to talk to you, but never had the courage. And then, suddenly, there you were in the teachers lounge that night. A chance encounter. I felt like the universe was finally making our paths cross. It was saying, 'Here's your chance, man. Take it or leave it.' And I took it. And before I knew it, we were friends. Your personality was even better than your looks." He raised an eyebrow. "And your looks are hard to top." Rose chuckled.

"Before I knew it, I had fallen in love with you. And when I found out someone had threatened you, called into question your parenting, I knew I couldn't let it stand. Because, Rose Coffey, you are the best person I know. I want nothing more than to spend the rest of my life with you."

He *was*. He was proposing. Rose felt like her body filled with helium. She could float. He reached into his pocket and took out a black velvet box, which he opened to reveal a stunning, sparkly wing, a diamond in the center and a colored stone — her birthstone — on either side. "Will you marry me?"

Rose nodded, said, "Yes! Of course I will!" And then she took his face in her hands and kissed him.

Celeste and Eleanor cheered while Mac slipped the ring onto Rose's finger.

Then, to Rose's surprise, Mac got to his feet and walked around the table to where Celeste still sat on Eleanor's lap. He knelt down next to them and took Celeste's hands in his.

"Celeste," he said. "I would be honored if you agreed that we could all be a family."

He pulled a second box from his pocket, and inside was a smaller version of the ring he'd given Rose. "Will you be part of my family?"

"You silly," Celeste said. "I already am! You didn't even have to ask."

She flung herself at Mac, who picked up up and carried her over to Rose. The three of them embraced, and Mac pulled in Eleanor.

"I think this calls for champagne," Eleanor said, her voice thick.

"I just happen to have some," Mac said.

While Celeste danced around the kitchen, Mac got out the champagne (and a bottle of sparkling cider) and poured them all drinks.

Everyone reached for a flute, and Mac raised his. "To family," he said.

"To family," Rose, Celeste, and Eleanor chorused.

"To love," Mac said, and again, they echoed his toast.

They all drank again, and Mac brought his lips, cool from the champagne, to Rose's. "To marriage," he said.

They kissed, and Celeste giggled and shouted, "To family!"

She thrust her flute into the air, and Rose, Mac, and Eleanor said, "To family!"

As the evening wore on, the mood remained celebratory, and Rose remained grateful. She couldn't believe she'd spent so long trying to be independent, when having a family — *this* family — was the best thing that had ever happened to her.

The End

About the Author

Hilary Dartt loves great adventures, whether she's writing, reading, or living them. The author of twelve novels, Hilary lives in Arizona's high desert with her husband, their three children, and her Weimaraner and running partner, Leia. She loves camping, exploring in the Jeep, and dance parties with her kids. Learn more and sign up for her newsletter at www.hilarydartt.com.

Preview: To the Moon

Book Three in the Love Under the Arizona Sky Series

To the Moon Chapter 1

Shane West wasn't living his ideal life, but jumping out of airplanes every day helped take his mind off that. At least, most of the time. One Monday morning, at ten thousand feet altitude, he grinned at his business partner, Roman.

"Ready?" Shane asked, and Roman gave him a nod and offered his fist for a bump.

They had a busy schedule that day — six jumps between seven a.m. and five p.m. — which meant Shane was in his happy place. Their first client, Debbie McIntyre, was celebrating her fortieth birthday with Jump Zone. From the light in her eyes as they got her suited up, Shane was pretty sure she'd become a skydiving junkie. But this was her first time, and she'd become a junkie only if Shane and Roman made it really special.

Shane would jump first, solo, and document Debbie's experience with his high-speed camera. Roman and Debbie would jump second, tandem. The two men took turns photographing and jumping, and Shane loved both tasks equally. He pulled open the door of the airplane and the wind rushed in, whipping around the cabin, making it difficult to hear.

"Ready?" Shane asked Debbie.

She gave him a thumbs up, the smile she'd worn all morning

now stretching into a grimace. Suddenly giddy, Shane gave Roman the countdown and jumped out. For just a couple of seconds, he free fell, gravity pulling him toward the earth at a spine-tingling rate.

"Amazing," Shane murmured to himself. The experience *was* amazing, every time. Every single jump felt like the first: thrilling, scary, dangerous. Exhilarating. He rotated his body so he could see the plane and the silhouettes of Roman and Debbie in the doorway. Good. He was in perfect position. He pulled his cord, knowing that as Roman watched his parachute unfurl, he'd be preparing to jump. Sure enough, a couple of seconds later, the pair came gliding past him. Shane had his camera ready and used it to capture as much of their descent as he could. Roman and Debbie landed first and Shane selected a spot on the other side of the field for his own landing. By the time he made his way over to the pair, the birthday girl was on her feet, arms raised in triumph. Shane lifted his camera and snapped a few photos as Debbie let out a wild holler.

"This is why we do what we do," Roman said as he unhooked his harness from Debbie's. "Happy birthday, Debbie."

Still breathless, Debbie said, "What a thrill! I'm hooked. Some people buy convertibles during their midlife crisis, but I'm going to be a serial skydiver."

"I thought you had that look about you," Shane said.

She threw her arms around him in a giant bear hug.

Back in the office, Shane pulled the memory card from his camera and popped it into the computer. The images from the jump came up on the monitor, and Debbie gasped, jumping up and down. "Oh my gosh! These are great! I look like a complete maniac!"

Smiling, Shane said, "These *are* great. Some of the better images I've gotten. Listen, because it's your birthday, I'll give you one print and all the digital images for free. Consider it our birthday gift to you."

"Really? You would do that?"

"Absolutely," Shane said. "It's not every day someone turns forty and celebrates with us."

Debbie came around the corner and gave him another hug. "Thank you so much!"

Shane printed her favorite image, a snap of her flying past him, giving the camera a double thumbs up and a wild smile, and she practically floated out the shop door.

"That was fun," Roman came to stand beside Shane. "When do you think she'll be back?"

"A month, tops."

"That's what I was thinking. What do we have next?"

Shane clicked over to the scheduling software just as the shop door opened. "You must be Patrick."

The packed day, end to end with takeoffs, jumps, photos, and landings, kept Shane's mind busy. Just the way he liked it. Only at six p.m. as he and Roman prepped the parachutes for the next day, tidied up the shop, and locked the door, did Shane have the mental space to think about anything else. First, he thought about dinner. He had some leftovers in the fridge. That idea made him groan as he got in his truck. Maybe he'd pick something up. A hot, juicy burger and French fries right out of the fryer would really hit the spot. He'd just make an online order and grab the food on the way home.

He took out his phone and despite his best efforts to keep his mind off her, he was forced to think about Jessie Monroe. Because there, on his screen, was a notification she'd sent him a text. He thanked his past self for removing her profile picture. Simply seeing the letters that comprised her name conjured images of eyes with their dark lashes and her full, pouty lips. The last thing he needed was that visual reminder. He opened her message.

Hey, Shane Train. The throwback to his childhood nickname and the memories it dredged up of her cheering for him at track meets made a lump form in his throat. *Would you give me a call when you get a chance?*

Shane rested his head against the headrest, scrubbed his face with his hands, took a deep breath. When would he ever get over her? He had no idea. One thing he did know, though, was that he wasn't going to call her on an empty stomach. He opened the app for Burger Barn and ordered a double cheeseburger and fries. Then he texted her back. *Just about to eat. I'll call you after.*

Suddenly deciding he didn't want to eat alone, Shane updated his order, doubling it, then texted Roman: *Burgers and beer, my place?*

The response came through right away: *See you in 15.*

"I wouldn't say eating a burger from Burger Barn is a religious experience, exactly," Roman said after digging in, "but it's pretty much as close as it gets."

Mouth full, Shane nodded. He grabbed several fries and swiped them through the ketchup he'd squirted on his burger wrapper. "Definitely a religious experience."

Shane's phone dinged again. He turned it over, looked at the screen, and swore.

"What's wrong?" Roman asked. "Another girl asking for a second date you don't want to go on?"

Shane didn't want to have a whole conversation about Jessie, so, without taking a break between bites, he stuffed the burger into his mouth again.

"Ah," Roman said. "I see. You don't want to talk about it. I take it it's that girl. Your childhood best friend. What was it, Judy? June? Jennifer?"

Rolling his eyes, Shane swallowed. Took a swig of beer. "Jessie. Jessie Monroe."

"That's a good name. She sounds like a —"

Shane held up a hand. "Don't even say it."

"What's the deal with her, man? Whenever she comes up, you act all weird about her. You never want to talk about it, but she definitely seems to have an effect on you."

As much as Shane loved the way he and Roman worked together — intuitively in sync, complementary — he hated that that relationship came with Roman's ability to damn near read his mind. He made a dismissive gesture. "You're right. I never want to talk about her."

"What does she want?"

"Your burger's getting cold. You should probably do less talking and more eating."

Roman laughed. "Fine. But I want you to know that I know

something's going on. And not to be all mushy or anything, but if you want to talk about it, we can."

"Thanks." Shane stuffed the burger into his mouth. "I don't."

For the next couple of minutes, he felt content with the silence as the two of them ate and drank. The only problem: it was during those silent moments that thoughts about Jessie crept in. Since he'd left their small hometown a few years before, he'd relived his last summer there dozens of times, each time questioning himself. Asking himself what he could've done differently.

"I was in love with her," he blurted out.

Roman, who had his beer bottle to his lips, raised his eyebrows, took a gulp of his beer, and then said, "I suspected that might be the case."

Shane shook his head. "I was in love with her for years. And she never knew. To her, I was just Shane West, the chubby, nerdy best friend. The confidant." Bitterness edged his voice. "I heard about every one of her crushes, endured questions about whether I thought they liked her. Listened to her pine away after them. Sometimes even had to stop her talking about what great kissers they were."

"Got any ranch?"

Shane pointed at the fridge, and Roman stood up. "Did you say chubby?"

Shane leaned back in his chair and rubbed his six-pack. "I did. I definitely did not have this rockin' bod before I moved here."

Having retrieved the ranch, Roman sat down at the table. "You're, like, the most ripped guy I know."

Chuckling, Shane said, "Yeah, well, that's new. Relatively."

"So, if you guys were best friends, don't you keep in touch? I mean, seriously. If she saw you now, don't you think things would be different?"

If they were going there, Shane needed sustenance. He took two long swigs of beer. "Nah. We still text, pretty regularly, but to tell you the truth, I've avoided seeing her. When I go down to Prescott, I choose weekends I know she's gone. I invited her up here once or twice when I first moved, and we hung out, just like always."

Because his voice threatened to crack, he grinned. "But that was before I got these guns." He pulled back his shirtsleeve and flexed his biceps. "But honestly, man, she never thought of me in that way."

His friend shook his head. "So, what did she text you about?"

Shane picked up his phone again and unlocked it. "Earlier, she asked me to call her. I told her I was about to eat and would call her back. Just now, let's see." He navigated to his texting app. "She says she knows I can inhale my dinner in about three-point-seven seconds. And wants to know why I haven't called yet. See? Still thinks of me as the chubby kid she knew back then."

Roman leaned back in his chair, mimicking Shane's posture. "Or, she has something important to tell you and doesn't want to stress you out."

Huh. Shane hadn't thought of that. "If it was that important, I guess she could call me, couldn't she?"

Roman shrugged. "I guess she could." A few beats of silence passed before Roman said, "Well, I guess I'll clear out. Leave you to it."

Shane took his time cleaning up. Not that procrastinating would change anything. In fact, procrastinating simply gave him more time to think about Jessie. He'd always loved her liquid brown eyes, too-big front teeth, and the dimples on the right side of her mouth. As a girl, and even a younger teen, she was cute. She wore bows in her hair and collared shirts with flowers on them. But then one day when they were fourteen something changed.

They ran into each other — literally almost collided — on the sidewalk in front of both of their houses. She laughed, the sound so familiar, the contrast between it and her new look shocked Shane. Her hair, typically in a high ponytail, curled gently around her face and over her shoulders. She wore a plain black v-neck shirt and high-cut jeans that accentuated her slender waist and generous hips. He was thinking, *You look different*, but he knew better than to say that — especially because of the way his body was responding to that difference. For the first time, he felt pure, unbridled lust for an actual girl. Not a movie star or a musician, but a real, actual girl. The girl next door. And because he didn't know what to do with that, he blurted out an apology, did an about-face, and hightailed it back to his house where he ran up the stairs and locked himself in his bedroom to sort out his thoughts. He'd always loved Jessie Monroe, but that was the day he fell *in* love with her.

Even though she looked different after that (she took a new interest in fashion and beauty magazines and implemented what she read), she was still the same, funny, sweet girl he'd grown up with. They still walked to school together, stopped by her house for snacks after school, and hung out on weekends, watching movies or doing science experiments. He knew he could never tell her how he felt. It would change things between them.

Then she started dating. *That* changed things between them, but she didn't even know. Completely oblivious to the things she did to him, she went about her life.

Sometimes, Shane would watch from his bedroom window — not in a creepy way, but in a sad, wistful way — as another guy picked her up for a date. His dad noticed (of course he did).

One night, just after Jessie climbed into Ranger Morrison's truck and the thing sped away with an earsplitting roar, Shane's dad, Alvin, knocked on his door. "Son? Why don't the two of us go out and do something fun?"

Even in his state, somewhat heartbroken, mad at himself for not being able to share his feelings with Jessie, Shane could see the value in his dad's idea and agreed to go. They wound up at the only arcade in town, just to find that Jessie and Ranger had come up with the same brilliant idea. For a little while, Shane and Alvin did their best to avoid Jessie and Ranger. They played a couple of rounds of Skee-ball and two games of miniature basketball. But when his dad saw him watching Jessie and Ranger compete in air hockey, he threw an arm around Shane's shoulders and said, "Come on. Let's go shoot some real hoops."

Back then, Shane wasn't athletic, but he and Alvin enjoyed shooting around at the park. After an hour, they were both sweaty and tired, and Shane admitted to his dad that he was feeling quite a bit better.

"Listen, son. I see the way you look at Jessie. And I'm sorry she doesn't look at you the same way — at least, not right now. I wish I could tell you she would come around, but it's possible she won't. There's just no way to tell the future. But I want you to know, she's the one who's missing out. You are a wonderful young man, and whoever you end up with will be a lucky woman."

Emotion clogging his throat, Shane said, "Thanks, Dad."

Although his dad spoke with authority, he'd never married — he adopted Shane when Shane was seven, and it was just the two of them after that.

As a teen, his heart aching for a young woman he couldn't have, Shane didn't give more than a passing thought to whether his dad might be speaking from experience. Instead, he wallowed in his own misery.

Fast forward to present day. He wasn't a teen anymore, but his emotions around Jessie still gripped him. The garbage from Burger Barn sat in the trashcan, along with Roman's empty beer bottle. Shane finished off his second beer while he scrubbed the kitchen counter, which gleamed, and the sink, which sparkled.

Having run out of things to do Shane picked up his phone, and sighing heavily, called Jessie.

"Took you long enough," she said, her voice coming through line with its normal playful tone. "What did you do, buy out the whole burger joint?"

Despite the memories he'd just relived, Shane found himself smiling. "How do you know I got burgers?"

"Something about the tone of your voice. Your text voice."

Shane couldn't help it. He pictured Jessie at home in her cute little craftsman-style bungalow, wearing baggy sweats and an even baggier t-shirt, her hair in that high ponytail he so loved. She'd probably already washed her face, which meant she was at her prettiest.

"For your information, I had just one burger. A double, but still."

"I knew it." Her tone had shifted, and Shane said, "So, what's up?"

The sound of her deep inhale and long exhale came through the earpiece. His stomach roiled with nerves.

"I don't want you to be worried," she said, and he said, "You know that by saying that, you've now made me worry."

Her laugh was just shy of authentic. "Sorry. Has your dad mentioned that he and I have been spending some time together?"

Weary all of a sudden, Shane sat down at the bar, his elbow on the counter and his hand rubbing his eyes. "He mentioned it." What Shane didn't mention was the sharp pang of jealousy he felt whenever his dad mentioned having lunch or shopping with Jessie, tasks he'd imagined doing with her.

"Shane — I'm just going to say it. I'm worried about your dad. I don't know that he should be living alone. Most of the time, his mind is there. Sharp as a tack. But he's been a bit forgetful. And he's gotten pretty frail. I do love hanging out with him, but the real reason we've been spending so much time together is because I'm checking up on him, and, to tell you the truth, helping him out quite a bit."

While she talked, Shane felt a tremor starting somewhere deep in his core. Alvin West couldn't get old. He couldn't be frail. He was the strongest man Shane knew. He gulped. "How bad is it?"

Another deep breath. "I mean, it's not too bad right now. But, for example, last week we got just the tiniest bit of snow, and the driveway was icy. He fell while he was going to get the mail." She chuckled. "I think he overestimates his abilities."

"He fell? Why didn't he call me? Why didn't *you*?"

"Everything was fine. And neither one of us wanted to bother you. You've made it pretty obvious that you're busy, and aside from a little bruising, he was none the worse for wear. We didn't want to worry you. But then, just yesterday, I went over there to bring him dinner and I noticed he'd left the stove on. No flame, just propane, leaking into the air. That's dangerous. I feel like it might be a good idea for you to come home, spend a little time, see what you think."